Dog Eat Dog

A MELANIE TRAVIS MYSTERY

by

Laurien Berenson

KENSINGTON BOOKS
Kensington Publishing Corp.
http://www.kensingtonbooks.com

KENSINGTON BOOKS are published by

Kensington Publishing Corp.
850 Third Avenue
New York, NY 10022

Kensington and the K logo Reg. U.S. Pat. & TM Off.

First Kensington Hardcover Printing: November, 1996
First Kensington Paperback Printing: November, 1997
10 9 8 7

Printed in the United States of America

Books by Laurien Berenson

A PEDIGREE TO DIE FOR

UNDERDOG

DOG EAT DOG

HAIR OF THE DOG

WATCHDOG

HUSH PUPPY

UNLEASHED

ONCE BITTEN

HOT DOG

BEST IN SHOW

JINGLE BELL BARK

RAINING CATS AND DOGS

Published by Kensington Publishing Corporation

This book is dedicated to the many wonderful members of the dog show community who have kindly and generously supported my efforts, in particular Anna Katherine Nicholas, Bo Bengtson, Dorothy Welsh, David Frei, Suzanne Hively, and Chris Walkowicz.

To Carol Hollands, David and Ellen Roberts, Nancy Chiero and Tim Garrison, thank you for your patience in answering my questions. I'm sure there will be more.

To Debbie West. You always make me laugh when I need it most.

And thank you to Doris Cozart for buying all the copies of my books in Texas.

Laurie Berenson
Ashlyn Miniature Poodles

☞❋ *One* ❋☜

Phone calls in the middle of the night never mean good news. Something's wrong, or somebody needs help. Otherwise they wouldn't be waking you up. The way I see it, any call you have to regain consciousness for is one you don't want to get.

I'm a mother, so when the phone began to ring on that cold March night, I was instantly awake. The fact that my son, Davey, is only five, and that I'd tucked him safely into bed right down the hall several hours earlier, didn't dull the maternal reflexes one bit. I was already reaching for the receiver before the end of the first ring.

To do that, I had to maneuver around Sam Driver, whose long, lean body lay between me and the phone on the night table. He opened one eye as I slithered across his chest and smiled appreciatively. Neither one of us had been asleep. We were just dozing contentedly; warm, satisfied, and utterly pleased with ourselves, enjoying a last few minutes of cozy harmony before Sam had to get up and go home.

I trailed a kiss across his chest and reached for the receiver. Before the phone was halfway to my ear, I could hear the insistent thump and twang of a lively country music tune. Immediately I felt better. It was a wrong number; it had to be.

"Hello?"

"Hey Mel, guess who?"

I had no intention of guessing, nor did I have to. I hadn't heard the voice in years, but I recognized it right away. It belonged to Bob Travis, my ex-husband.

I glanced at Sam. He lifted a brow. I levered my weight up off him, yanked the cord until it stretched to the other side of the bed, then sat up and clutched the blanket to my breasts.

"Melanie? You there?"

Could I say no? I wondered. Was there any possibility of getting away with that? Probably not.

"I'm here."

"It's been a while, huh?"

He was shouting into the phone, probably to make himself heard over the music blaring in the background. A woman, her voice tinny like it was coming from a juke box, wailed about losing her man. The Bob I remembered had been a rock and roll man. Country western? No way. But then a lot could have changed in four and a half years.

"A while," I agreed. There was a moment of silence and I let it hang.

If Bob had something to say, let him figure out how to start. I wasn't going to make it easy for him, any more than he'd made things easy for me when he'd packed up the car and run away from home one day when Davey was just ten months old. Bob had made his choices; among them, child support payments that had dried up in the first six months, and a presence in his son's life that was limited to a small framed picture on the kitchen shelf. As far as I was concerned, he was on his own.

I heard the soft pad of footsteps in the hallway and the door to the bedroom pushed open. It wasn't Davey, but rather our ten month old Standard Poodle puppy, Faith. She sleeps on Davey's bed, so I knew he was okay. If he'd been awake, she wouldn't have left him.

Faith trotted across the room and leapt up to land lightly on the bed. Sam loves dogs and has Poodles of his own. He patted the mattress beside him, where I'd been lying happily only moments before. The big black puppy turned twice, then laid down.

"Have you been missing me, darlin'?" said Bob. "I've been missing yew."

He had to be kidding. I wondered if he was drunk. And where had he gotten that accent? I'd heard he'd gone to Texas, but somehow I couldn't picture button-down Bob turning into a good old boy. Maybe after a few beers, the lyrics from the juke box had gotten stuck in his head and the only way he could think to get rid of them was by calling me up and passing them along.

Sam tugged at the blanket to get my attention. "Who is it?" he mouthed silently.

"Bob," I said.

Sam frowned.

"Right here, darlin'," the voice on the phone said cheerfully.

"Stop calling me that!" I said, irritated. This aspect of my relationship with Sam was new enough to still feel fragile. I'd hate for him to think that I made a habit of fielding late night calls from my ex-husband. "What's the matter with you? Are you sure you have the right number?"

"I could hardly be calling all the way to Connecticut by mistake, now could I?"

"I don't know, Bob. It's been a long time. I really don't know anything about you anymore."

"Well darlin', that's about to change. In fact, that's the reason for my call."

Behind him, the music subsided. "Hey Bob!" yelled a voice. "You standin' us another round?"

"Hell yes!" Bob roared and a lusty cheer went up.

Now I knew he was drunk. The Bob I'd known hadn't been much of a drinker, and certainly not one to buy a round for the house. Perversely, that made me feel better. With any luck, this call was nothing more than an alcohol induced trip down memory lane. In the morning he'd wake up and remember that we hated each other, and everything would be fine.

"Bob," I said gently. "I think maybe you've had enough to drink."

"Nah," he disagreed. "The party's just getting started. We're celebrating."

"Lucky you." It was time to wind this call down. Actually way past time, if the look on Sam's face was anything to go by. "I won't keep you from it—"

"Melanie, wait!"

I was already inching back across the bed toward the night stand. Faith's tail thumped up and down on the blanket as I passed. "What?"

"You didn't even give me a chance to tell you my good news. I struck oil!"

I'm a teacher. I work with eight year olds, so I'm used

to dealing with tall tales. This one, however, seemed a mite taller than most. My guess was that Bob was going to have one hell of a hangover in the morning.

"You couldn't have struck oil, Bob. You're an accountant."

"Well sure, but I own a well."

He owned a well. My brain received the message, but flatly refused to process it.

"Not a whole well. Actually a share of one." Bob was talking faster now, as if he was afraid I might hang up before he'd gotten out everything he wanted to say. The Texas twang was becoming less and less pronounced. "A friend of mine was buying up old mineral leases and drilling wildcat wells. Just speculating, you know? He didn't have any money, but he needed someone to do the books. So we made a deal."

He paused as if he expected me to say something. No chance of that. All the words I could think of were stuck in my throat.

"I never expected anything to come of it. I just thought I was doing a friend a favor. Then this morning Ray comes flying into town to tell me he'd brought one in. Can you beat that?"

No, I thought, I certainly couldn't.

"What's the matter?" asked Sam, looking at the expression on my face. He leaned closer, cocking an ear toward the receiver.

"It seems Bob owns an oil well."

"A share in a well," my ex corrected. I heard him take a swig of beer. It must have sharpened his perception. "Hey," he demanded, after he'd swallowed. "Who's that you're talking to?"

If there was any easy answer to that question, I certainly didn't know what it was. Nor did I owe Bob any explanations. "Nobody," I said firmly.

That went over well. Sam glared and pulled back.

Bob dropped the phone. At least that's what it sounded like. There was a loud thunk and a sudden increase in the decibel level of the music. Now a man was wailing about love gone wrong. "Hang on, darlin'!" Bob yelled.

Sure. Like I had nothing better to do.

When he didn't return in a few seconds, I put the receiver down on the blanket. Unless Bob had used a credit card, I figured the long distance operator would probably disconnect us soon anyway.

"I didn't mean that the way it sounded," I said to Sam.

"I hope not." He pushed back the covers, easing Faith gently aside, and got up.

I knew he had to go, but that didn't stop me from wanting to reach out and pull him back. Instead, I drew my legs up under the covers and wrapped my arms around them. On the bed beside me, the phone was silent.

"It was none of his business, that's all I was trying to say."

"I guess you made your point." Sam glanced at the receiver. "Where'd he go?"

I shrugged as if it wasn't important, which it wasn't. Bob was my past. I thought of him sometimes as a stage I'd gone through, like Farrah Fawcett hair or disco. If it wasn't for Davey, I'd have said we had no reason to ever speak to each other again.

Up until now, Bob had played almost no part in his son's life. That had been his choice. Mine was that he keep it that way.

Faith reached out with one large black paw and batted the receiver gently. It rolled over several times and lodged beneath a pillow. Good place for it.

Though the bedroom was dark, the moon outside was nearly full. Sam crossed the room, passing through a shaft of silvery light. He walked with the easy grace of a man who was comfortable with his body. And no wonder. A bit over six feet tall, he was trim and tightly muscled. Downy golden hairs covered his chest and legs, matching the thick, often unruly thatch on his head.

At thirty-four, he was in his prime. Three years younger, I found myself cultivating crow's feet and battling the effects of gravity. Biology's a bitch.

I watched as Sam slipped on his jeans and a long sleeved thermal tee. The weathered denim shirt he buttoned over it was the same color as his eyes. My eyes are hazel, a middle of the road shade. So's my hair. It's brown and hangs straight to my shoulders. But when Sam turned and looked at me in the moonlight, I felt beautiful.

"I wish you didn't have to go," I said.

"So do I."

He came back and sat on the edge of the bed. The mattress dipped beneath his weight. Both of us left the rest unsaid. He had dogs at home that needed to be taken care of. And I had Davey.

It wasn't that Sam and my son weren't friends. But Davey had never known his father, and I was wary of his forming too deep an attachment to Sam. Maybe I was wary of doing the same thing myself. Davey had never woken up to find a man sitting at the breakfast table. I wasn't sure either one of us was ready to start.

Sam reached over and brushed his lips across mine. I

reached out my hands and ran them up over his shoulders. The blanket slipped down, pooling around my knees. The cool air made my nerve endings tingle.

"Hey Mel!" the receiver squawked suddenly. Faith cocked her ears and nudged it with her nose. "You still there?"

Sam drew back. Slowly I did the same.

"Aren't you going to pick that up?" he asked.

"I guess." I sighed and lifted the phone to my ear. Talk about a mood breaker. "Now what?"

"Sorry about that," said Bob. The twang was back. "Billie Sue just spilled a few beers. Wasn't her fault. If Jocko hadn't goosed her, she'd have been okay. I guess I've had my bath for the night."

"Bob—"

"Now listen darlin'. There's a reason why I called."

I figured there might be.

Then he told me what it was and I felt my whole world tilt, ever so slightly, on its axis. I wanted to rant and rave and tell him no. I wanted to slam down the phone and pretend that the call had never happened. I wanted to run into Davey's room, gather him in my arms and hold him tight against whatever was to come.

Instead, I scarcely moved at all. I simply listened until Bob had finished speaking, then hung up the receiver, placing it gently back in the cradle without saying another word. Around me, all was dark. I could feel the warmth of Faith's body pressed along my leg, and the slight rise and fall of her even breathing. I wondered if I sat very still I could convince myself that it had all been nothing more than a bad dream.

"What?" Sam demanded.

Funny, I'd almost forgotten he was there.

"He's coming."

"Where?"

"Here," I said quietly. "Bob's coming to Connecticut to get to know his son."

≈* *Two* *≈

The next morning I overslept. If it hadn't been for Faith, who wandered in at seven-thirty and licked my face until she got a response, Davey and I might never have made it to school.

I ran downstairs first thing and let the puppy outside. Poodles are extremely smart and once they learn something, like housebreaking, they hate to make a mistake even if—especially if—it's not their fault. Faith is a Standard Poodle, the largest of the three varieties. She stands twenty-four inches at the withers, has a beautiful head and expression, long legs, a high tail-set, and a dense coat of long black hair. I've just started taking her to dog shows and according to my Aunt Peg, when Faith matures, she should do very well.

If anyone should know, it's Margaret Turnbull. She's Faith's breeder, and owner of the Cedar Crest Poodles, one of the top Standard Poodle kennels on the east coast. She and her husband had been involved in breeding and showing for nearly thirty years, until his death the summer before. Now Aunt Peg was carrying on alone.

She's an imposing woman, with keen intelligence and a boundless supply of common sense. She's almost sixty, but that hasn't slowed her down a bit. At half her age, I sometimes have trouble keeping up, especially when Poodles are involved.

I opened the back door and Faith bounded down the steps. There were still six inches of snow on the ground from a storm the week before. Freezing temperatures overnight had covered it with a thin film of ice. I watched long enough to make sure that the puppy could handle the footing, then turned on the coffee maker and got out a box of instant oatmeal for Davey's breakfast.

"Mom!" Davey called from upstairs. "Where are my clothes?"

At five, my son has yet to master the art of choosing an outfit. Left to his discretion, he invariably ends up dressed in the same color from head to toe. Last time it was red. He looked like a misplaced Christmas elf. I work at Hunting Ridge Elementary, where Davey goes to school, so I have to watch things like that. It's hard to inspire confidence in other parents when your own child looks to be sorely in need of adult guidance.

"Be right there!"

The coffee was starting to drip; Faith was waiting at the back door to come in. If only I'd had a third or fourth hand, I'd have switched on the TV and tried to find the weather. March in southern Connecticut always leaves you guessing. I opened the door for Faith and threw down a bowl of dry kibble, then grabbed a cup of scalding coffee and ran back upstairs. I could only hope the day's forecast wasn't critical.

Davey and I made it to school by the second bell, but just barely. The last of the big yellow buses was parked at the curb when we pulled into the already full side lot and designated our own unmarked parking space.

The ride to school had taken less than ten minutes, but in that time Davey had managed to shed both his hat and his mittens. I had his backpack on the front seat next to me or he probably would have unpacked that, too. Organization isn't a strong suit with him. He gets that from his father.

It was only a stray thought, but it stopped me where I sat. A chill washed over my head and neck. For a moment I thought it was an omen; then I realized Davey had opened the Volvo's back door.

He got out and jammed his hat on his head. "I thought we were late."

"We are."

Still I didn't move, except to smile as I gazed at my impatient child. My son. In the space of an instant, his birth had transformed everything I thought I knew about love.

Davey's cheeks were pink with cold, his breath coming in small puffs of steam. He'd gotten the green knit cap on crooked, covering one ear but leaving the other bare. Sandy hair stuck out from beneath the rim. He had mink-brown eyes much like his father's. They were heavy lidded and rimmed with long dark lashes. Someday he'd be a heartbreaker, I had little doubt of that. He already held my heart in his hands.

For five years, I'd been the focus of Davey's world and

he of mine. I'd always thought I wanted Davey to have the opportunity to get to know his father; but now that it seemed he would, suddenly I was apprehensive about the prospect. When Bob reappeared, everything would change. I wasn't sure I was ready for that.

"Come on," Davey said insistently. He wasn't allowed to cross the parking lot alone. "Hurry up!"

"I'm coming." I gathered up my things from the seat, got out and locked the car behind me.

"Race you to the door!"

"Davey, wait! Take my hand!"

Fat chance. We hit the school running and went inside to start the day.

My formal title is Learning Disabilities Resource Room Teacher. What that actually means is I'm in charge of special education. I work with all the elementary school grades at Hunting Ridge, taking aside in small groups any children who are in need of extra help.

My job is varied, hectic, and often rewarding. On a usual day, I can barely cram everything I need to do into the time allotted. Tuesday was no exception. I had a small mountain of paper work still sitting on my desk when the last bell rang, and a Pupil Placement Team meeting scheduled for after school.

Davey was going home on the bus with Joey Brickman, a friend from down the street. I'd arranged for him to stay through dinner, as that evening was the monthly meeting of the Belle Haven Kennel Club. I was too new to dogs to be a member, but Aunt Peg had invited me to attend the meeting as her guest.

Peg Turnbull can be hard to say no to under the best of circumstances. When she thinks she's doing something for your own good, she's apt to roll over opposition like a Humvee in low gear. I had only the vaguest notion of what went on at a kennel club, and no idea at all why anyone would want to join one, but it seemed I was going to find out. Aunt Peg was picking me up at six.

When I got home, Faith was waiting at the door. I threw my gear in the hall, snapped on the puppy's leash and took her for a long walk around the neighborhood. Flower Estates is a small sub-division in north Stamford: compact houses on tiny plots of land, built in the fifties and meant to appeal to the young parents who were busy producing the generation of children that would come to be known as baby boomers.

Those families are long gone now. Luckily for us, Flower Estates remains. With its outdated design and air of weathered practicality, the neighborhood is a haven of relatively affordable housing on Connecticut's gold coast.

We'd completed our walk and I was in the kitchen mixing Faith's dinner when the puppy ran from the room, raced through the hall and skidded to a stop by the front door, barking wildly. That's one benefit of getting a dog: guests never arrived unannounced. Aunt Peg was already letting herself in by the time I got to the hall. Standing five foot eleven and swathed in scarves and gloves and boots, she bore more than a passing resemblance to Nanook of the North.

"Cut out that racket!" she said to Faith. "It's me, your grandmother."

Dog-talk for breeder. Immediately the puppy stopped barking and wagged her tail. As Aunt Peg doffed gloves and hat and unwound her scarf, Faith danced on her hind legs, offering to help. What a pair.

"You're early," I said. "I'm just feeding Faith."

"Six," Aunt Peg said firmly. "I'm right on time."

My watch said ten to, but it wasn't worth debating.

Aunt Peg followed me back to the kitchen. "Where's Davey?"

"At a friend's house for the evening. I told Joey's mom I'd be by around nine. We'll be back by then, won't we?"

"If we're lucky." Aunt Peg watched with a critical eye as I added a dollop of cottage cheese and some canned meat to Faith's kibble, then set the dish on the floor. "Sometimes these meetings go on until all hours. It depends how much arguing everyone wants to do."

"About what?"

"Anything and everything. The members of the Belle Haven Kennel Club are a diverse group, nearly all with different breeds and strong opinions about what's best for each of them."

I considered that. Faith was the first dog I'd ever had. In many ways, I was still feeling my way around Poodles. I knew even less about what went on in the other breeds.

"Actually," I told her, "you never did explain exactly what a kennel club is."

"It didn't occur to me. You know what the American Kennel Club is, of course."

I did. The A.K.C. was the largest registry of purebred dogs in America. From its offices in New York City and North Carolina, it registered puppies, issued pedigrees, and sponsored more than a thousand dog shows every year.

"Local clubs are a little different, both in their goals and their make-up. They serve a variety of functions, one of which is to give breeders in a particular area a chance to get together, socialize, and compare notes."

That seemed obvious enough. "What else?"

"A well-run club can act as a liaison between dog owners and the community. Club members take their dogs to visit nursing homes and hospitals. They put on programs in schools. They sponsor clinics, do breeder referral to help people who are shopping for puppies, and many now have rescue services, which take in unwanted pets and find them new homes."

"It sounds like a lot of work."

"It is. And that's only half the job."

Faith finished her food, and looked up. When Aunt Peg patted her leg, the puppy ambled over obligingly. Never one for subtlety, Peg ran her hands over Faith's body; checking, no doubt, to make sure that I was keeping her grandchild in good condition.

I picked up the empty stainless steel bowl and carried it to the sink. "What's the other half?"

"The kennel clubs put on the dog shows. One per year, for most clubs." Apparently satisfied, Aunt Peg straightened from her inspection and scratched Faith under the chin. "That's their most visible function, and certainly most profitable. If a club knows what it's doing, the show can support club activities for the rest of the year."

"Does Belle Haven know what it's doing?"

"Overall, I'd say yes. Like most dog clubs, we have a core group of dedicated members who do the lion's share of the work. Most of us have been in the dog game a long time. Which is not to say that we always get along. I'll say one thing for Belle Haven's meetings. They're seldom dull."

I opened the back door and let Faith out into the yard. When I let her back in a moment later, Aunt Peg's gaze went pointedly to the clock over the sink. "We wouldn't want them to start without us."

"The meeting starts at six-thirty. It takes twenty minutes to get there." Ten, with Peg driving, but I didn't bother to mention that. "We have plenty of time."

"So we'll be a bit early." She was already leading the way to the front hall. "That means we'll get the best seats. On the way, you can tell me all about what's new with you."

She meant with me and Sam. I knew that perfectly well. Aunt Peg had met Sam Driver before I had, decided he and I were meant for each other, then spent the next six months pushing us together at every opportunity. I'd retaliated by telling her next to nothing about how our relationship was progressing.

It's childish, I know. But sometimes you have to make use of whatever tools are at hand. Aunt Peg was ever resourceful, however. The week before I'd caught her pumping Davey for information.

Wait until she heard what I had to say now.

I got my good wool coat out of the closet. Gloves were stuffed inside the pockets. I figured I'd skip the scarf and hat. "Do you remember anything about Bob?"

"Bob who?"

It was as good a start as any.

∾❀ *Three* ❀∾

A silver moon hung low and full in the clear dark sky. Its light cast a shadowy glow over the great stone mansions and post-and-rail bound fields of back country Greenwich. I'd enjoyed the view many times. With Aunt Peg driving, I kept my eyes on the road.

She had headed west from Stamford and was now going south, navigating the twists and turns of the dark roads with speed and easy familiarity. As always when riding as Peg's passenger, I put on my seat belt, checked the clasp twice, then sat braced, ever so slightly, for impact. That was a psychological problem—mine—and I was trying to overcome it. As far as I knew, she had yet to have an accident; but that didn't stop my life from flashing before my eyes every time she flew around a blind curve or rolled through a stop sign.

"Bob who?" Aunt Peg repeated, once we were under way.

"Travis. My ex-husband."

"Oh." She bore down hard on her horn. A driver planning to pull out of a side street thought better of the idea and waited. "Max and I must have gone to your wedding, didn't we?"

"I think so. I doubt that you stayed very long."

"Probably not," Aunt Peg agreed.

Max had been her husband, and my father's brother. When Bob and I married, there had been a rift in the family caused by the division of my grandmother's estate. For years, the two sides had barely spoken and done little or no socializing.

Peg closed her eyes briefly, as if trying to summon a memory. I kept mine open and got ready to grab the wheel if necessary. "No," she said finally. "I'm afraid I don't remember your husband at all. Is there a reason that matters?"

"Ex-husband," I corrected firmly. "And unfortunately, there is. He called last night from Texas. It seems he's coming for a visit."

"I see."

She didn't really; she couldn't possibly. Aunt Peg and I hadn't been close until we'd worked together to find her missing dog the summer before. By then, Bob had been gone for years. Nobody within the family, not even my brother, Frank, knew how devastated I'd been by the circumstances of my divorce.

Aunt Peg flipped on her signal and careened around a turn. "What does Davey think about that?"

"He doesn't know."

"Why not?"

"Because I haven't told him." I could hear how defensive I sounded. With effort, I moderated my tone. "Unfortunately, I imagine Davey will probably be thrilled to know that his father is coming to see him."

"And that upsets you."

I struggled to explain how I felt. "The whole situation upsets me. Bob's been gone nearly five years. I've built a life without him. I've gone on. Davey and I are happy. We don't need him back."

"That doesn't change the fact that he's Davey's father."

"I know . . ." My voice trailed away unhappily. "The two of them should have the chance to get to know one another. It's just that I don't want anything to change."

"Sometimes change is good."

"And sometimes it ruins everything."

We rode in silence the rest of the way. Our destination was a steak house down by the Sound called Francisco's. Aunt Peg bypassed the long hill of Greenwich Avenue with its trendy shops and nouveau-everything restaurants. Even at that time of night, the center of town could be slow going. We drove under the railway bridge, past the Bruce Park entrance, and into Francisco's driveway.

"When is Bob coming?" she asked as we got out and locked the car.

"He didn't say. In fact, I might be worrying over nothing. Follow-through never was Bob's strong suit. With luck, he might not show up at all."

Aunt Peg snorted softly under her breath. Apparently she didn't believe that any more than I did.

Francisco's is a big, old fashioned, family owned steak house. According to the sign by the door, it had been in operation for more than forty years. If, in that time, the owners had read any reports on the dangers of cholesterol, it was not reflected by changes they'd made to the menu. The steaks still came in two sizes—large and truly monstrous. Baked potatoes smothered with butter and sour cream accompanied them and the side salads were covered with crumpled gorgonzola cheese. Proving what everyone already knows—that most Americans would happily sacrifice good health for great taste—a loyal clientele kept the dining room full.

In the front room, the hostess stepped forward to greet us, then evidently recognized Aunt Peg. "The kennel club, right?"

We both nodded.

She waved toward a stairway just beyond the cloak room. "You're in the front room tonight, right at the top of the stairs. Looks like it should be a pretty good turn out."

We left our coats, then headed up. At the top of the stairs, an elderly couple stood uncertainly, blocking the doorway to the meeting room.

"Paul? Darla?" Aunt Peg stepped up beside them. "Is something the matter?"

"Oh no, not at all." The man turned and smiled. He was mostly bald and the small amount of gray hair he had was carefully combed over his freckled scalp. Though he wore a thick, fisherman knit sweater it added scant substance to a torso that had shrunken with age. "We're just waiting for the waitress to finish setting out the ashtrays. Last time we sat down too early and ended up on the wrong side of the room."

"Paul coughed all night," said Darla. She was small and

frail, with skin like crepe and cloudy blue eyes. "It was just terrible."

Aunt Peg grasped my arm and thrust me forward as she performed the introductions. "Paul Heins is our club vice-president," she added.

He laid his hand limply in mine and left it to me to shake. "Welcome to Belle Haven. Your aunt is a valued member of our board."

Was she? I hadn't known that. Then again, knowing Aunt Peg, I should have guessed.

She fielded my glance and said, "Recording secretary. I do the grunt work. I think we can all go in now."

"High time," said Paul. With a stride that belied his age, he marched on ahead. "What's holding up this show, anyway?"

The meeting room was big, square and plain. The only decoration was an overly ornate chandelier that hung down from the center of the ceiling, illuminating the area so brightly that the white tablecloths made me squint. Long tables, set end to end around three sides of the room, formed a horseshoe with seating for about thirty. A few of the places were already taken; others had their chairs tipped forward against the table to show that they were being saved.

Paul and Darla Heins headed for the far side of the room. I started to follow, but Aunt Peg steered me in another direction.

"Yoohoo Peg! Over here!" A heavyset woman with improbably red hair stood up and waved. She gestured toward the chair beside her. "There's an empty seat right here."

Aunt Peg hesitated fractionally; if I hadn't known her

well, I wouldn't have noticed it at all. "Sorry Monica, we need two seats. This is my niece, Melanie. She's my guest this evening."

Monica gave me a long, assessing look. She wore big round glasses with brown tortoise-shell frames. As if to compensate for the fact that they hid so much of her face, she'd applied a great deal of make-up. Her cheeks and lips were a matching shade of bright pink.

"I'm sure we can make room." Monica turned to look, her gaze straying two seats down where a wool-lined Burberry raincoat had been folded neatly over the back of a chair. "Maybe Louis can move."

"I don't think so," a deep voice said firmly. The man who came up behind us was mid-forties, tall and slender, and holding two glasses. Scotch on the rocks, I guessed for one; the other was frothy and had an umbrella on top. He had a wide brow, a neatly trimmed black beard, and wore a tweed sports jacket with leather elbow patches.

"Did I hear Peg say you're her niece?" he asked. "Louis LaPlante, club treasurer. I hope you're planning on joining Belle Haven. We could certainly use some fresh blood. My wife and I have Yorkies. What's your breed?"

Joining? Fresh blood? I was barely two feet inside the door. Beside me, Aunt Peg was grinning like a magpie.

"I have a Standard Poodle. She's only a puppy. Actually I'm just getting started—"

"Poodles, of course. I should have known." He set down both drinks. The scotch went beside the raincoat. The other he set in front of a woman with frosted, shoulder length hair who was sitting one place down. She had a leather purse the size of a knapsack in her lap and was pawing through it with great concentration.

"Honey," said Louis. "This is Melanie. She has Poodles."

I got a distracted wave, but no eye contact.

"My wife, Sharon." He cast her a fond gaze. "She's always looking for something. She'll surface about the time the salad arrives."

"Look!" said Aunt Peg, pointing suddenly. "Two seats together. I think we better go grab them."

"Nice meeting you." I'd barely gotten the words out before I was being hustled across the room.

Aunt Peg homed in on the seats in question, tossing her purse on one and waving me toward the other.

"I take it we didn't want to sit with Monica or Louis and Sharon?" I asked in an undertone.

"Louis and Sharon are fine. He's a lawyer in town, and he's recently applied to judge. Dogs, that is; not people."

Aunt Peg busied herself with getting settled. "Monica Freedman's the one we're avoiding. She'll talk your ear off, telling you every single solitary thing she's done in the last two weeks. Then she'll expect you to reciprocate, and she'll have an opinion about everything you have to say, most of them annoying. Just the thought of having a conversation with that woman wears me out."

"Does she hold a position in the club?"

"Corresponding secretary."

"I thought that was your job."

"Almost, but not quite. I'm recording secretary. The secretary position involves a tremendous amount of work, so most clubs split the job in half. Monica handles all the club mailings. I'm responsible for the minutes of the meetings." She opened her commodious purse, pulled out a pen and a fat notebook, and laid both on the table in front of her.

"I see you're all ready to get started, Peg. As usual." The

comment could have been innocuous, but the tone in which it was delivered had just enough edge to give it sting.

The woman speaking tipped back the chair on the other side of Aunt Peg and sat down. She had small, sharp features and dark blond hair, liberally streaked with gray. A covered rubber band gathered it into a careless pony tail at the nape of her neck.

Judging by her clothes—a chunky cardigan sweater and a heathered wool skirt that fell to beneath her knees—she might have spent the afternoon walking the Scottish moors. I'd have guessed her age at fifty, but with the frown lines that seemed permanently etched on either side of her mouth, it was hard to tell.

"Punctuality is a virtue, Lydia." Aunt Peg glanced at her watch meaningfully. "One you might try a little harder to cultivate."

The woman managed to laugh without sounding the least bit amused. "There's no starting a dinner meeting on time at the Belle Haven Kennel Club. Everybody knows that. You may as well relax and have a drink, Peg. They won't even start bringing up the salads until everyone's seated."

The room was filling rapidly now. One by one, most of the chairs were being taken.

Aunt Peg leaned back in her seat, so that I could see across in front of her. "Melanie, this is our club president, Lydia Applebaum. She breeds Miniature Dachshunds and she's the person in charge of this melee. If you have any complaints, you must take them directly to her." Aunt Peg's dark eyes gleamed mischievously. "Lydia, my niece, Melanie Travis."

"Complaints?" Lydia snorted. "With friends like these, what could anyone possibly have to complain about?"

On my other side, the chair pulled back. A stocky woman with a ruddy complexion sat down. "You're new," she said. "I know everyone who belongs to Belle Haven, and I've never seen you before."

"Melanie Travis," I said. "First time." I stuck out my hand and it was firmly shaken.

"Joanne Pinkus. I sell insurance. Let me give you my card."

I started to demur, but it was already too late. "You never know when you could use some extra coverage," she said as she handed over the card. "I have Norwich Terriers. Want to see a picture?"

It seemed pointless to say no; I didn't even bother. Joanne opened a large, white cardboard envelope, and pulled out several eight by ten glossy photographs. Win pictures from dog shows.

"This is Camille," she said, passing the top one. "And this is Rupert."

Beside me, Aunt Peg rolled her eyes.

I was still thumbing through photographs five minutes later when the waitress came by to take our drink order. I'm not usually much of a drinker. Then again, I'd never been to a Belle Haven Kennel Club meeting before.

I pulled out my wallet and ordered a double.

∾❀ *Four* ❀∾

I had assumed that the purpose of a dinner meeting was to hold the dinner and the meeting simultaneously, but it turned out I was wrong.

"We eat first," Aunt Peg told me, digging eagerly into a steak that looked like it weighed more than a pound. "The meeting's after. Much more practical than trying to chew and argue at the same time."

Only for people who didn't have young children waiting at home with the neighbors.

I tried to remember that I was a guest and not be grouchy. Because of the size of our party, orders for the food had been made in advance, which meant I was in Aunt Peg's hands. My plate held a sirloin nearly the size of her own. The potato next to it oozed sour cream. I didn't see a sign of vegetables anywhere.

The club members fell to eating like a pack of carnivores who'd just chased down the weakest member of the herd. I pushed my steak around my plate and let my gaze wander. Seated on one leg of the horseshoe was a squat, broad shouldered man with a carefully cultivated tan and profuse white hair. His movements seemed awkward and after a moment I figured out why. He was eating his steak one-handed.

The other hand—wide and beefy, with short, blunt fingers—was resting on that of the woman seated beside him. Her manicured nails were rose tipped. From the look of boredom on her face, I suspected if he hadn't been holding her fingers they'd have been drumming. Her plate of chicken appeared untouched.

I nudged Aunt Peg. She was nosing around in the bread basket, having discovered to her delight that it contained garlic bread. I wondered where I'd been when God was handing out fast metabolisms. Aunt Peg had obviously passed through that line twice.

"Who's that?" I asked. "The man with the white hair. Next to the blond."

Aunt Peg nudged the wedge of bread onto the edge of her already full plate, then had a look. "Cy Rubicov. The woman next to him is his wife, Barbara."

"What's their breed?" The question made me feel very smug. See how fast I was catching on?

To my surprise, Aunt Peg stopped to consider. That was the type of information she could usually supply off the top of her head. "I guess you'd have to say it was Dalmatians," she said finally.

"You don't sound too sure."

"That's because the Rubicovs aren't actually breeders in the sense that most of the people in this room are. They don't have a breeding program, and they're not committed to a particular breed of dog."

"What do they do?"

"They show dogs."

"You show dogs, too," I pointed out.

"Yes, but in their case, it's different. Every time I breed a litter, I'm hoping to come one step closer to producing the perfect Standard Poodle. Each of my puppies is the culmination of years of planning. I'm proud of my Poodles and I enjoy showing them off in the ring, but it's the breeding that's the important part. Winning at a dog show is just the icing on the cake."

Over the last ten months, my exploration of the dog show world had taught me that few people had as pure an attitude toward the breeding of dogs as Aunt Peg. Many people would have called her old-fashioned, if not downright out of touch. Dog showing and dog breeding was big business, with the sky-high handling fees and flashy advertising campaigns to prove it.

"I take it the Rubicovs take winning a little more seriously than you do?"

"I should say so." She piled some baked potato on her garlic bread and took a bite. "The Rubicovs aren't interested in breeding good dogs, only in owning them. They're much more apt to buy than breed, the purpose being to sponsor the dog's career in the show ring."

"You mean they pay all the expenses?"

"Precisely."

"That must take a lot of money."

"It does. On that level, showing dogs is a very expensive hobby. Then again, so is owning a football team. And there seem to be plenty of people who are eager to do that. For some people, it's all about associating your name with a winner. As to the cost, I don't think the Rubicovs are particularly concerned about that."

I snuck another look down the table without trying to be too obvious about it. The Belle Haven Kennel Club had its headquarters in Greenwich, so I guessed that a number of its members would come from money. Still, for the most part, the attitude and dress around the table was casual. Barbara Rubicov was the lone exception.

Seated, she appeared to be several inches taller than her husband. Her sleek blond hair was bobbed to chin length, and her navy blue Donna Karan suit fit as though it had been tailored specially for her. An abundance of gold jewelry glittered in the light from the chandelier, and the diamond on her left hand must have been blinding at close range. Her age could have been anywhere between forty and fifty, although I guessed she was closer to the latter, with good grooming and skillful attention to detail holding the years at bay.

Beside me, Aunt Peg was busy cleaning her plate. She chose clothing with an eye toward utility, not style. I doubted if she'd noticed Barbara Rubicov's outfit, or if it would have made an impression on her if she had. The records of the Rubicovs' dogs, however, were another matter.

"I've heard mention of an Irish Setter," she was saying. "And they did a fair amount of winning with a Dalmatian last year. Spot, his call name is. Have you ever heard anything so ludicrous? Crawford Langley handles it for them."

"Crawford? I thought he was a Poodle handler."

"He is, primarily. But the coat care with Poodles is a lot of work. By comparison, Dalmatians are a breeze. And since the handlers get paid almost the same no matter what kind of dog they take in the ring, you can see why he might be just as happy to branch out."

Aunt Peg used her fork to push the last piece of steak around her plate, sopping up the remaining drops of juice. The acquisitive glance she cast at my uneaten sirloin wasn't even subtle.

"That's going home in a doggie bag," I said firmly.

Aunt Peg's look was filled with injured innocence. "Did I say a word?"

"No, but you thought it. If you're looking for leftovers, you might try Cy's wife. She doesn't seem to have touched her food."

"Barbara never does. She thinks eating at a steak house is beneath her. And as for dining with the rest of us . . ." Peg chuckled gleefully. "I think she'd sooner break bread with Pygmies. At least there might be some charity value in that."

"Then why does she come to the meetings?"

"For Cy. It makes him happy. And it makes him think she's a good sport, even if everybody else knows that she's anything but."

Two seats down, Lydia Applebaum finished eating and rose to her feet. Immediately Joanne, on my left, picked up her spoon and began tapping it against her glass. Lydia sent her an annoyed look as the room quieted.

"While they're clearing and serving coffee, I'd like to go ahead and call the meeting to order," the club president said. "We have plenty of business on the agenda and we don't want to be here all night."

"Here! Here!" cried Paul Heins.

"In lieu of roll call, we've passed around a sign-up sheet.

Everybody, please be sure to sign in. As the minutes from the last meeting were published in this month's newsletter, perhaps someone would like to make a motion to dispense with reading them?"

I gathered this was a procedure they'd followed many times. Lydia looked around the room expectantly as several hands shot up. The motion was made, seconded, and carried.

I surreptitiously checked my watch. It was already past eight o'clock and the meeting was just beginning. I wondered if there was any way I could slip out and call Alice Brickman and tell her I was going to be a little late picking Davey up. And on a school night, no less.

The waitress plopped a slice of half melted ice cream cake roll down on the table in front of me. "Regular or decaf?" she inquired brightly.

"Regular."

I added a dollop of half and half and took a cautious first sip. The coffee was hot and strong, just the way I like it.

"We'll move on to the president's report then," said Lydia. "And I'm afraid I have to start off with some bad news. It appears that the dinner checks collected at last month's meeting are missing."

There was a moment of shocked silence, then everyone was speaking at once.

"Missing?" cried Monica Freedman. "As in stolen?"

"They were probably just misplaced," said Cy.

"Order! Order!" said Lydia. I got the distinct impression she would have loved having a gavel to pound. "The chair has the floor."

Several hands around the room came up. Lydia ignored

them and turned to the club treasurer. "Louis, since you were directly involved in what happened, perhaps you'd like to explain further."

Reluctantly, Louis nodded. "You're all familiar with the routine. If you're going to attend the meeting, you make your reservations in advance with Monica, then pay for your dinner when you arrive. I write a check to the restaurant from the club account when we leave. The checks you've given me are put in a pouch and I deposit them in the account, usually sometime during the following week."

"I'm sure I paid last month," a woman at the end of the table said belligerently.

It seemed to me she was missing the point. I lifted a brow at Peg.

"Penny Romano," she whispered, shaking her head slightly.

"We paid too!" said Darla Heins.

Others around the room nodded in agreement.

"I'm sure we *all* paid," Aunt Peg said in a loud voice before anyone else could speak up. "Now let's let Louis tell us what happened."

Lydia shot Peg an irritated look. Clearly she didn't like having her authority usurped. Complacently, Aunt Peg ignored her.

"Yes, well . . ." Louis cleared his throat and consulted a note on the table in front of him. "I had collected a total of four hundred and sixty-eight dollars, including twenty-three checks and eighty-four dollars in cash. The collection took place before the meeting and I placed the money in the pouch as usual."

"Then where did it go?" Monica demanded and earned another stormy look from Lydia. I was just as pleased she'd spoken up; I wanted the story to move along too.

"That's just it. I don't know. When I opened my briefcase the next morning, the pouch was gone. I don't know how to explain it. Nothing like this has ever happened before."

Beside me, Joanne sat up straight. "Maybe it was taken from your house," she suggested.

Sharon LaPlante shook her head. "It couldn't have been. There's nobody home but the two of us. Unless you count the dogs, of course . . ." Her voice trailed away in nervous laughter.

"Then you're saying it must have been taken by one of us," Monica pointed out unnecessarily, and once again the room erupted in a babble of voices. This time Lydia let the private conversations run their course.

"That's very odd," Aunt Peg said in a low tone. "The eighty-four dollars in cash is certainly negotiable. But the checks wouldn't be. They should have been made out to the Belle Haven Kennel Club. It seems like someone went to a lot of trouble for very little gain."

"Clearly this is all Louis's fault." One voice, loud and accusing, drowned out all the rest. Aside from Lydia, all the club members had spoken from their seats. Penny Romano, however, rose to her feet. She swayed slightly and the man beside her put up a steadying hand. "Louis is the club treasurer, and we trusted him to take care of our money. He should have been more careful."

"Now Penny." Louis's voice sounded sad. "I followed the same procedure I always have."

"I think we've had enough discussion," said Lydia, reasserting her control. "Especially since this is an issue we're not going to be able to resolve. I propose we wait and see what happens. Perhaps the pouch will turn up." She looked slowly and meaningfully around the room.

"What if it doesn't?" asked Monica.

Lydia didn't give an answer.

I wondered if she had one.

☞❋ *Five* ❋☜

With that excitement behind us, the meeting moved on to more mundane matters.

By eight forty-five, I'd finished my second cup of coffee and checked my watch three times. The club members were arguing over whether or not to raise the entry fees for the following year's show. The topic had come up under the heading of "Unfinished Business" and had all the earmarks of an old fight.

It was also the fourth disagreement that had arisen in less than twenty minutes. The other three had gotten themselves talked into the ground and then tabled for future discussion. Clearly none of these people had ever heard of compromise, not to mention closure. At this rate, it was looking as though I should have packed pajamas in Davey's backpack in case his play date turned into a sleepover.

Beside me, Aunt Peg was smiling contentedly. She'd leapt into the fray twice so far, both times on behalf of motions that had gone on to pass their votes easily. No doubt she was pleased with the way things were proceeding.

"Higher entry fees *do* make a difference," Monica was insisting. Most members seemed to join into a discussion when the topic was important to them. Not Monica. She had something to say about everything. "Not everybody who shows dogs is made of money."

She wasn't looking at Cy and Barbara, but I got the distinct impression that the comment was aimed in their direction. Neither rose to the bait. Cy was adding sugar to a new cup of coffee; Barbara seemed to be examining the glossy shine on her nails.

"We're only talking about a dollar or two," Lydia said reasonably. "Most other clubs in the area have already raised their entry fees and the revenue could make a big difference to us."

"Unless the higher fees cost us exhibitors," Penny interjected hotly. "Some of us show dogs on a budget, you know."

Louis spoke up from the other side of the table. "I think Lydia was merely trying to point out that when handling fees and expenses are taken into account, the entry itself is the least expensive item associated with showing dogs. Perhaps—"

"Perhaps we should make the little guy pay, as usual!"

"Here! Here!" cried Paul Heins. So far, his contributions to the meeting had been limited to those two words.

Louis LaPlante threw up his hands eloquently.

"Penny," said Lydia, sounding tired. "I think you've made your point. Perhaps we'd better table that topic until the next meeting."

Penny smiled triumphantly. The man seated beside her leaned over and whispered something in her ear. She shook her head impatiently and pushed him away.

Husband and wife, I decided. They had to be. In the way of some long married couples, they had even begun to look alike. Both had brown hair, worn short, and pleasant, if unremarkable, features. Penny wore no make-up; a watch, a plain wedding band, and a simple pair of stud earrings were her only jewelry. The man beside her had on a tie, one of the few in the room. It disappeared down into the neck of a wool vee-neck sweater that creased across the beginnings of a paunch.

"That's Penny's husband, Mark," Aunt Peg leaned over and whispered. "They breed Dobermans."

"Penny certainly seems to have a lot to say."

"And none of it useful. If you ask me, the woman is a pain in the butt."

I swallowed a laugh. Aunt Peg had been raised in gentler times. Coming from her, that was a world class insult.

"You haven't touched your dessert," she pointed out.

I shook my head. The mound of ice cream cake roll was now fully melted, which meant that it looked even more revolting than it had when it arrived. By contrast, Aunt Peg's dessert plate looked as though she'd licked it.

"It's all yours."

I leaned back in my chair and crossed my arms over my chest as the meeting limped along. "Unfinished Business" turned into "New Business." With the club's show only six weeks away, we got to listen to reports from the various committee heads. Then Lydia announced that on the first Sunday in April she'd be hosting a reception for a former club member who'd moved away, but who was returning to judge in the area that weekend. Yippee.

If I remembered my Robert's Rules of Order correctly, that meant adjournment was next. And none too soon, either. By now, Alice was probably picturing me dead by the side of the Merrit Parkway. In my brain-numbed state, I wasn't sure that wasn't a preferable alternative.

Aunt Peg finished her second piece of cake roll and sighed with satisfaction. I read once that people lose their taste for sweets as they grow older, but not Aunt Peg. If she was running true to form, she had a brownie stashed in her purse for the ride home.

"Do I hear a motion to adjourn?" asked Lydia.

I was so excited, I almost raised my own hand. Luckily, several actual club members quickly filled in. Nine-fifteen, and another twenty minutes to get home. All I could offer was an abject apology and a promise to take Joey the next eight times Alice got stuck. Hopefully, she'd accept.

I pushed back my chair and stood up. Aunt Peg was chatting with Lydia. Briefly I considered kicking the leg of her chair. Unfortunately, good manners won out.

"I'll pick up your coat," I said instead.

"Yes dear, go ahead. I'll be along in a minute."

I'd heard that before. When Aunt Peg gets going, she's one of the world's great talkers. Maybe after I'd gotten her coat, I could bring it back up and drape it over her head.

Joanne Pinkus was standing as well. "I can't believe he's doing that in here," she said, sounding truly disgusted as she gazed across the room.

"Who?" I turned to look. "What?"

"Louis. Smoking that awful pipe. He knows how much everybody hates it."

Around the table, everyone was packing up. Some, closer to the door, had already left. Sharon, Louis's wife, was searching the top of the table, pushing aside the bread basket and checking under napkins. I wondered if she was looking for her glasses, which were hanging around her neck. My mother used to do that all the time.

While he waited, Louis had pulled out a meerschaum pipe. He tamped the tobacco in the bowl several times with his thumb, then flicked on a lighter and sucked the flame down through.

"At least he waited until the meeting was finished," I said.

"He didn't have any choice about that. Since we're in a private room, we make our own rules. And pipe smoking is definitely out."

We moved across the room and joined the crush of people at the top of the stairs. The surprisingly sweet aroma of Louis's tobacco eddied around us. There were several wrinkled noses and almost as many frowns.

Farther down the steps ahead of us, Louis seemed oblivious. He was talking to a strikingly attractive redhead. I'd noticed her earlier sitting at the table, but she hadn't had much to say during the meeting. Now, in the crowd on the stairs, she was standing so close to Louis that his lips were almost touching her hair. The pipe smoke didn't seem to bother her a bit. Several steps back, Louis's wife trailed along behind.

"Who's Louis talking to?" I asked Joanne as we began our descent.

"Alberta Kennedy. Everybody calls her Bertie. She's a handler, or at any rate, she'd like to be."

"What's stopping her?"

"Not enough clients. Not the best clients. She hasn't been at it that long, and she's still pretty much at the bottom of the heap."

"She and Louis look like good friends," I said innocently.

"Bertie's good friends with anyone she thinks can help her along. If you know what I mean."

It wasn't hard to figure out. Tall and curvy, Bertie was dressed in a clinging blue silk jumpsuit whose low vee-neck accentuated two of her best features. Her shoulder length auburn hair was layered becomingly around a face that Botticelli could have painted—porcelain skin, full red lips and luminous green eyes. God had given this woman a plenitude of assets and when she pressed herself against Louis's arm as she leaned across him to take her wrap from the coat check, I realized she wasn't wasting any of them.

"That's really gross," Monica said in a loud voice.

I thought she was talking about Bertie and Louis, but when I turned to look, I found her glaring at Barbara Rubicov. Cy had just handed his wife a full length mink he'd retrieved from the coat check.

"I can't believe anyone would have the nerve to wear a pile of dead skins to a dog club meeting."

"Oh be quiet, Monica," said Bertie. Her voice, like the rest of her, was soft and pleasing. "You're probably just jealous because you can't afford a fur."

"I don't want a fur!" Monica snapped. "Unless it's attached to a live animal where it belongs."

Cy linked his arm though his wife's. For a moment, I

thought the two of them would simply sweep past Monica as though she didn't exist. But Barbara was made of sterner stuff.

"This coat is made of ranch mink," she said in a loud voice. "The animals were bred and raised for that purpose, much like the cow that provided the steak you ate tonight."

"But . . ." Monica sputtered. "There's a difference!"

"There's no difference," Barbara said complacently. "Except in the minds of ill-intentioned trouble makers like yourself."

"Good for you!" Louis muttered under his breath.

Sharon, now beside him, jabbed him in the ribs.

Heads held high, Cy and Barbara left the restaurant. Never a dull moment indeed.

I got in line and by the time I had our coats, Aunt Peg had appeared. We walked outside together. The night air was crisp and cold. I could smell the water of Long Island Sound, less than a dozen yards away beyond the parking lot.

"There now," said Aunt Peg. "That wasn't so bad, was it?"

"Compared to elective surgery, possibly not. That doesn't mean it's something I'd like to do on a regular basis."

"Oh pish. That's just because you don't know anyone yet. Once you get involved . . ."

I'd probably want to strangle myself.

"Be honest," I said. "You can't tell me you think of those people as friends."

"Well, maybe not all of them."

I harrumphed softly under my breath. Aunt Peg has

good ears. She probably would have caught that if a chorus of loud, keening howls hadn't suddenly filled the air.

"Good Lord!" I said, the hair standing up on the back of my neck. "What is that? Did somebody run over a dog?"

"Beagles." Aunt Peg frowned. "They make a frightful noise when they're excited."

"Excited? It sounds like they're being tortured."

As I spoke, a pair of the small tricolor hounds came flying around the end of the row of parked cars. Both wore sturdy leather leashes and they were dragging club secretary Monica Freedman in their wake. All three passed through a circle of light from the overhead beams, then disappeared into the next row. The Beagles had their noses pressed to the cold macadam. In hot pursuit of leftovers no doubt.

"Don't tell me Monica brought those dogs with her again," Lydia said, coming up behind us.

"I'm afraid so." Peg shook her head. "Why on earth she'd think they'd want to spend all night waiting for her in the van is beyond me."

"You'd think they'd get cold," I said.

Aunt Peg gestured toward a minivan parked at the end of the row. "This time of year, she's got all sorts of blankets in there. That car is a dog mobile."

As if hers wasn't.

"I just hope she's cleaning up after them," Lydia said critically. "This club doesn't need to get any grief because her dogs left a mess behind in the parking lot."

We reached Aunt Peg's station wagon and stopped.

"Two weeks?" Lydia said to Aunt Peg. "Same place? Same time? One final meeting of the committee heads and the show should be all set."

"Right," said Peg. "I'll be here."

The howling had tapered off. Now it rose once again to a new crescendo. The sound had all the appeal of a banshee screeching in the wind. Tiny hairs kept bristling at my nape.

Imagine, they got to do this all over again in just two weeks. And I thought school teachers had all the fun.

☞❋ Six ❋☜

That weekend the weather finally broke. For the first time since mid-January, the thermometer climbed high enough to awaken hopes that spring might actually be on the way. The snow in our yard turned to slush and then mud. Davey and Faith loved it. Speaking as the floor washer, dog groomer, and the one who did the laundry, I was somewhat more ambivalent.

Saturday morning, Davey and Faith were outside playing hide-and-seek, my son's favorite game. With the puppy for a playmate, the exercise has a whole new wrinkle. Davey hides, and Faith seeks. This saves me all kinds of time. As a mother who's mislaid her son in more situations than she cares to count, being excluded from the challenge is positively gratifying.

I opened the back door and stuck my head out. "Want to go to the park? It's much too nice a day to spend sitting around here."

"Yea!" cried Davey. "Can Faith come, too?"

"Of course." Faith was a member of the family now. It

hadn't occurred to me to leave her behind. Too bad Sam was in the middle of a week long jaunt to London, otherwise we could have invited him as well.

"How about Joey Brickman?"

"Let's make a call and see."

Alice, Joey's mother, had not only forgiven my tardiness Tuesday evening, she'd understood. The woman was a saint. Then again, she'd been coping for years with a husband who worked all hours at a law firm in Greenwich. She was used to dealing with the temporally challenged.

What she wasn't used to dealing with was chicken pox. Joey's little sister, Carly, had them and was thoroughly miserable.

"No problem," I said. Davey and Joey had gone through a bout together two years earlier. "I'll pick Joey up and he can spend the day here. The night too, if you like."

"No, just the day would be great. Joe should be home later."

Joe was her husband. Neither one of us mentioned that it was Saturday, when most fathers were home all day.

"You're a lifesaver," Alice said gratefully.

"Just call me Supermom." I laughed at my own joke. So far, my motherhood skills seemed to consist mainly of the muddling through variety. Fortunately, that didn't make me any different than most of the other mothers I knew.

I loaded dog and child into the Volvo and we swung by the Brickmans' to pick up Joey. Alice waved from the door as Joey came tearing down the walk. He threw open the back door and flung himself onto the seat like Rambo on a terrorist raid.

Faith yelped and hopped up to join me on the front seat.

I didn't blame her a bit. That boy must watch too many cartoons.

"Seat belt," I said.

He was already reaching around to strap up.

"Check out the odometer," Davey told his friend proudly. Cars are his passion. Everything about them fascinates him. "Pretty soon, it's going to be all zeros."

"What's a 'dometer?" asked Joey. He had a thatch of dark curly hair, freckles everywhere, and he'd recently lost his first tooth.

Davey showed him where to look as I pulled away from the curb. I'd pointed out the day before that the meter was approaching all nines and Davey was delighted with his new knowledge. "That's how you measure how many miles your car has gone."

"Cool." Joey looked at the large number. "How many is that?"

"Ninety-nine, ninety-nine hundred," Davey said importantly. "Pretty soon it's going to say a hundred thousand."

Actually he'd missed a digit. It was going to say two hundred thousand. But who was counting? Probably just me, and the happy mechanic we all but kept on retainer down at Joe's European Motor Cars.

"Wow," said Joey. "Way cool."

Way cool. Are five year olds easy, or what?

Apparently I wasn't the only mother who thought the park would be a good idea on a beautiful early spring day. When we arrived, the playground area was filled with children. Almost immediately, Davey and Joey were drawn into a boisterous game of freeze tag, whose sound effects had all the resonance of heavy artillery.

I found a bench in the sun and sat down to watch. Faith hopped up and draped her front paws across my legs. At forty plus pounds, she still thinks of herself as a lap dog.

I threaded my fingers in behind her ear and scratched her favorite spot. The puppy danced happily in place. Poodles are generally very well behaved. Their main ambition is to please their people, which makes them a delight to live with. Faith was still at the stage, however, where a puppy's exuberance often outweighed common sense—and things like putting two big muddy paws into someone's lap could seem like a good idea.

Since she was there anyway, I ran my fingers through her neck hair, checking for mats. At ten months, Faith's thick black coat was growing rapidly; and to create maximum effect in the show ring, she'd need every inch. The hair on the top of her head and the back of her neck had never been cut, but it would still take another year for her to grow out a full show coat. During that time, the hair was washed and conditioned, then either banded or wrapped to keep it out of the way.

Faith lifted her nose into the wind, wuffing softly. I tickled beneath her chin and her tail wagged slowly from side to side. Before Aunt Peg had given us Faith, I'd never pictured myself as a dog lover; now I couldn't imagine the family without her.

"Hey Mom!" cried Davey. "Look at this!"

He was hanging upside down by his knees from the highest bar on the playground apparatus. As if that wasn't exciting enough, he had Joey pushing him so that he swung wildly from side to side.

"Very nice," I called back.

One thing I have to say for motherhood. It has given me nerves of steel. After five years with Davey, almost nothing fazes me. Threats to life and limb are commonplace; anything less serious I scarcely notice.

I leaned back against the bench, closed my eyes and turned my face up into the sun. Faith was warm and heavy in my lap and the sound of children's laughter filled the air. When I was younger, I'd dreamed of this. I'd pictured myself right here—a working mother who was busy but very content, watching her children at the playground on a Saturday afternoon. This was where I'd thought I was heading when I married Bob.

Too bad I was wrong.

Bob and I met while we were in college, stayed together through graduate school, and then married almost immediately thereafter. Two incomes enabled us to swing the house. Bob mowed the lawn; I cooked the meals. Sometimes after dinner we'd hold hands like teenagers and walk around the neighborhood; more often, we'd hold hands and not go anywhere at all.

Bob worked in White Plains and I started part-time at a school in Stamford. I had visions of the two of us growing old together like Ozzie and Harriet. In my case, it turned out that love was not only blind, it was deluded as well.

Looking back, I realized that Bob and I had never really talked, at least not about the things that mattered. I wanted a baby; Bob wanted to wait. Six months later, I found out I was pregnant. Though the pregnancy wasn't planned, I was thrilled. Bob would change his mind, I'd thought. He'd have to.

We shopped for a crib and a layette, and turned the second bedroom into a nursery. If Bob began working late more as my due date approached, I didn't really blame him. I had mood swings even I didn't want to be around.

When I went into labor, Bob was with me all the way. He coached, he breathed, he blew. After the doctor, he was the second person in the world to hold our child. He was utterly captivated; I knew it just by watching him.

The bubble burst ten months later. In the intervening time since he'd first held his perfect baby boy, there'd been too many sleepless nights and take-out meals, curdled milk stains on his clothes and a diaper pail that needed emptying when he'd rather have been out with his friends.

One day when Davey and I were at the supermarket buying formula, Bob had packed up his clothes, the stereo, the VCR, and moved out. I read the note he'd left on the kitchen table. It explained nothing; at least not in words I could understand.

I might have cried, but with Davey sitting on the kitchen floor, stacking cans and tupperware around my feet and waiting for his lunch, there wasn't time. So I picked up my son and set about building a life for the two of us.

Courts had hammered out the details of our divorce. I'd kept the house—mortgaged to the hilt. Bob had agreed to pay child support. After the first few months, the checks stopped coming. When I called the phone number he'd given me, I found out why. Bob had gone off to find himself, his roommate told me. He felt he needed a little time and space.

Tell me about it.

And now he was coming back to see his son. I sat up and gazed out over the playground. Davey and Joey were on the swings, their small legs pumping mightily to carry them ever higher.

Davey had unzipped his sweatshirt; the bright red tails were flapping in the wind. His sneakers and jeans were streaked with mud, as were the small, sturdy hands that clutched the chains holding up his seat. He was laughing out loud as the swing arced upward; his mouth opened in a round "o" of delight as it swooped back down toward earth.

Pride and love swelled together in my heart.

Bob was going to be very proud of his son.

But what would Davey think of his father, a man he'd never known? Would they build a relationship; and was it a good thing if they did? What would happen to Davey when his father left again?

There was so much I'd tried to protect Davey from, and for the most part I'd succeeded. But there was nothing I could do to shield him from the threat I feared was looming now. As if sensing my thoughts, Faith snuggled closer. I tangled my fingers in her hair and she leaned into the caress.

"Hey Mom!" Tired of the swings, Davey and Joey came running. "We want to take Faith on the slide."

At the sound of her name, the puppy jumped up, ready to join in the game.

"I don't think dogs are allowed on the slide."

"I bet Poodles are. Poodles can do anything."

Aunt Peg had been coaching him. I just knew it.

Faith leapt up and braced her paws on the front of Davey's shirt. Standing like that, they were almost the same size. Davey wrapped his arms around the puppy's neck and gave her a hug. "You're the best dog in the whole world," I heard him whisper in her ear. "We're pretty lucky."

Worries about what was to come faded. On a sunny Saturday in the park, who could argue with a sentiment like that?

☞ ❖ *Seven* ❖ ☜

We stopped for ice cream on the way home, then dropped Joey off at his house. Alice opened the door, looking frazzled and distracted. Her daughter was in her arms. Carly's delicate skin was pock marked with dozens of small red blisters.

"Let me know if you need anything," I said.

"You know I will."

As soon as we got home, I headed Davey straight upstairs to the bathtub. His clothing was stiff with dried mud, and the parts of him I could see weren't any cleaner. Faith followed me out to the kitchen, trotting directly to the cabinet where I keep the biscuits.

Whenever Davey and I come back from school or shopping, Faith gets a reward for staying home alone. This time, however, she'd come along and shared in our fun. The interesting thing about Poodles is that you never really know just how smart they are. Had she forgotten that treats were for when she'd been left behind, or was she hoping to con me into forgetting?

"All right." I opened the cabinet door and the pom pon on the end of her tail whipped back and forth. "Just one."

As I'd been shown in handling class, I held the biscuit up for a minute and made Faith pose before getting her reward. The exercise is called baiting, and it's tremendously useful in the dog show ring. A dog that will stand on its own looking pretty, is vastly more appealing than one that must be constantly manipulated into the right position by its handler.

Finally I tossed the biscuit and Faith plucked it happily out of the air. As she carried it over to her crate in the corner, the phone began to ring. Davey's at the stage where he likes to talk to everybody. I hurried around the counter and snatched up the phone before he could decide this was a good excuse to emerge, dripping wet, from the tub.

"What are you up to?" asked Aunt Peg. Opening pleasantries just get in her way; she often bulldozes right past them.

I pulled out a chair at the kitchen table and sat down. "Trying to figure out the best way to get mud out of a show coat."

"The *best* way is not to get mud in the coat in the first place."

"Too late."

She sighed, and made sure it was loud enough so I could hear. "Legs or topknot?"

"Legs and stomach."

"Could be worse." Peg stopped to consider. Inside the crate, Faith finished her biscuit and stood up to paw her bedding into a lumpy mass. "When's her next bath?"

"Uhh . . ." Poodles that were growing hair for the show ring were supposed to be bathed weekly. The problem was that with a coat like Faith's, the bathing and the blowing dry that followed took at least three hours—a chunk of time that I was often hard pressed to find.

"Definitely in the future." Trying hard to factor in honesty, it was the safest answer I could come up with.

"I should hope so. Is the mud wet or dry?"

"Mostly dry by now."

"Just toss her up on the table, and brush it out. That's probably the easiest way."

By table, Peg meant a grooming table. They're collapsible, stand waist high and are covered with rubber matting. Every Poodle, whether it's going to be shown or not, learns at an early age how to sit on one and be groomed. At the moment, my table was folded up in the basement, along with a box filled with brushes, combs, scissors, and all the other grooming paraphernalia I was gradually acquiring.

"That doesn't sound too hard."

"It's not," Peg agreed briskly. "Now listen. What are you doing Thursday?"

Experience with Aunt Peg had taught me to be wary. I wracked my brain for a ready excuse. "Teaching school?"

"Not then, later. At night."

"Well . . ."

"Good. Belle Haven's holding its committee heads meeting that night at Francisco's. It's very convenient."

For people who lived in Greenwich and were committee heads. Neither of which seemed to apply to me. "I thought that meeting was next week."

"It was, but there was a mix-up in the booking at the restaurant, and we lost our room. It's not that big a group, but if we're to get any work done, we need to be set apart. Lydia rebooked us for Thursday."

"I'm not a committee head," I pointed out. "I'm not even a member."

"Yes, but I am." The patience of a saint was there in her voice. "And I need a ride. My car's going to be in the shop."

"You just bought that car." I thought of my old Volvo, which had weathered more than a decade. "Don't tell me it broke down already."

"Twenty-thousand mile check-up. When you show dogs, the miles add up quickly. The service was already scheduled and when I called to change it, they said they couldn't fit me in again for a month. Imagine!"

I did. Knowing the way Aunt Peg got around, by then she'd be due for the next check-up.

"It's a week night. I don't know if I can get a sitter."

"Already done," Peg said smugly. "I called Frank. Did you hear he has a new job?"

Frank is my brother, younger by four years chronologically; and by eons, if maturity were taken into account. He lives in an apartment in Cos Cob, a fifteen minute car ride from here, tops. Even so, we never seem to spend much time together. Some siblings are born friends; others develop the relationship later. Though the death of our parents six years earlier had brought us somewhat closer, Frank and I were still in the process of finding our way.

Meanwhile my brother, who had yet to choose a career path in life, changed jobs with regularity. On the whole, he was just as likely to be unemployed as he was to be working. He called it keeping his options open. To me, it looked like swinging on a trapeze without a net. But then, I've always played the ant to his grasshopper.

"He's tending bar," Aunt Peg told me. "It seems he sees

this as the first step up the ladder in food services management."

I thought of all the comments I could make, but didn't say a word. After all, stranger things have happened. Look at me. I was trying to find three hours in my schedule to blow-dry a dog.

"Don't bartenders work at night?" I asked. There was an out here somewhere. I just had to find it.

"Frank's got the weekend shift. So he has Tuesday, Wednesday, and Thursday off. It all worked out perfectly. Frank will be at your house by six, and you can come straight here. I've explained to Lydia and made your reservation. You're having the sirloin."

"Great," I said with notable lack of enthusiasm.

"I knew you'd be pleased."

Like hell she did. Maybe I should bring some school work with me. I could use the time to get caught up. . . .

"Listen," said Aunt Peg. "I've been thinking."

Uh oh. A sure sign of trouble.

"You really don't have anything to do with the planning for the show, but since you're going to be at the meeting anyway, maybe you could snoop around a little—"

"Do what?" I yelped and woke Faith up. She lifted her head and cocked an ear inquiringly.

"Those dinner checks are still missing, you know. And I mentioned to Lydia that you were pretty good at figuring things out."

"Oh no I'm not," I said quickly. The last thing I wanted to do was get involved in another of Aunt Peg's projects. "I'm often baffled and confused. Even the smallest things confound me."

"Don't be ridiculous. This whole business is very odd,

you have to admit that. Nobody can cash those checks, so what could they possibly have hoped to gain by taking them?"

"Maybe someone was having cash flow problems. They'd written a bad check and didn't want to be found out."

"You see?" cried Aunt Peg. As soon as I heard her triumphant tone, I knew I'd been had. "That's just the kind of thinking we need."

"I'll go to the meeting," I said firmly. "But that's all."

"Of course you'll go to the meeting, dear. I'm counting on you. See you Thursday!"

As soon as I hung up the phone, it rang again. At this rate, with Faith still to brush through, Davey and I would be lucky to eat dinner by midnight. I picked up once again.

"Mel? It's me."

I should have known. Back when we were together, Bob and I had always sensed when one of us was thinking about the other. It was an uncanny connection, one that transcended time and distance. I'd be home thinking of Bob and he'd call from work. Now I'd spent the afternoon dwelling on our time together and here he was.

"Hi Bob." I went back to the kitchen table. My chair was still warm. "How are you?"

"I'm okay. Actually, I'm pretty good. I need to ask you something . . ."

There was just the slightest hint of a southwest accent, but the twang I'd heard the week before was gone. Actually, Bob sounded rather sheepish, and that wasn't like him at all.

"What?"

"Did I talk to you the other night?"

"More or less."

"Then I did call?"

I grinned, glad he couldn't see me. "You don't remember?"

"To tell the truth, that night's a bit hazy. I was out with some friends."

"It sounded like you were out with half of Texas."

He chuckled softly. "That's the way my head felt the next morning, too."

"You didn't used to be much of a drinker."

"I'm still not. We were, ah . . . celebrating."

"You said something about an oil well."

"Did I?" He sounded surprised. "I wish I could remember. What else did I say?"

As I wondered how to answer that, Faith stood up, shook out and came sauntering out of her crate. She walked over to the counter and cast a meaningful glance at her empty food bowl. Her message was perfectly clear. In fact, her communication skills were so good, I thought it was a shame I couldn't put her on the phone and let her talk to my ex-husband.

"Not much, really." If he didn't remember what he'd said about coming to visit, I certainly wasn't going to remind him. I stood up and headed over to the counter. "Do you really own an oil well?"

"I own a share. A quarter, actually. Still, it should pay off pretty well. Listen I've been thinking. Actually this has been on my mind for a while . . . What I'm trying to say is, maybe it's about time—"

I dumped three quarters of a cup of dry kibble into the

stainless steel bowl, then carried it to the sink and ran hot water over it. "What?" I said as I set the food aside to soak. "I couldn't hear you."

"Of course you couldn't hear me. It sounds like you're running a gravel pit up there. What was all that racket?"

I reached down and ran a hand along the side of Faith's neck. "I was making a bowl of dog food."

"Dog food? When did you get a dog?"

"You've been gone four and a half years, Bob. Lots of things have changed."

There was a long moment of silence on the line. "Yeah," he said finally. "I guess they have."

I opened the refrigerator and got out the cottage cheese and a can of meat to use as mixers when the kibble was ready.

"So how's my boy?" asked Bob.

"*Davey?*" It just popped out, I swear. *His* boy?

"Of course, Davey. Who else would I mean?"

"I don't know," I said, swallowing a breath. "Davey's fine."

"He must be getting big."

"He is."

"Like he can walk, and talk . . ."

He'd been doing those things for years. But then how would Bob know? The last time he'd seen his son, Davey had been wrapped in a swaddling blanket.

"He can do all of that," I said curtly. "He goes to school, too."

"Jeez, Mel. You're not making this easy, you know?"

"Easy? Why on earth would I want to make things easy for you? Do you think they've been easy for me?"

"You're angry," he said softly. "I guess I can see that."

"I guess you'd damn well better." I almost hung up on him. My finger was poised over the "off" button when I thought better of it. I put the receiver back to my ear.

"Look," Bob was saying. "I don't want to fight with you. And certainly not over the phone. I'll admit I haven't been the best father."

You haven't been *any* father. That's what I wanted to say. But he was right. What was the point of arguing now?

"That's about to change. I'm coming to Connecticut. I want to see you and I want to see Davey. I want to get to know my son."

"When?" I asked quietly.

"I'll have things wrapped up here by mid-week. I've got some vacation time saved up. I figured I'd pack up the car and drive."

Pack up the car and drive. Well that brought back memories.

"I'll probably get there sometime next weekend. Will you be around?"

"I guess."

"Good. I'll call you when I get in. And Mel?"

"Hmmm?" All right, so I was distracted. Could I help it if the possibility of taking Davey and Faith and making a run for it had crossed my mind?

"Put Davey on for a minute, would you?"

"On? On the phone?"

"Yeah, sure."

"No," I said firmly. "Not a chance."

"Mel—"

"Don't even think it. He doesn't know you, Bob. He barely even knows that you exist."

It was a lie, plain and simple. Not only that, but it was

hitting below the belt. But all at once I was just so afraid. I was hurting, and I wasn't even sure why. On some level—small and mean, somewhere deep inside—I wanted Bob to hurt, too.

"Bob, I'm sorry—"

"No, you're right. Maybe I deserved that. I'll see you next weekend, okay?"

"Davey does know who you are," I said, hurrying to get the words out before it was too late. "Really he does. And I know he's going to be pleased to have a chance to get to know his father."

"Good." Bob cleared his throat. "I guess that gives us something to build on. Tell him I love him, okay? And I'll see you next week."

Slowly I hung up the phone. Faith nudged her nose against my leg and steered me toward the counter. She likes her food crunchy; the kibble had soaked too long and gotten mushy. I threw it in the garbage and started another batch.

"Mom!" Davey called from upstairs in the bathtub. "Will you bring me my pajamas?"

"Be right up," I called back.

I had to tell him. And now I had a deadline. One short week. No matter how much I tried to downplay Bob's visit, I knew Davey would be excited. Hell, he'd be thrilled.

But what would happen when Bob left again? How do you explain to a five-year-old that just because your father says he loves you, it doesn't mean he wants to be a part of your life?

⌒❀ *Eight* ❀⌒

Every day that week I seemed to find a different excuse for not telling Davey about his father's visit. Sam was back, and I'd talked it over with him. He was inclined not to see what all the fuss was about. Then again, he'd never been a parent.

My brother, Frank, arrived a few minutes early Thursday evening. I was putting a meatloaf in the oven. Faith and Davey were in the living room trying to figure out where in the world Carmen Sandiego was. They sat, side by side, on the couch, my son lifting up the long flap of the puppy's ear and whispering the clues inside. Don't knock it. Together, they've made some pretty amazing solves.

Both took time out from the show when the doorbell rang. Guests arriving at my house have learned to beware. Davey and Faith make a formidable welcoming committee. I figured that if I could reach the front hall before Davey got the door open, there was a chance Frank might still be on his feet.

Too late.

All three were on the floor together. The only part of my brother I could see was a pair of blue jean clad legs sticking out from beneath child and puppy. The front door behind them was standing wide open, releasing all the heat from the house. Faith was barking; Davey, shrieking. I couldn't hear Frank at all.

I stepped around them and shut the door. "Frank, are you alive under there?"

"Possibly." The voice was muffled, but didn't sound too unhappy considering he was outnumbered.

Suddenly Frank's hands came snaking out of the pile. He grasped Davey around the waist, fingers tickling mercilessly. Davey squealed with helpless laughter; Faith fell back to regroup. My brother saw his chance and scrambled to his feet.

"Whew." He pulled off his coat and scarf and flung them over the banister. "Some greeting."

"Be glad they like you," I said mildly. "You should see the alternative."

"No thanks." Frank was grinning. He raked his fingers back through his hair, an old habit because there isn't much to rake at the moment.

He and I have the same hair, medium brown and stick straight. Mine hangs to my shoulders; currently, Frank's is cut short and combed back. He stands a good deal taller than me, which isn't hard; and there's an appealing gawkiness to his frame, as if he hasn't quite grown into himself yet.

My attitude toward my little brother veers wildly, ranging anywhere from outraged to over-protective. For the most part we tread, somewhat uneasily, on middle ground. Actually the same could be said of our whole family.

The Turnbulls are a contentious clan, and over the years a variety of issues have created family rifts. Recently, loyalties had shifted once again when Aunt Peg's husband, Max, died about the same time his sister, Rose, left the Convent of Divine Mercy to marry a former priest. All this was complicated by the fact that Rose and Peg have hated each other for years. Since Frank usually takes Rose's side, while I tend to champion Peg's, we try not to let our differences cause too much disruption.

"Something smells great." Frank was already heading toward the kitchen. "Don't tell me you cooked."

"Of course I cooked. What kind of a mother do you think I am? I'll have you know your nephew eats a balanced dinner every night." I had my fingers crossed, but I was walking behind my brother. There was no way he could have seen them.

"Right." He opened the oven and had a peek, then went to the refrigerator and got out a beer. "What about the pooch? Does she get meatloaf, too?"

"Faith's already eaten. Just try not to let Davey give her too much food off his plate. We'll be at Francisco's in Greenwich. The number's written down, and I don't think we'll be too late."

"Francisco's, huh? Did Aunt Peg tell you I'm working there now?"

I frowned. "She told me you were tending bar."

"Right, at Francisco's. She's the one who told me about the opening. I just started last week, and the tips are great. It sure beats selling men's clothes in the mall."

And for this, he got a college education. I bit my tongue and didn't say a word.

My coat was draped over the back of the kitchen chair. I picked it up and put it on. "Davey goes to bed at eight-thirty. He'll protest some, but he usually caves right in if you're firm."

"Got it."

"If Faith goes to the back door, just open it and let her out. The yard's fenced—"

"Go," said Frank. He took my arm and walked me to the door. "We'll be fine."

"I won't be late."

"You said that already." He had the door open and was pushing me out.

I can't help it. He's my little brother, so I worry. "If you need me—"

"We won't."

The door slammed shut in my face.

"Hey Davey!" I heard Frank yell as I started down the steps. "Let's paaarty!"

He was kidding. At least I hoped he was.

The restaurant had given us the same room as last time. This evening the tables were arranged in a single long line down the center. In a quick glance, I counted fourteen seats, about half of them already filled when we arrived.

Nearly all of the faces around the table looked familiar. It seemed that most of the people who held an office in the club or had voiced an opinion at the meeting, were also show committee heads. Aunt Peg had mentioned that there was a core group of members whose participation involved every facet of club activity. Here they were.

Lydia, wearing the same gray cardigan she'd had on the meeting before, had saved us two seats. Aunt Peg sat down next to the club president and I found myself squeezed between her and Cy Rubicov.

He held out a hand. "You were here last time, but I don't believe we met. Cy Rubicov. And this is my wife, Babs."

"Barbara," she corrected with a cool smile. Her suit was spectacular, in an understated way. I was guessing Armani. "You must be a new member. Don't tell me they've got you working on the show already?"

"No, actually I'm not a member at all. Margaret Turnbull is my aunt, and she needed a ride. I'm just here as transportation."

Cy frowned. He reached around behind me and tapped Peg on the shoulder. "Why didn't you call us if you needed a ride? You know we're right over in Conyers Farm. We could have swung by and picked you up."

"Why Cy, what a nice offer. Next time I'll think of you first."

I wondered if he knew her well enough to read the subtle nuances in her tone. Aunt Peg was smiling, but she was picturing hell freezing over.

Cy turned back to me. He lifted a beefy hand and rested it on my shoulder in a friendly fashion. "Now listen, Mel . . . It's Mel, right?"

"Actually, it's Melanie. The only one who calls me Mel is my ex-husband."

Barbara's gaze flicked in my direction, then skimmed away once more.

"As I was saying, if you do want to get involved in the show, you just let me know. I'm in charge of hospitality and we can always use some extra hands."

"I'll do that," I said. What the hell. He hadn't read Aunt Peg's tone. He probably couldn't read mine either.

As soon as we were settled in our seats, a waitress came around to take our drink orders. The last dinner had been for socializing; this one was for work. While we were waiting to be served, business got underway.

As club president, Lydia had run the last meeting. This time Louis LaPlante, the show chairman, was in charge. He started by asking each of the various committee heads to give a report. Bertie Kennedy, who was handling the advertising, went first.

She bent down to the floor beside her chair, picked up a notebook and placed it on the table in front of her. For anyone else, the movement would have been mundane; Bertie managed to make it look distinctly sensual. There was the obvious shift of her breasts beneath the cream silk blouse, the toss of her head to flip back the hair that had fallen forward as she leaned over. Biting her full lower lip, she used one manicured fingertip to skim through the notebook until she found her place.

A quick scan of the room confirmed that all male eyes, even those belonging to Paul Heins, who was old enough to be her grandfather, were riveted. After that, the report itself was almost anticlimactic.

"Excellent, Bertie," Louis said when she was done.

Others around the room were nodding. Advertising sales were up by more than twenty percent over the previous year. For all the physical assets on display, Bertie was obviously no ball of fluff.

Raising her hand, Monica Freedman volunteered to report on the raffle next. She settled her large glasses firmly on her nose and bounced to her feet like an over-age cheer-leader. Monica spoke with great enthusiasm about the prizes she'd solicited, the tickets she expected to sell, and the profits she was sure the raffle would make.

But try as she might—and I got the impression Monica was trying very hard indeed—she couldn't command the room's attention as Bertie had done so effortlessly. While she spoke, the salads were served and another drink order taken. Water was poured from the pitchers on the table, salt was passed, silverware clinked.

"Well," Monica said brightly at the end of her report. "I guess that's it."

Louis nodded vaguely in her direction. "Who'd like to go next?"

Looking disgruntled, Monica found her seat as Cy Rubicov began to talk about hospitality. His wife, who was doing the judges' lunch, followed. The entrees were served. I dug into my steak while Mark Romano, grounds committee, went into a long winded explanation of the difficulties of preparing an outdoor site for an April show date. Judging from the expressions on the faces around the table, they'd heard it all before.

Penny Romano was in charge of decorations. After her husband spoke, she simply waved a hand through the air and assured the members that she had everything under control. Louis LaPlante looked unconvinced. Aunt Peg, assistant show chairman, was frowning. But she didn't say a word when Louis turned to Lydia and asked how publicity was coming along.

The waitress came around for a third time and offered to refresh our drinks. No mystery where this restaurant's profit margin lay. Most club members waved her away; Penny Romano handed her an empty glass and placed another order.

I ate about a third of my sirloin, which was still more red meat than I normally eat in a week. Beside me, Aunt Peg was ladling sour cream onto her baked potato. All this, and she still had dessert to look forward to.

No wonder she enjoyed coming to these meetings. It certainly couldn't have been because of the scintillating discussion. Listening to Paul Heins, who was rambling on about concession space, I was quite certain of that.

Seated beside him, Paul's wife, Darla, smiled sweetly at everything he said. I wondered how long they'd been married. Longer than I'd been alive, probably.

As dessert was served—vanilla ice cream, topped with a rapidly congealing brown sauce—Joanne Pinkus gave the last report on the trophy committee. I took one look at the bowl the waitress set in front of me, and passed it directly over to Aunt Peg. She's never turned down a sweet yet, and as usual, she didn't disappoint.

"Joanne," Monica said loudly. "Did you look into that foundry I told you about in Woodbury? The one that was doing such nice things in pewter?"

"I sent for a brochure." Joanne's ruddy complexion flushed even redder. She looked down and consulted her notes. "But in the end I decided that with the amount of money we had to spend, our needs would be better served by crystal."

"Glass, you mean." Monica sniffed. "That's really all it is. Surely a club like Belle Haven could afford to offer trophies that are a cut above the norm."

"In the past, maybe so. But trophy donations were down this year. Even in an affluent area like Fairfield County, people are cutting back."

"Not according to Bertie," Penny Romano yelled out. "She pulled in more money than ever."

"Yes, but . . ." Joanne flipped through the papers in front of her, looking flustered. "In some ways, that's precisely the problem. People allot a certain amount that they're going to give, and they know that with advertising, they'll see a return. There's a page in the catalogue with their dog's picture on it. On the other hand, a trophy donation is really just that . . ."

"We see your point." Louis sounded ready to move on. "I'm sure the trophies you've picked out are lovely."

"Well, I'm not," Monica snapped. I wondered if this was her way of getting back at the membership for not making a bigger fuss over her presentation. "I made a suggestion and Joanne ignored it. Those trophies represent our club. Why should she get to choose what they look like?"

"Because that's her job," said Aunt Peg, speaking up firmly. "Heading the trophy committee is a great deal of work, I've done it myself. Joanne seems to have everything under control. Monica, if you're dissatisfied, perhaps you'd like to volunteer to chair the trophy committee for next year's show."

"Maybe I would. It's not like doing the raffle is easy."

Abruptly, Lydia pushed back her chair and stood. She wasn't a tall woman, but she had presence to spare. Even though this wasn't her meeting, it didn't take long before she had everyone's attention.

"None of these jobs are easy," she said. "Running a dog show takes a great deal of work and this club is very fortunate in the number of dedicated members it has who are willing to volunteer their time and energy to make it happen."

Lydia moved her gaze slowly around the room, until each person felt that his or her own contribution had been recognized. It was a masterful stroke of gamesmanship and I could see why she'd been elected president. With this group, there was probably a lot of call for her peace making skills.

"Now then, Louis," she said, ceding the floor gracefully to the show chairman, "is there anything else you wanted to cover?"

"No, I think that about does it." His meerschaum pipe was already out, sitting on the table beside his empty coffee cup. "From what I've heard here tonight, I think this year's show is going to be our best ever. Keep up the good work, and we'll see you all in three weeks at the regular monthly meeting."

Class dismissed. Chairs scraped back; belongings were gathered. This time, I'd hung my coat over the back of my seat. Aunt Peg had done the same, so we were near the front of the group as we emerged from the restaurant. The parking lot seemed colder and darker than it had been the week before. Looking up, I saw that two of the overhead spotlights were out.

I blew out a breath in a long puff of steam and dug in my pocket for gloves. "Just when you think spring might finally be coming, Mother Nature turns around and takes you back to square one."

"Oh pish," said Aunt Peg. "A little cold air is good for you, especially after all that stuffiness inside."

"The room?" I inquired archly. "Or the people?"

Before she could answer, I heard a van door slide open and Monica's Beagles began to howl. It didn't matter that I knew what they were—the eerie sound coming out of the quiet night still sent a shiver slipping down my spine.

"Good Lord," said Aunt Peg. "Not again. Doesn't she ever leave those dogs home?"

As we came up beside the Volvo I heard the scramble of running feet, the dogs' nails scraping on the hard macadam. I was fitting the key to the lock when they ran by. It took me a moment to grasp that something was wrong. Then I realized what it was—the Beagles were running loose.

No leashes, no collars. No Monica.

"Oh that woman!" Aunt Peg cried in exasperation. "What is the matter with her? In the dark, with all these cars driving every which way. How *could* she let them get away from her?" Hand going automatically to her pocket for treats, she took off in pursuit of the loose dogs.

Shortly after her first call, I heard several other club members chime in. All were dog lovers, and all immediately realized the potential danger inherent in the situation. The Beagles were near a busy road, in a strange place at night. The sooner Monica had them back under control, the better.

Thinking the Beagles might circle back, I started down the row of cars in the direction from which they'd come. It seemed strange that Monica hadn't come running after the dogs; stranger still, that with all the voices now calling out in the night, hers didn't seem to be among them.

The door to her van was open. As I drew near, I saw that the interior held two built-in crates. A tangled pair of leashes trailed off the top of the higher one. Why hadn't Monica taken them with her when she went after her dogs?

Then I reached the van and saw that Monica hadn't gone anywhere. She was sprawled on the ground; her body half beside the minivan, half underneath it. Her face was turned away, and her hair looked absurdly red against the black macadam. Something dark and thick seemed to be matted through it.

"Monica?" I leaned down to touch her shoulder, then drew back quickly. A sickly sweet, metallic scent hung in the cold air. I'd smelled it before and I knew what it was. Blood.

"Oh God."

"What's the matter?" said Bertie, coming up behind me. She took in the situation in a glance. "Did she faint? I know CPR."

"I don't think it'll help," I said.

That's when Bertie saw the blood. I heard her swallow heavily. My own meal was rising in my throat.

Gingerly, Bertie leaned down and felt for a pulse. Wrist first, then throat. By then, I'd already guessed it was too late.

"I've got one of the little scoundrels," Aunt Peg said triumphantly, coming up to join us. "I think Mark managed to nab the other." She was cradling a wiggly Beagle in her arms.

Aunt Peg looked from my face to Bertie's, then back again. "What?"

"It's Monica," I said, and stepped aside so she could see. "She's dead."

The Beagle in her arms lifted his nose to the cold, pale moon and howled.

ᗡ❊ *Nine* ❊ᗡ

It's a good thing Frank was staying with Davey, because by the time the police finished questioning all of us it was nearly midnight. They talked to us separately, but afterward we grouped together in a small pool of illumination provided by one of the overhead lights. Nobody seemed in a hurry to leave. I think we were all in shock.

It just didn't seem possible that Monica was actually dead. Even worse was the thought that had immediately crossed my mind: that the list of likely suspects began and ended with the members of the Belle Haven Kennel Club. One look at Aunt Peg's face, and I knew she was thinking the same thing.

The police had cordoned off the area around Monica's van, firmly rebuffing Aunt Peg's attempt to retrieve the Beagles' leashes. She'd piled the two little hounds onto the back seat of the Volvo—without asking, I might add—where they were now scratching at the windows and howling mournfully. The windows, firmly shut, muffled most of the noise.

One patrolman was videotaping the proceedings. Other members of the police force were in and around Monica's van, gathering up bits and pieces of what they hoped was evidence. A stiff breeze blew in from over the water; but cold as it was, none of the club members recommended that we move inside the restaurant. Our comfort seemed a secondary consideration in the face of what had been done to Monica.

"I just can't believe it," Joanne Pinkus said for what had to have been the tenth time. "How could this have happened?"

"Easy," Bertie snorted. "Someone snuck up behind Monica, bashed her over the head with a rock, then went off to join the hue and cry about the loose Beagles."

"A rock?" Aunt Peg and I asked simultaneously.

Bertie nodded. "When I was speaking with Detective Shertz, one of the other policemen brought it over. I think he'd found it under the van."

"I saw it too," said Cy. "The medical examiner was comparing it to the depression in the back of Monica's skull. Of course when I asked about it, they wouldn't tell me a thing."

"I think this whole business is positively horrid!" said Barbara. Snuggled into her mink, she was probably the only one among us who wasn't feeling the cold. "In Greenwich, of all places. Is nowhere safe anymore? And then we're all questioned as if we might have had something to do with it."

"We *were* all out here," Aunt Peg pointed out, sounding as if she'd like to ask a few questions herself.

"Surely you're not thinking of us as suspects!" Penny Romano glared at Aunt Peg, and her husband slipped a comforting arm around her shoulder.

"I'm sure that's not what Peg meant," Louis said sooth-ingly.

I thought that was exactly what Peg had meant. Wisely, I kept my mouth shut.

Standing beside her husband, Sharon LaPlante spoke up. "If anyone saw anything, it was probably Peg's niece. Melanie, isn't it?"

I nodded as all eyes turned my way.

"You were the first to reach her. What did you see?"

"Nothing," I replied honestly. It seemed like a woefully inadequate answer. "The door to Monica's van was open. I saw the leashes on top of a crate, and thought it was odd she hadn't taken them with her. Then when I got closer, I saw her lying on the ground."

"There you go," Lydia said firmly. "None of us saw a thing, which isn't surprising when you consider how dark it is out here, and that we had the loose Beagles to distract us. For all we know, this was just a random act of violence, like we're always hearing about on the news. It had noth-ing to do with any of us."

Baloney, I thought, wondering if Lydia actually believed what she was saying. She sounded sincere, but how hard was that? Unless I missed my guess, the murderer was standing in the circle among us.

"What happened here was a terrible shame," Lydia was saying. "Monica was a valued member of the Belle Haven Kennel Club, and we shall all miss her dearly. Perhaps someone would like to prepare a small tribute to Monica for the next meeting?"

I never saw so many gazes drop so fast. Feet shuffled, mufflers were pulled more tightly around throats. No-body stepped forward to volunteer.

"We'll all think about it. How about that?"

That idea seemed to go over somewhat better. At least it was accompanied by a bit of eye contact. But it didn't look to me as though Monica Freedman was going to be getting a tribute from the Belle Haven Kennel Club any time soon.

After that, everyone began to drift away. Joanne, who ran the club's rescue service, agreed to take the Beagles home with her. Monica had apparently lived in Banksville with her widowed mother, and nobody wanted to chance reaching Mrs. Freedman before the police could explain what had happened.

"This is a fine mess," Aunt Peg said unhappily, when we were finally alone in the Volvo. "As recording secretary, I'm in charge of writing up the minutes. You don't suppose I have to put this in, do you?"

It wasn't funny, but she sounded so disgruntled I almost laughed. Right now, Aunt Peg's defense mechanisms were in full gear. Tomorrow, she'd probably be horrified by what she'd said.

"No." I put on my signal and turned out of the lot. "The meeting was already over by then."

Peg lapsed into silence. Concentrating on the road a good deal harder than was necessary, I did the same.

Aunt Peg didn't speak again until we pulled into her driveway. She lives on a large piece of land in an updated farmhouse whose roots go back more than a century. It has a gabled roof and a wrap-around porch. A Japanese Maple, the same vintage as the house, stands stately guard near the front door.

Six Standard Poodles, all retired champions, live in the house with her. Another six or so, in various stages of growing coat for the show ring, are housed in a small kennel building out back. Aunt Peg had left on plenty of lights and as the Volvo coasted to a stop near the front steps, I could see the house Poodles, their heads bobbing in the windows as they stood up on their hind legs and heralded our arrival.

With that much activity going on, I thought Aunt Peg would go right in. Instead, she sat right where she was and said, "Random act of violence, my fanny!"

I turned off the car and turned to look at her. "Why didn't you say something when Lydia trotted out that preposterous theory?"

"Why didn't you?" she countered quickly.

"It wasn't my place. It's not even my club. Besides, I was the one who found Monica. Under the circumstances, I figured the less I said, the better."

"That was just Lydia's way. She's the consummate politician—always trying to put the best possible face on things. I'm sure she thought it would make everyone feel better."

"Including Monica's killer. He or she was probably standing right there among us."

"I know." Aunt Peg gave a small shiver. She didn't look frightened though. Instead, illuminated by the small amount of light coming from the dashboard, she seemed positively invigorated. "So who do you think did it?"

"How should I know?" I threw up my hands.

If I'd had any sense, I'd have held them up in self-defense; or maybe in the shape of a cross to ward off a curse. I knew what was coming next. I just knew it.

"It's obvious you're the perfect person to figure this out."

"Why me? Two weeks ago, I'd never even met any of those people. I still know next to nothing about them."

"So you'll be objective. With the added benefit that I can give you the inside scoop. You have to admit, we make a pretty good team."

She had a point. The truth of the matter was, we did work well together. The summer before, she'd plucked me up out of a serious case of single-mother, lost-my-summer-job, boyfriend-eloped-with-somebody-else doldrums, dusted me off, and launched me out on a search to find her missing stud dog. I wouldn't say that my new-found relationship with Aunt Peg had revitalized my life; but it had certainly given it an extra dollop of spice.

Besides, nobody said no to Aunt Peg. She simply didn't allow it.

"Who do *you* think killed Monica?" I asked, throwing the question back to her.

"If that woman annoyed everyone as much as she did me, I'd say the field is wide open."

"Because she talked so much?"

"Monica didn't just talk. She also knew how to listen. She had a way of offering just enough of a sympathetic shoulder that people opened up and told her a little more than they'd intended. She loved being the person who was in the know. She enjoyed having that sort of edge on everybody else."

"Do you think she knew more than somebody wanted her to?"

"It's just a guess," Aunt Peg said with a shrug. "For all I know, Monica was having an affair with Cy and Barbara decided to take matters into her own hands."

"With a rock?" I laughed. "I doubt it. A pearl handled revolver seems more her style."

"See?" said Peg. She opened the door and slid out. "You might find you know these people better than you thought. In the morning, I'll take a trip down to the police department and see what they've come up with."

"In the morning, I'll be in school." I turned the key in the ignition. The car had been stalling all day, and it took three tries to catch. "After that, I've got to figure out a way to tell Davey that his father's coming this weekend."

"This weekend as in day after tomorrow? You'd better hurry."

Of course she was right. That was why, even though I still felt like I was floundering, I sat Davey down in the kitchen as soon as we got home from school the next afternoon, fortified him with a double dose of milk and his favorite shortbread cookies, and got down to business.

Faith had already been out for a quick run in the back yard. Now she was dancing impatiently around Davey's chair. Usually when we got home, she had his undivided attention. Clearly she couldn't figure out what was holding him up. After a moment, she ran into the living room and returned with a soggy tennis ball that she dropped at Davey's feet.

"In a minute, Faith," I said. Tail wagging, the puppy hopefully nudged the ball my way. I kicked and sent it flying into the dining room. Paws scrambling for purchase on the linoleum floor, Faith followed.

"Davey, I have something important to tell you."

He stuffed a whole cookie into his mouth. "What?"

"You know how your daddy had to go away when you

were still a baby, even though he loved you very much. Right?"

"Sure." He washed the cookie down with a swig of milk. "You're not going to tell that story again, are you?"

"No. Not exactly. But it turns out . . ." Stop waffling, I thought. At this rate, I'd never get the words out. "I heard from your father the other night. He's coming to visit us this weekend."

"He's coming to see me?" Everything he was feeling—delight, excitement, wonder—it was all there in his voice. Just the expression on his face was enough to break my heart.

"Yes honey, he's coming to see you—"

"Hooray!" Davey leapt up and spun in an excited circle. "When will he be here?"

When we'd gotten home from school Wednesday, there'd been a message on the machine. Bob knew I worked. He should have realized there'd be no chance of reaching me at home during the day.

"He's coming tomorrow, late in the afternoon."

"Tomorrow?" Davey yelped. Faith came flying back into the kitchen to see what all the fuss was about. He grabbed the puppy around the neck and the two of them went down on the floor in a heap. "Did you hear that? My daddy's coming home!"

"Honey," I said quietly. "It's just a visit—"

"My daddy's coming home!"

"He wants to see you Davey, and he wants to get to know you, but he's not going to be able to stay—"

"I'm going to have a real daddy again!"

Faith barked as if she understood. Giggling, Davey

whispered something in her ear. No doubt they were already making plans for Bob's arrival.

Maybe I should have insisted that Davey listen to what I was trying to say, but I didn't. Unfortunately, I imagined his bubble would burst soon enough.

Damn.

⌒✳ *Ten* ✳⌒

Sam came over later that evening. Davey and Faith greeted him at the door with their usual exuberance.

"Guess what?" my son demanded, before Sam had even had a chance to take off his coat.

"What?"

"My daddy's coming to our house tomorrow. He called on the phone and everything!"

Sam hunkered down until he and Davey were at eye level. "That's pretty exciting, isn't it?"

"Sure thing!" cried Davey. "Do you think he'll bring me a toy?"

"I don't know. He might."

Davey grinned slyly. "Did you bring me a toy?"

"Enough," I said, grasping my son by the shoulders. "You have plenty of toys. You don't need to be begging for any more from our guests. Why don't you take Faith out to the kitchen? Her food's ready, and you can put it on the floor for her."

"Okay. Come on, Faith." The two of them headed full-speed down the hall. It was already seven o'clock. I wondered if their batteries were going to run down any time soon.

Sam enfolded me in a hug. "A guest? Is that all I am?"

"A welcome guest?" I cocked one brow and insinuated my body close along the length of Sam's, hips pressing firmly to his. "A *very* welcome guest?"

"That's better." He chuckled softly, his fingers tangling in my hair.

My body felt as though it were floating, filled with millions of tiny champagne bubbles. I slipped my hands inside Sam's sheepskin jacket and circled them around his waist. Then I tipped my face up and lost myself in his kiss.

"Gross," said Davey.

We pulled apart slowly.

My son was standing beside us, hands on his hips. "Are you going to kiss daddy, too?"

I felt Sam start, ever so slightly; but my gaze was trained on Davey. "No honey. Your daddy and I are divorced, remember?"

"You're not married to Sam, and you're kissing him."

Things were so much easier when he was three. Come to think of it, they were even easier before he could talk at all.

"Kissing's fun," said Sam. He stepped back, shrugged out of his coat and threw it over the banister, then held out a hand. Davey slipped his much smaller one inside. "People like to do it whether they're married or not. But first they have to be really good friends."

Together, they headed off toward the kitchen. "What's your mom cooking us for dinner?"

"Chicken. It's in the oven. But there isn't any stuffing."

"No stuffing?" Sam asked gravely. "What should we do?"

Did they want to hear from me, these two males who were the most important part of my life? I supposed not. Otherwise, I might have mentioned that I'd all but witnessed a murder less than twenty-four hours earlier, spent a full day in school, broken the news to Davey about his father's imminent arrival, then felt guilty enough to take him and Faith for a walk around the neighborhood.

They were lucky to be getting chicken, much less stuffing.

"Try complaining," I grumbled under my breath, trailing along after them. "Just try it."

"Smells great," Sam said when I reached the kitchen. He was getting two beers out of the refrigerator and his grin told me he knew exactly what I was thinking. "I hope you haven't worked too hard."

"I'll survive."

Faith's food bowl had been licked clean and she was standing by the back door. While I let her out, Sam dug around in the cabinet for glasses, popped the tops on the beers and poured. Davey had wandered back into the living room where he was building a city out of Legos.

"So tomorrow's the big day?"

"Apparently so." I took the glass Sam offered and sat down at the butcher block table. "Davey's been wild ever since he found out."

"This is a big deal for him."

He sounded as though he was feeling his way, trying to say what he thought I wanted to hear. That irritated me. As well as we knew each other, did he really think I needed to be coddled that way?

"Of course it's a big deal. I just wish I had a better idea what Bob had in mind. He said he wants to get to know his son, but after all this time, why now?"

"You'll find out tomorrow."

"I guess."

"Do you want me to be here?" His hand reached across the table and covered mine. "I'm good at moral support."

All right, maybe a little coddling wasn't a bad thing. I squeezed his fingers gratefully. "I know you are. And I appreciate the offer. But I think this is something Bob and I had better figure out for ourselves."

"Whatever you think is best. But if you change your mind, let me know."

"Will I be calling you?" I asked in a sultry tone. "Or nudging you?"

Sam grinned. Tiny lines radiated outward from those oh-so-blue eyes. "Did I mention I've been looking into getting a pet-sitter who could spend the night with my dogs?"

"No, you didn't." I thought for a moment. The idea had definite merit. And it gave me something to look forward to. "Keep me posted."

"I will," said Sam. "Believe me."

Stuffing or no, the chicken was a success. I'm not a great cook, but I have a repertoire of half a dozen meals that I've cooked so many times, I could probably prepare them blindfolded. Sam *is* a great cook. He's also very diplomatic. So far, he's eaten everything I've put in front of him.

I waited until Davey was in bed—bathed, pajamaed, and accompanied by his favorite Standard Poodle puppy—before bringing up the subject of Monica Freedman's murder. I can't protect my son from everything, but he doesn't have to be privy to a discussion of violence that took place almost in his backyard.

Sam lives in Redding, which is in northern Fairfield County. There isn't a lot of major crime in this area, and the event had made his morning paper. Aside from telling him that Aunt Peg and I had been there, however, there wasn't much I could add to what he already knew.

We wrapped up the conversation quickly. With Davey asleep, Sam and I had better things to do.

Aunt Peg called first thing Saturday morning. Sam, having perfected his middle of the night vanishing act, was long gone by then. Peg has a soft spot in her heart for Sam. She's determined to nurture our relationship like a rare violet she's trying to coax into bloom. I could have sworn she was disappointed that he hadn't picked up the phone.

"I thought you were seeing Sam last night," she said.

"I did."

"And you're not feeding him breakfast . . . ?" Aunt Peg let the suggestion dangle. Where subtlety was concerned, she and *Geraldo* had a lot in common.

"And who would have been taking care of his Poodles?"

That shut her up. Like Peg, Sam's hobby is breeding Standard Poodles. She would never have left her own dogs unattended overnight, and could fully understand why Sam wouldn't either. I never even had to mention the fact that with Bob about to reappear, I'd decided that the less change there was in other areas of Davey's life, the better.

"Speaking of Sam," I said. "How come you haven't been dragging him along to these Belle Haven meetings?"

"Sam's a very busy man. He knows the club's there. When he's ready, he'll take steps to join."

Well that made me feel about two years old. As if she trusted Sam to make decisions about his own life, but not me. I don't usually sulk. In fact, in most situations I'd say I'm much too mature for behavior like that. But sometimes Aunt Peg has a way of bringing out the worst in me.

"Listen!" she said cheerfully. "I've got a great idea."

If there's one thing worse than sulking, it's having nobody notice.

"Why don't you and Davey come along to the Rockland show today? It's not far, just across the Tappan Zee Bridge. I'm showing Hope," she added as an incentive.

Hope was Faith's litter sister. Since Aunt Peg knew what she was doing, her Standard Poodle puppy had more hair and was better trained than mine was. She was also being shown more. Faith wasn't entered again until the end of the month. In the meantime, I was delighted to have the chance to see her sister in the ring.

"Sure," I said, then stopped. "Oh wait. I forgot. Bob—"

"Is arriving late this afternoon. Isn't that what you said? Frankly, I can't think of anything worse than sitting home all day waiting for him."

Now that she mentioned it, neither could I. We made plans to meet in the grooming area, and I went off to get Davey dressed and break the news to Faith.

Aunt Peg has a theory about Standard Poodle puppies and dog shows. Because so much of the emphasis in the ring is on animation and showmanship, she feels it's vitally important that puppies never think of going to a show as anything but fun. Which means they're never simply thrown in the car and taken along for the ride.

Aunt Peg wanted Faith to think of dog shows as a special treat, an activity where most of the attention would center around her. Since that wasn't the case today, the puppy was staying home.

The Rockland County dog show is held in the field house at Rockland Community College. There's lots of room to park, and plenty of space inside for concession stands and large rings. A portion of the room was set aside for grooming. Even in a spacious facility like Rockland's the area was crammed with crates, exercise pens, and portable tables.

Davey's getting to be an old hand at going to dog shows. He used to point and stare at all the different breeds, and once tried to talk himself into ownership of an Old English Sheepdog. Now he's able to walk by even the wrinkly skinned Shar-Peis without comment. I hate to think that at the ripe old age of five, he might be getting jaded.

Exhibitors tend to cluster together by breed in the grooming area. That makes it easier to talk to your friends, and it was no surprise when we found Aunt Peg holding court in the middle of the Poodle section. I'd met many of the breeders and professional handlers the summer before when I was looking for Aunt Peg's missing stud dog; and since I'd started showing Faith, they'd accepted me as part of the group.

"Not showing your pretty puppy today?" asked Crawford Langley as Davey and I passed by on our way to Aunt Peg's set-up.

Crawford was a professional handler, once among the best in Poodles. Now getting older, with a career that was winding down, he still knew how to play the game just about better than anybody. He had several Standard Poodles out on top of tables, as well as a Maltese and three Papillons.

"No, I came to watch the rest of you work."

"Fine by me." Crawford smiled. "That's one less for me to beat."

Aunt Peg had her things set up in the next aisle over. I boosted Davey up on top of Hope's empty crate and opened the bag we'd brought with us, filled with things I hoped would keep him busy for the next several hours. I had let Davey do the packing. True to form, there were toy cars, picture books about cars, and a fire engine coloring book. At least he was consistent.

"Do you need any help?" I asked Aunt Peg, just to be polite. I couldn't imagine any dog show situation she wouldn't have well in hand.

"I'm fine." Hope was lying quietly on her side on the grooming table, while Aunt Peg line brushed through her coat with a pin brush. "If you ask me, Crawford's the one who could use some extra hands. His assistant's in the Yorkie ring and Papillons go in five minutes. How's he going to show all three at the same time?"

Crawford inclined his head slightly in our direction. "Do I hear the sound of someone volunteering to help?"

"Sure." I left Davey to his coloring book and what I hoped was Aunt Peg's watchful eye. "What do you need?"

"I've got two dogs in the Open class," said Crawford. "The older one only needs a major, so I doubled entered in case the numbers didn't make it. It turned out to be a major on the nose, so now I've got to show them both."

Nine months earlier, that all would have been gibberish to me. But now I knew just what he was talking about. Dogs who have not yet attained their championships are entered in shows for the purpose of accumulating points. Breed classes are divided by sex and points are won by beating others of the same sex.

Fifteen points makes a champion, with the proviso that along the way each dog must have two "major" wins; that is, it must defeat a substantial number of its peers at a single show. The number of dogs necessary to make a major varies from breed to breed and from one part of the country to another. Crawford hadn't intended to have to show two of his clients' dogs against each other, but the way the entries had turned out made it impossible for him to do anything else.

He looked over my shoulder and scanned the area. "I've got someone coming to handle the other dog. But if you could bring the bitch up to ringside for me, it would be a big help."

As he spoke, Alberta Kennedy came hurrying across the room. "Corgis ran late," she said breathlessly. "Am I in time?"

"Just made it. We're going up now." Crawford picked up the female Papillon and placed her carefully in my arms.

Bertie picked up one of the males. Her dress today was dove gray, high-necked, and fell to mid-calf. I'd have looked like a nun wearing it. Bertie looked like Miss America trying to go incognito.

Crawford, who picked up the third Pap and led our procession toward the ring, didn't spare her a glance. Considering he was gay, that wasn't surprising. But since

Bertie's obvious assets were lost on him, I figured either he had to be desperate to ask her to handle one of his dogs, or else she was good at what she did.

Standing ringside during the Open Dog class, I decided on the former. Bertie was perfectly competent, but with none of the spark that set the truly talented handlers apart. Indeed, from my vantage point, her attention seemed centered less on her dog than on someone standing outside the ring.

There were five dogs in the class and Crawford's Papillon was quickly moved to the head of the line. The judge glanced at Bertie's entry and she favored him with a dazzling smile. The next thing I knew, her Papillon was standing second.

Whatever works, I thought.

Bertie cast a surreptitious glance over her shoulder and I homed in on whom she was looking at. Cy Rubicov was standing ringside, watching the judging.

One thing I've discovered about dog shows: sometimes there's a surprising amount to be learned just by keeping your eyes and ears open. Some people might call that nosiness. I think of it as practical—kind of along the same lines as Bertie wearing a push-up bra.

We were both just making the most of the gifts God gave us.

∽❖ *Eleven* ❖∽

Crawford's Papillon went on to win the Open class. He stayed in the ring to vie with the winners of the other dog classes for the title of Winners Dog and the points that went with it. That accomplished, Crawford came out and exchanged the dog for the bitch I was holding.

"I won't win again," he said. "Winners Dog was my piece for the day. But he needs to go back in for Best of Breed, so stay close, okay?"

I nodded, and Crawford hurried back into the ring.

With the dog classes over, Bertie's duties were finished. The Papillon she'd handled for Crawford had gone Reserve, and wouldn't be needed for further judging. If she wished, she could return the dog to Crawford's set-up and be on her way.

As I waited by the gate, however, I saw that Bertie was in no hurry to leave. Cradling the little dog in her arms, she'd sidled through the crowd at ringside and was now engaged in animated conversation with Cy Rubicov.

As her height topped his by several inches, Bertie was

leaning forward ever so slightly to bring herself down to Cy's level. The fact that the move pressed her breasts together and thrust them forward was, I'm sure, lost on nobody. Her long fingers, with their brightly polished nails, stroked the toy dog's silky hair.

I was too far away to hear what they were saying, but the body language was eloquent. Cy was rocking back on his heels, chest puffed out, a broad smile on his face—a man supremely aware that the best looking woman at ringside was with him. I remembered Aunt Peg telling me that Cy backed a lot of top winning dogs, among them a Dalmatian being handled by Crawford Langley, and wondered if it was a coincidence that Bertie had made herself available to help out.

As Crawford had predicted, he quickly lost with the bitch. We switched Paps at the gate, and he went back in the ring to show the dog for BOB. When I looked back to where Cy and Bertie had been, only the handler remained. She was staring off into the distance, a distracted frown on her face.

Tucking the bitch under my arm, I went to stand beside her. "Must be tough," I said.

"Hmm?"

With Cy around, Bertie had sparkled; now the wattage was turned way down. She'd been the first person to reach Monica after me. I wondered if she'd simply been running in that direction, as I had. Or could she have been with Monica, wielded the rock and run, then doubled back to see what would happen next?

"Drumming up new clients," I said. "It must be tough trying to build a business."

"I do all right," Bertie said carefully. "I don't have a big string yet, but then I don't take just any dog. Some handlers don't mind being seen in the ring with all kinds of garbage, as long as they get paid. That's not for me."

"I guess that's why getting the right kind of client is so important."

"It's everything. A good dog, with the right kind of money behind it, is a big winner. Unfortunately, there aren't nearly enough of those to go around."

"Good dogs, or big money clients?"

"Both."

I imagined that Cy Rubicov, with his buying power, would qualify on both counts. Clearly, Bertie would love to have one of his dogs to show. I wondered how he felt about the prospect; and what, if anything, Monica Freedman might have known about their relationship.

"The other night when Monica was killed, I was near the road when the Beagles came by. I ran to the van from that direction. Where were you?"

"The next row of cars over." Bertie frowned. "I never saw the dogs at all. I just heard that infernal racket, and went over to tell Monica to shut them up."

"As you approached the van, did you see anyone else?"

"I saw you."

That was the truth, certainly. But I wondered if it was all of it.

"We came from two different directions," I said slowly. "The murder had just taken place. How do you suppose the murderer managed to slip away so quickly without anybody seeing him?"

"We were all questioned by the police," said Bertie. "If I'd seen anything, I'd have told them."

"The police weren't there. But we were. All of us, members of the Belle Haven Kennel Club, were right there when it happened."

"You're not a club member." She lifted one manicured hand to flip her hair back over her shoulder. "Is that why you're so interested in pinning this on someone who is?"

"I'm not trying to pin anything on anybody—"

"Sharon told me you solved a murder before."

"I guess I did."

"So now you think you're going to solve this one?" There was no mistaking the sarcasm in her tone.

"Look," I said. "What I told you a minute ago is true. We were all there. Fourteen of us, including Monica. Now she's dead. Doesn't that make you curious about what the rest of us were up to?"

"Not at all. Nobody liked Monica much. You probably won't find even one club member who's sorry she's gone. Besides, it has nothing to do with me. And I try not to worry about things that don't concern me." Her lips lifted in a smile that was smooth and vacuous. "Wouldn't want to get wrinkles, you know."

Right. The Barbie doll act might work with some people, but I'd already glimpsed the intelligence that lay beneath the surface. It was interesting, though, that Bertie thought she had to try. What did she know about Monica's death that she felt she needed to hide?

"All done." Crawford came up behind us. The third Papillon was under his arm, the blue and white striped ribbon for Best of Winners in his hand. "Ladies, thank you for your help."

"Any time," Bertie purred.

She deposited the dog she was holding into the crook

of his other arm. As Bertie headed off toward the next ring, Crawford and I started back to the grooming area.

"I met Bertie the other night at a kennel club meeting," I said, falling into step beside him.

Crawford grunted softly under his breath.

"She seems very nice."

This time he didn't bother to grunt.

"Is she is good handler?"

His gaze shifted in my direction. "Why do you want to know?"

"Just curious." I tried to inject the enthusiasm of the eager novice into my voice.

Judging by the look on Crawford's face, he wasn't buying it. He'd been involved with dogs for more than three decades, and by now he knew where all the important skeletons were buried. He also knew enough not to gossip with eager novices.

"Bertie still has a few things to learn. But she's young yet. She'll get there."

I'd met more than one new handler who'd sought to establish himself by taking other handlers' clients. If that was the case with Bertie, Crawford certainly didn't seem worried. Then again, I'd seen the way Bertie acted around him—all sweetness and innocence. I hoped for his sake he'd taken the time to peer beneath the glossy exterior.

"You're back!" Davey cried, as we came into view.

I slipped the Pap into the crate Crawford indicated and hurried back to Aunt Peg's set up. Not long ago, perching Davey on top of a high Standard Poodle sized crate had been enough to keep him in one place. Now he set aside his coloring book, eyed the distance to the ground, and launched himself over the edge.

I leapt to catch him and missed by about a foot. Luckily there was no crunch of broken bones when he landed in a heap on the hard floor. Davey scrambled quickly to his feet.

"Lunch time!" he announced.

I checked my watch. "It's ten-thirty."

"It can't be ten-thirty. We've been here for *hours.*"

Half an hour. Maximum. But then I'd already learned that my five year old son's perception of time and mine were vastly different. I think he was living his life in dog years.

Aunt Peg had Hope lying on the grooming table with her left side—the side that would face the judge in the ring—facing upward, which meant she was almost finished brushing. "You could try the food concession," she said. "I bet they have doughnuts."

"Yea!" cried Davey. "I want jelly!"

Just that quickly, without even being consulted, I was outvoted. I slipped my hand firmly over Davey's and we set out.

The concession booths ran along the two opposite sides of the building. Davey and I cut across the middle of the big room, past rings filled with Bulldogs, Irish Setters, and then at the far end, Beagles. I found myself slowing, then stopping all together, despite Davey's efforts to drag me on.

Beagles, like Poodles, come in more than one variety and are divided by size. In their case, the two classifications are thirteen inch and fifteen inch, with the height being measured at the withers.

The fifteen inch Beagles were in the ring, being judged

by a plump woman with neat, gray streaked hair and a firm hand on a dog. None of these Beagles pulled at their leashes, and there wasn't a howl to be heard. Nonetheless, I couldn't help being reminded of Monica's dogs, probably the last thing she'd seen before the killer snuck up behind her and snuffed out her life.

"It makes you think, doesn't it?"

I looked up and found Mark Romano standing next to me. His shoulders were slumped; his hands, shoved in his pockets. The most interesting thing about his bland features was his frown. "I can't seem to stop thinking about what happened to Monica. The funeral's tomorrow, did you hear?"

"No, I hadn't. I didn't really know Monica. I'd just met her briefly at the last two club meetings."

Mark nodded. "Speaking of the club, I hope someone's made arrangements to send flowers. Monica was our corresponding secretary. In the past, that would have been her job."

Davey gave my arm a sudden yank. "Mommy, come on! It's time to go."

"My son," I said, introducing him to Mark. "His manners could be better."

"What a fine young man," said Mark.

"A *hungry* young man," Davey stated rudely, giving another yank for good measure.

If I hadn't known he would disappear, I'd have been tempted to let go. As it was, I settled for pulling him back to my side a little harder than was strictly necessary. He hung on my arm like a forty pound dead weight.

"About the flowers, maybe my Aunt Peg would know.

I know she and Monica split the secretary job between them. She might have sent an arrangement on behalf of the club."

"I hope so," Mark said. "It would look terrible if we neglected to send our condolences."

"I'll check into it—"

Davey's foot trod heavily on mine, and I yelped.

"Are you all right?" Mark asked solicitously.

I nodded, not trusting myself to speak.

"Goodbye," my son said loudly. "Nice meeting you."

Fine time to remember the social niceties.

"Davey!" With that much warning in my tone, he should have backed down. He didn't.

"But I'm hungry!" he wailed. "You said I could get a doughnut!"

"All right, we're going. In one minute." I looked at Mark apologetically. "Do you have kids?"

"Not yet," he said. "We're still hoping."

Probably with less enthusiasm after today's exposure.

Mark pointed out where he and Penny were set up in the grooming area and I promised to find out about the flowers and get back to him. Dobermans weren't going to be judged until afternoon, so there was plenty of time.

I wasted my breath lecturing Davey about his behavior the rest of the way to the food concession stand. A better mother than I might have enforced her point by canceling the trip for doughnuts all together. But then I'd have to explain to Aunt Peg why she was going hungry, too.

Sometimes this business of parenting is enough to make you nuts.

❧❋ *Twelve* ❋❧

We bought half a dozen assorted doughnuts and a king-sized coffee for me. I justified the whole thing by deciding that life was just too short to spend arguing.

Back at the set-up, Aunt Peg had Hope on her feet. The puppy was standing on the table while Peg scissored her coat, resetting the lines of the trim and smoothing out the finish. This was one of those things that looked deceptively easy, but took years of practice to truly master.

Aunt Peg has put in the time. When she was finished with Hope, the puppy looked as though she'd been created from blown glass. So far, my novice attempts at scissoring Faith have ended up looking more like papier-mâché.

When Aunt Peg took a break from her preparations and sat down with a doughnut, I asked her whether she'd arranged to send flowers to Monica's funeral.

Mouth full, she settled for a nod.

"Mark Romano was wondering. He said the funeral's tomorrow."

"That's right. Lydia called me. The club will have to elect another corresponding secretary, but in the meantime I've agreed to fill in."

I glanced around to see what Davey was up to. Placated by sugar, he'd clambered back up on top of Hope's metal crate and was coloring happily in his book.

"Did you ever have a chance to talk to the police?" I asked in a low tone.

"For all the good it did me," Aunt Peg sniffed. "They told me they were pursuing various avenues of investigation. As if any fool couldn't figure that out."

"What about the rock Cy and Bertie saw? Did you at least find out if that's what killed Monica?"

"It was," Aunt Peg confirmed. "Which narrows down the field not a whit. Presumably it was lying near the parking lot. Any one of us could have picked it up."

"It is interesting, though. It means the murder had to have been a spontaneous act. Someone saw his chance and took it."

Aunt Peg nodded. "Think back to the meeting that night. I wonder if something happened that we've overlooked, maybe something that could have set the murderer off."

"Monica argued with Joanne."

"Monica argued with everybody. That was nothing new. And we've already established that all of us had the means. What we need to do is narrow down motive and opportunity."

No small task. But Aunt Peg didn't seem too perturbed. She's always enjoyed a challenge. Not that she was about to let this one get in the way of showing her puppy.

She stood up, brushed a few crumbs off the front of her

apron, and dug around in her tack box for the equipment she'd need to put in Hope's top-knot: comb, spray bottle, knitting needle for parting the hair, and a baggie filled with tiny round black rubber bands. "Time to get back to work. Come hold her head, would you?"

Hope knew what was coming next. Lying on the table, she rested her muzzle in the palm of my hand while Aunt Peg unfastened the big, loose top-knots she wore for comfort at home, then banded the hair on her head into smaller, tighter ones that would look better in the ring. When they were in, Peg used her fingers to pull the front top-knot forward, creating a small bubble of hair over the puppy's eyes.

She leaned back to study her handiwork. "That will do. How would you like to go up to the ring and get my armband?"

Going to a dog show with Aunt Peg was somewhat akin to signing up to herd cattle on your vacation. It usually turned out to be more work than play.

"Sure. Is there time for me to stop by and see Mark?"

"Just about." Aunt Peg checked her watch. "I'll be spraying up. Don't dawdle."

Spraying up referred to putting hair spray in the hair on the Poodle's head and back of the neck in order to make it stand up and look as plush and full as possible. Another Poodle technique that sounded a great deal easier in theory than it turned out to be in practice.

At the Poodle ring, I gave Hope's name and picked up Aunt Peg's numbered armband. Then I skirted back through the grooming area. Mark's set-up was just where he'd said it would be. There were two big wire crates; one with a black Doberman Pinscher asleep inside. The other had a platform on top with a second Doberman lying on it.

Penny was holding a bowl of water up to the dog on the crate. She was dressed in a loose jumper that did nothing to flatter her slender frame, and her short hair looked as though it had been pushed into place with her fingers. Mark saw me coming and waved.

"I checked with Peg," I said as I drew near.

"Peg who?" Penny asked, looking at me suspiciously.

"Honey, you remember Melanie, don't you? She's about to become a new member of Belle Haven."

Mark was stretching my credentials, but it didn't seem to matter. Penny was still staring as though she couldn't quite place me. I turned to her husband.

"Peg says Lydia asked her to act as corresponding secretary until the club can elect a replacement. She's already taken care of sending flowers."

"Good. I'm glad to hear it."

"Who are we sending flowers to?" Penny set down the water bowl, and came to join us. She ended up standing a good foot closer to me than I thought was necessary. I could smell the liquor on her breath.

"Monica Freedman," I said, angling myself back. "The flowers are for her funeral."

"Oh, yes." Penny frowned. "Of course."

One thing I'd learned about dog people, the way to their hearts was through their pets. I stepped around Penny and approached the Doberman on the crate. "May I?"

"Certainly," said Mark. "Ben loves the attention."

I held out my hand and was politely sniffed. I ran my fingers down the Doberman's long, smooth neck, feeling solid muscle beneath. Talk about low body fat.

"He's beautiful."

"Thank you." Penny moved to stand beside me, cradling the dog's head in her arms. "You're just a big baby, aren't you?" She cooed the words an inch from his nose, but Ben didn't seem to mind. His stumpy tail was wagging like mad.

"You should have brought Davey with you," Mark said, gazing at his wife. "Penny loves children."

"Davey?" asked Penny.

"My son. He's five."

"And very sure of his opinions," said Mark. "They're wonderful at that age."

"They're wonderful at any age," said Penny.

It didn't take a genius to figure out that she wasn't a mother.

"I was wondering if I could ask you both something. The other night after the meeting, where were you when Monica's Beagles got loose?"

"I was just coming out of the restaurant," said Mark. "One of them came flying by. I heard everybody yelling and grabbed him."

"The two of you were together?"

"No, not then." Penny left the dog, picked up a catalogue that was lying on a chair and consulted the judging schedule.

"I'd left my scarf," Mark explained. "And I had to go back to get it. Penny went on ahead. She was going to get the car and drive around to meet me at the entrance."

"Except I didn't," said Penny. "I heard all the commotion and I was trying to figure out what was going on."

If she'd had as much to drink that night as she had today, it was no wonder she was baffled, I thought snidely.

"Then the waitress found my scarf and came running out after me," said Mark. "So I didn't have to go back upstairs after all. When I came out, there was the Beagle running like the devil and baying his little heart out."

"So neither of you was near Monica's van?"

Mark and Penny both shook their heads.

"Don't worry," said Mark. "The police were there. They'll figure out who did it."

Except that the police had arrived after the fact. Fourteen of us had been there at the moment the murder occurred. Just like Aunt Peg said, it all came down to means, motive, and opportunity. Only one of us had had all three.

By the time I got back to Aunt Peg, she had Hope ready to go. I rolled the rubber band up her arm and slipped the armband underneath. Davey helped us clear a path through the spectators, so that the puppy's carefully coifed hairdo arrived at the ring intact.

Hope won the Puppy class. As she was ten months old and in full bloom I thought she might have a shot at the points. Evidently Aunt Peg did, too. She did everything she could think of to draw the judge's attention her puppy's way, but Winners Bitch went to the white who had won the Open class, handled by a pro named Barry Turk.

When it comes to the competition at dog shows, Aunt Peg is usually pretty fair. But she doesn't like being beaten by a Poodle that she doesn't think is as good as the one she brought. She came out of the ring looking decidedly huffy and walked in silence back to the set-up.

She hopped Hope back up on the grooming table and began fishing around in her tack box. She'd spent more than an hour scissoring, putting in a topknot, and spraying up. Now a further chunk of time would be needed to undo everything she'd put together.

Davey looked at Aunt Peg, getting out brushes and combs. Then he looked at me. He seemed to be weighing the chances that one of us might come up with something exciting for him to do. Clearly, it didn't look good.

"Now it's lunch time," he said.

"You just had doughnuts."

"That was *hours* ago."

One, maybe.

"I'm hungry again," said Davey.

I thought teenagers were supposed to be the ones who ate everything in sight. Davey was only five. I hated to think what life was going to be like when he worked his way up to full capacity consumption.

"Good idea," said Aunt Peg, putting down her brush. She gave Hope a pat on the head and left her lying on the table. "I could use a break. Let's go eat."

Unless I was mistaken, she'd been munching on doughnuts, too. As for me, I'd had low-fat cereal and skim milk for breakfast. Just in case you were wondering.

"Will Hope be all right on the table?" I asked.

"Fine. She's table trained. Nearly all Poodles are."

The jibe struck home as Aunt Peg had known it would. Poodles spend a lot of time at the shows being groomed on their tables, and they are never tied in place as many of the other breeds are. Hope seemed to understand the need to stay put without even being told. I was still working on instilling the same level of obedience in Faith.

"Lunch it is," I said, happy to change the subject.

As at many dog shows, our culinary choices were limited: hot dog, hamburger, meatball sub. Davey angled for a meatball sub and ended up with a hamburger. Aunt Peg and I opted for the same. The first bite tasted like hot and greasy cardboard. Little ketchup packets provided the flavor we'd been missing, and we headed back to the set-up as we ate. No wonder so few of the truly great chefs are American.

On the way, we passed the ring where Yorkshire Terriers were being judged. Aunt Peg paused, and Davey and I stopped with her. The little blue and tan dogs were adorable, with tiny bows on top of their heads and hair so long it trailed on the ground. Even so, if Aunt Peg had an interest in Yorkies, this was the first I'd heard of it.

"What are we looking at?" I asked, when a minute went by and she still hadn't moved on.

"Louis."

I scanned the faces of the handlers quickly. "Where?"

She lowered her voice, proper ringside etiquette. "He's judging."

So he was. I moved in closer so that I could whisper too. "How can he be judging already? I thought you said he just applied for his license."

"It must be a sweeps." She checked the schedule posted by the gate and nodded. "Licensed judges are required for the breed competition where points are awarded. But Yorkies are having a specialty today, so there's also a sweepstakes, which is a fun competition for young dogs. The specialty club has some leeway on who judges and it's not unusual for a prominent breeder to be asked."

I glanced back in the ring. Louis LaPlante looked much the same as he had at the Belle Haven meetings: tweed jacket, creased pants, beard neatly trimmed. A small Yorkie was trotting away from him on the diagonal mat, and he studied the puppy's movement with great gravity of expression.

"Is Louis a very prominent breeder?"

"I should say so. He and Sharon have been in Yorkies for at least twenty years. Together, they've bred more than forty champions."

That was a big achievement. I looked around, scanning the ringside. Sharon was sitting near the gate in a canvas folding chair with the words "LouShar Yorkies" stenciled across the back. Like many exhibitors, the LaPlantes had apparently created a kennel name by combining syllables from their own names. As Louis arranged the puppies in the order he wanted them and awarded the ribbons, his wife nodded in approval.

"What about Sharon?" I asked.

"What about her?"

"If she and Louis have been breeding together for all that time, presumably she's as knowledgeable as he is. Doesn't she want to judge, too?"

"You know," Aunt Peg said thoughtfully. "I have no idea. Judging is the sort of intellectual exercise that appeals a great deal to some people and not at all to others. Louis has always seemed to be the brains of that pair. Not that Sharon might not be smart, I really don't know her well enough to say one way or the other. But she's always played the supporting role."

"She certainly supported him at the meeting when he had to explain about the missing checks."

"Precisely. You get the impression that whatever Louis is doing, you'll always find Sharon standing two steps behind. She's the perfect corporate wife—good at small talk and totally non-controversial. Both of them are highly respected. Which makes this business about the dinner checks seem all the odder."

She slanted me a look. "By the way, I thought you were going to look into that."

I'd been hoping she wouldn't remember. "I was thinking about it. Then Monica's murder put the whole thing right out of my mind."

"Maybe they're connected," Aunt Peg said hopefully. "Then you could solve both problems at once."

Her belief in my abilities was gratifying. It was also self-serving, manipulative and hopelessly naive. But it had the intended effect. As long as she kept prodding me, I'd keep asking questions.

When we got back to the set-up, Aunt Peg decided to band Hope's ears, take her home and undo the rest there. Davey and I helped her pack up her car and we all left.

It was just as well we hadn't made a day of it at the dog show. Bob had said to expect him in the late afternoon; but as usual, his timing was off.

When we pulled into the driveway, there was already a car there. A cherry red Trans-Am, with an irate ex-husband leaning against the hood.

❧❀ *Thirteen* ❀❧

He hadn't changed much.

He still had the same lanky build and casual grace I'd always admired. And I remembered those dark brown eyes, fringed by a row of even darker lashes. The laugh lines were new, creasing either side of his mouth. On him, they looked good.

Bob had been leaning stiff-legged against the hood of his car, booted feet crossed at the ankles, arms similarly crossed over his chest. You didn't have to be a psychologist to read those signals. As the Volvo coasted to a stop, he levered himself up.

Davey had been staring with rapt fascination at the bright red Trans-Am. Now he seemed to notice Bob for the first time. "Wow," he said. "Who's that?"

"He's your father."

Silence. I'd expected screaming. Judging by the response I'd gotten earlier, I'd thought Davey would launch himself from the car and wrap his arms around Bob's legs. But now that the time had finally come to meet his father, my son was feeling shy.

"Let's get out," I said.

But Bob was already there. He opened Davey's door and leaned his head inside. I saw him start to reach for his son, then hesitate. If I wasn't such a cynic, I'd have sworn there were tears in his eyes.

"Davey?" He swallowed heavily. "I'm your Dad."

"I know." Davey's tone was matter-of-fact, but he still hadn't moved.

"Do I get a hug?"

Davey thought about that. He looked away and made a show of unfastening his seat belt. Then, when Bob withdrew, Davey climbed past him and out of the car. Standing beside his father, he looked up.

"You're pretty tall," he said.

"So are you." Bob knelt beside him and held out his arms. "How about that hug?"

Decision made, Davey threw himself forward. An embrace like that would have knocked me over, but Bob stood firm. He wrapped his arms around my son—around his son—and held on tight.

I got out and slammed my car door. Just for effect.

The two of them broke apart. Bob walked over and fished through a worn canvas back-pack he'd left sitting on the ground.

"Look what I brought." He held out a shiny toy car that looked much like the Trans-Am sitting in the driveway. "Do you like cars?"

"Wow!" cried Davey, snatching it away. In seconds, he was zooming it down the driveway.

I watched, not happily. It was flat out bribery. Not only that, but it was working.

Inside the house, Faith was jumping on the front door, barking to be let out. As Davey came zooming back, he heard her, too. "Hey!" he cried. "We have a dog, a real live Standard Poodle. Want to see?"

"Sure." Bob grinned. "Where is he?"

"It's a she, and her name is Faith. She's in the house."

"Here Davey." I handed him the keys. "Why don't you let her out for a run in the backyard first? Bob and I . . . Your father and I will be along in a minute."

"Okay!" Holding his new car carefully, Davey snatched the key-ring and ran for the steps.

That left the two of us. Standing there. Staring at each other. It wasn't until that moment that I realized that on some level, I'd been half afraid that there'd still be some sort of a spark.

There wasn't. I held out my hand. "Hi, Bob."

"Mel!"

He ignored my outstretched hand. Two long steps was all it took and I found myself wrapped in Bob's arms just as Davey had been. Maybe with his convenient memory, my ex-husband had forgotten how we parted, but I certainly hadn't. I stood stiffly until he let me go.

"Yes, well . . ." He stepped back awkwardly. "It's been a long time."

"Years," I said succinctly.

To my surprise, Bob had the grace to blush. I felt myself softening. "How did you know about the toy car?" I asked.

"What do you mean?"

"Davey loves cars. You brought him his favorite thing."

"Lucky guess," Bob said, shrugging. "I was nuts about them when I was his age."

Father and son. Maybe even after all this time apart, the bond was stronger than I had guessed. Or cared to admit.

An uncomfortable silence fell. We were on my turf. I figured that meant I didn't have to break it.

Left to his own devices, Bob cast around and settled on the first thing he saw. "Don't tell me you're still driving this old heap." He patted the Volvo's worn gray fender. "You got that car when you were in college and it wasn't new then."

I knew he was fumbling. A nicer ex-wife would have helped him out. Maybe one who hadn't been abandoned with a ten month old child.

"As opposed to what?" I let my gaze drift in the direction of his shiny sports car. "Something like that, maybe?"

He swallowed and I knew he saw the trap coming. It still didn't stop him from putting his foot in it. "Well, yeah."

"Cars like that cost money, Bob." I smiled sweetly. "So does food. Sometimes it's all a matter of priorities."

"Give me a break."

He looked up at the small cape behind me, yellow with green shutters. They were white when he lived here, but I'd since taken them down and repainted them. I'd also planted a new row of rhododendron bushes out front. Neither improvement totally disguised the fact that the house itself needed painting and the driveway was beginning to crack.

"I left you the house," said Bob, working hard to sound like an aggrieved good Samaritan.

"You left me the mortgage."

"You had a job."

"Part-time."

"And a graduate degree. You could have taught."

"I *do* teach. That's why we're not out on the street."

Bob frowned, pulling his denim jacket more tightly around him. It didn't look as though it would offer much warmth. "Look, I didn't come here to fight, okay?"

"Maybe we have to get the fighting out of the way first. Maybe after that I'll be able to be civil."

"Jeez Mel. Do we have to go back over all that? It's been four years."

"Did you think I'd forget how you left me?"

"Maybe I just hoped you'd be over it by now." Bob sighed. "Look, do you mind if we continue this inside? I'm freezing out here."

I came around and closed Davey's door. The anger was fading, I could feel it draining away. Bob was right, what had happened was in the past. It belonged to a totally different part of my life, one I was happy to have left behind.

"Sure, let's go in. But I don't want to argue in front of Davey."

"Suits me fine." Bob paused on the walk so I could precede him to the door. "He looks like a good kid, Mel."

"He's a great kid. The best."

"You've done a good job."

"In spite of—" Hand on the door knob, I stopped. Put it behind you, I told myself firmly. I looked back and gave Bob a small smile. "Yes, I have. Thanks."

On that note of cautious rapprochement, we found Davey and Faith in the kitchen. The new toy car was on the counter. The back door was sitting open so I guessed the puppy had already been out. Davey was pouring himself a glass of milk and they seemed to be sharing a box of shortbread cookies.

Faith takes this guard dog business very seriously. She took one look at Bob, a stranger in her house, and leapt toward him, barking ferociously.

"Good God!" Bob stumbled backward. "That's not a Poodle. That's a bear!"

I looped my arms around Faith's neck and caught her mid-pounce. "It's really mostly hair. And she's very friendly once you get to know her."

Bob righted himself in the doorway, trying to look nonchalant, as if an oversized Poodle puppy hadn't just scared him off his feet. He stared at Faith, who was now sniffing his legs.

"Do you realize she's wearing earrings?"

"Yes." Like I hadn't heard that before.

"Ear wraps," Davey said importantly. Aunt Peg must have been teaching this child more than I'd realized. "They're for keeping the hair out of the way. Faith's my dog. Isn't she great?"

"Great." Bob smiled at his son.

"You couldn't have gotten him a German Shepherd?" he mouthed at me, over Davey's head.

"Trust me," I said. "You had to be there."

Bob glanced at the refrigerator. "Do you suppose . . . ? I got up in Pennsylvania this morning and drove straight through. Is there any chance you could make me a sandwich?"

"Not much," I said. Fostering domestic independence in the male half of the population had begun to seem important to me lately. Probably because I was raising a male who seemed to think that his every wish should be catered to. "But you can help yourself. I'm pretty sure there's some turkey and swiss."

As soon as the words were out, I regretted them. Turkey and swiss. Bob's favorite. Now he'd think I'd remembered that on purpose; when it was really just a fluke, fate's way of having a good laugh at my expense.

Bob dug around in the refrigerator, then laid the supplies he'd found on the counter. "Bread," he muttered, crossing the kitchen and pulling open the right drawer. I cringed inwardly at his familiarity. Too bad I was such a creature of habit. It would have been nice to see him fumble around. Instead, getting out a plate, silverware, and a napkin to go with it, Bob looked right at home.

"Hey!" cried Davey. "How come you know where everything is?"

Bob slathered a heavy coating of mayo onto a slice of bread. "I used to live here."

"When I was a baby," Davey prompted.

Bob nodded.

"When I was only this big." Davey held his hands about a foot apart.

Piling turkey onto the bread, Bob nodded again.

"You used to be my daddy. Then you went away."

Bob stopped what he was doing and turned to face his son. "You're right, I did."

"Mommy said you had to go."

Bob spared me a glance, then hunkered down in front of his son. "At the time I thought I did."

"Why?"

"Because I was confused. Because I was scared. Because

suddenly it seemed as though my whole life was rushing by and I was just standing there watching it."

I wasn't sure Davey would grasp all that, and he didn't. Instead he walked over to the counter and picked up his new car. Then he looked at Bob's sandwich and said, "Can I have a bite?"

"Sure, when it's ready." Bob stood up and went back to work.

I stared at my ex-husband's back, frowning. Davey may not have understood, but I did. Communication had never been a strong point between us. That was the first time I'd ever heard him voice the feelings that had driven him away. Having gone through something similar myself recently, I knew how he must have felt.

That didn't make me like what he had done, however. Nor did it make me forgive. But it did lessen the hurt, just a little bit.

"You must be hungry." Bob had offered Davey half the sandwich and watched as his son bit off a piece a good deal larger than he could comfortably chew.

"We ate lunch at the dog show," Davey informed him, talking happily around his full mouth. "With Aunt Peg."

"Aunt who?"

"Do you remember my father's brother, Max?" I asked.

"Not really."

"He died last summer. Peg was his wife."

"She has Standard Poodles," said Davey. "A whole house full. And even more in a kennel out back."

"Standard Poodles as in . . ." He nodded in Faith's direction.

"You got it."

"Aunt Peg takes us to dog shows," Davey announced. "And she let me drive her car."

Bob and I both stared.

"She did not," I said.

"Did too." If he hadn't still been chewing, he might have stuck out his tongue.

"She sounds like an interesting woman," said Bob.

"She is."

I pulled out a chair at the kitchen table and sat down. "So, how long do you suppose you'll be staying in Connecticut?"

"How long?" Bob repeated. "Didn't I mention that?"

Something—intuition maybe—curled in the pit of my stomach. "Mention what?"

"I figured on a couple of weeks, or so. After that, I've got to be heading back. I guess I didn't get around to telling you. I'm getting married at the end of next month."

ᢒᢥ *Fourteen* ᢥᢒ

After that major bombshell was out of the way, the rest of the afternoon went remarkably smoothly.

Bob finished his lunch and let Davey take him for a tour of the house. I doubt that it looked much different than it had when he'd left; but Bob managed to comment with appreciation on each point of interest my son highlighted. Trailing along behind, I discovered that these included the back yard, the dining room table, and what was probably the largest toy car collection in the entire western world.

Davey had gotten over his initial shyness, but I noticed he hadn't gotten around to calling Bob "Dad" yet. Nor did he refer to him by name. For the time being, "hey" seemed to be serving as the attention-getter of choice. It wasn't as polite as I might have hoped for, but I liked the fact that Davey was dealing with things at his own speed.

Faith, meanwhile, was shamelessly easy. Having been slipped a piece of turkey from Bob's sandwich, she'd decided she'd made a new friend. When Bob and Davey went out back to throw a baseball around, she accompanied them happily. I stood at the kitchen sink and watched the three of them out the window. We could have been any happy suburban family sharing a quiet Saturday afternoon.

In the twilight zone, maybe.

Meanwhile I was fielding phone calls. The first, not unexpectedly, was from Aunt Peg. She said she wanted to check and make sure we'd gotten home okay.

Right.

Aunt Peg's curiosity ranks right up there with her sweet tooth—it takes a lot to satisfy her. And when she heard that Bob had already arrived, nothing short of all the gory details would do. She loves crash-and-burn adventure stories so I left her mulling over the notion of Bob's upcoming nuptials. It was the closest I could come.

Sam checked in a few minutes later. At least his motives were more altruistic. I assured him everything was fine, and tried to sound more convinced than I felt.

Bob and Davey progressed from baseball, to checking out the Trans-Am, to coming back inside for a game of Nintendo. I did my best to keep an eye on things and stay out of the way at the same time. To all appearances, Davey was simply having a play-date, albeit with a much bigger friend. They might not have been tackling the larger issues, but on the other hand, I wasn't seeing any emotional trauma either. Anxious as I'd been about Bob's coming, even I had to admit, things seemed to be going well.

I was mixing Faith's food that evening when Bob announced he was taking us all out to dinner.

"Yea!" cried Davey. "McDonalds!"

"Think again," I told him.

"Pizza!"

"You got it," said Bob, the big spender.

"Go find your shoes," I told Davey. The first thing he does upon entering the house is kick them off. You'd think that would mean they'd be by the door, but for some reason it never does.

As Davey bounded from the room, Bob leaned back against the counter. "You've been avoiding me all afternoon."

"No, I haven't." I looked up, surprised. "You told me you wanted to get to know your son. I was trying to leave you alone so you could do that."

"And you haven't asked me anything about Jennifer."

"I don't even know who Jennifer is." I could guess, but I said it anyway.

"The girl I'm going to marry."

"Girl? Don't you mean woman?"

I thought his consciousness might need raising about the status of women in the nineteen-nineties, but it turned out I was wrong.

"Maybe. She's not that old."

This time I stared. "How old, Bob?"

"Twenty. Almost twenty-one."

"My God, she can't even drink yet. How can she marry you?" I didn't mean it the way it sounded. I swear.

"If you don't want to talk about it—"

"No, I do," I said quickly. "I really do. How did you two meet?"

"I was doing some work for her father. He owns a sporting goods store. One day she came by to drop off some information I needed."

Twenty years old. Working for her father in his sporting goods store. At least she wasn't a student, I suppose that was something.

"Have you known her long?"

"We met right before Christmas. It's been about three months."

Three months. I needed a beer. I went to the refrigerator, got two out, and offered the other one to Bob. I could hear Davey rummaging through closets upstairs. He'd never put away a pair of sneakers in his life. Why he thought he'd find them there, I had no idea.

"That seems kind of fast, doesn't it?"

Bob popped the top on his can and took a long, slow swallow. "When it's right, I guess you just know it."

Not necessarily. Otherwise, he and I wouldn't have been standing here having this conversation.

"Was this before or after your oil well came in?"

"Before. At least that's when we met. But when we found out I'd have some money coming in, it just seemed to make sense to start talking marriage."

At least to Jennifer, obviously. Was I the only one who saw a giant neon sign flashing the word G-O-L-D-D-I-G-G-E-R?

Apparently so, because Bob said earnestly, "She's really a nice girl. I think you'd like her. And she just adores kids . . ."

He let that thought dangle, as if I was meant to respond. Did that mean I had Jennifer to thank for Bob's sudden interest in his son? If so, I'd rather not.

"We figured we'd wait a while before starting a family though. After all, Jennifer's pretty young. And besides, that will give her more time to get to know Davey first."

More time to . . . "*What?*"

"She'd like to get to know Davey, Mel. He's going to be part of the family, too."

My fingers grasped the edge of the counter behind me. I could feel my knuckles turning white. I fought for calm, hoping I'd misunderstood.

Speaking as slowly and clearly as I knew how, I said, "Davey's going to be part of what family?"

"Mine, of course." Bob set down his beer. "Now that I'm going to be getting married, I figured we'd work out some sort of joint-custody arrangement."

"Impossible!"

"Mel, just think about it—"

"I don't want to think about it." What I really wanted to do was throw something. Preferably something large and heavy and aimed at Bob's head. "It's not going to happen."

"I don't think that's your decision to make," Bob said evenly.

"It *is* my decision. Every decision concerning Davey is my decision. You left them all to me four years ago when you walked out."

Waves of anger, of outrage, flooded through me. I don't know which appalled me more—that Bob had had the nerve to make such a suggestion, or that he actually thought he might be able to pull it off. I sucked in a deep breath and struggled to control my feelings. Surely if I could keep my temper and outline the situation for him in a calm and rational manner, he'd see the lack of logic in what he was suggesting.

"Davey's five years old, Bob. This is the only life he's ever known. You live in Texas, two thousand miles away. There's no way we could share him across that distance.

Besides, Davey's only just met you. For him, that's enough of an adjustment all by itself."

"I don't think you're giving him enough credit. Kids are resilient—"

"How the hell would you know?"

He didn't even try to answer, which was just as well. At least when Davey came trotting in the room a moment later—shoes on the wrong feet, laces knotted—we weren't yelling at each other.

"All set," my son said brightly. My wonderful, laughable, lovable son. He looked back and forth between us, and it was all I could do not to pull him to my side. Instead, for his sake, I forced a smile.

"We'll finish this later," said Bob.

He could count on it.

I've never considered myself much of an actress, but it was amazing how civil I managed to be for the rest of the evening. Bob stayed until Davey went to bed. He had booked a room at a hotel in Stamford; but before he left he assured Davey that he'd be back the next day, and that they'd be seeing plenty of each other over the next several weeks. My son was delighted, and why not? He now had two parents doting on him: one with nefarious plans a five year old couldn't begin to fathom, and the other who was scared half to death.

Sunday, we went to the Bruce Museum in Greenwich. We'd barely gotten back when Bob suggested taking in the new Disney movie downtown. I had papers to grade, laundry to do, and a stop at the supermarket wouldn't have hurt.

Davey begged. Davey pleaded. In the end, I caved in and let them go by themselves.

Until the moment my son ran out to the driveway and climbed gleefully into the front seat of Bob's red Trans-Am, I hadn't thought of this as a competition. I hadn't realized I needed to. But in Davey's eyes, Bob was fast metamorphosing into the perfect parent: one with a flashy car, no rules, and plenty of money and free time to devote to anything a five year old might want.

Faith and I stood in the doorway, watching them leave. I waved goodbye, but Davey never even looked back.

I got four restless hours of sleep Sunday night.

I truly wanted Davey to have the opportunity to get to know his father. I wanted Bob to feel that he had free and easy access to his son. Desperately, I was hoping he'd come to his senses and consider that enough.

When Bob showed up Monday after school, I let him in. Tuesday, I gave him his own key. If he was going to be around so much, I figured he might as well be keeping Faith company, too.

Neither one of us brought up the issue of custody again. Bob probably thought he was giving me time to get used to the idea. Fat chance. I was hoping it would go away.

Bob could be selfish, I knew that. But he wasn't stupid. Surely in time he would have to realize that Davey was happy and well-adjusted just the way things were, and that for him to remain with his mother in Connecticut was the only possible alternative.

As if I didn't have enough to think about, Detective Shertz stopped by on Tuesday afternoon to ask a few more questions. Bob and Davey had taken the Trans-Am to the car wash. After that, they were planning to wax it themselves. If Bob had cared for his wife as well as he cared for his car, we'd probably still be married.

I'd brought plenty of work home from school but, absurdly, with the house so quiet, I wasn't able to concentrate. When the detective showed up, I was just as happy to be distracted. It turned out he mostly wanted to go over the same ground we'd covered the night of the murder. Where was I standing? Who was I with? What had I seen?

Then he asked if I knew anyone in the club who'd harbored a special animosity toward Monica. As I wasn't a member, which I'd already mentioned twice, I could only repeat what Aunt Peg had told me, that Monica hadn't been popular with anyone. Judging by the detective's expression, I doubted my answers satisfied him, or advanced his case in any way.

Nor did the answers he gave to my questions satisfy me. I asked him if the police were restricting their investigation to the members of the Belle Haven Kennel Club and he assured me that no possibilities were being ruled out. I asked if he had come up with any plausible motives for murder among those present that night, and he declined to comment.

He did admit that no fingerprints had been recovered from the rock that had killed Monica. That didn't surprise me. It was freezing that night; we'd all been wearing gloves.

Finally, I asked if he'd figured out who'd been closest to Monica when the murder occurred. He gave me a long, assessing look. Apparently, consensus among the other members was that *I* had been.

"Too bad," said Detective Shertz. "Because you seem the least likely to have had a reason for wanting to harm her.

According to your earlier statement, you and Monica Freedman had just met."

"That's right," I said evenly.

That left both of us without a clue. I saw the detective to the door and wished him good luck.

At the rate he was going, I figured he was going to need it.

༒ ❖ *Fifteen* ❖ ༒

Wednesday afternoon, Aunt Peg stopped by. Unannounced, uninvited. Just the kind of visit she likes best.

I was inside the house, doing all the paperwork from school I hadn't gotten to the day before. Bob and Davey were out front. My son, bless him, had decided that with the Trans-Am clean and freshly waxed, the Volvo deserved equal treatment. Much as I appreciated the thought, I hoped Bob and Davey didn't rub my old car too hard. I was afraid something might fall off.

It was Faith who alerted me to Aunt Peg's arrival. The puppy was lying beneath the dining room table, where I'd spread out my work. She got up and ran to the door. When she didn't come back after a minute, I went and had a look.

By that time, Peg was standing in the driveway, introducing herself to Bob. The reason for her visit, no doubt. I opened the front door and hurried out.

"Imagine that," Aunt Peg was saying. "Texas. And you drove all this way just for a visit?"

"I thought it was about time," Bob replied.

"About time?" Her tone could have peeled paint. "You must have a very slow watch."

Bob reddened beneath his tan. As I approached, his gaze swung to me in mute appeal. Even if I'd wanted to help him, there wasn't anything I could do. Once Aunt Peg gets rolling, I'd sooner try to stop a herd of stampeding elks.

"I imagine you won't be staying long," she said briskly.

"I'd planned on a couple of weeks."

"Lucky you, to have a job that can spare you for such a length of time."

"They've been very understanding," Bob mumbled.

"Take advantage of that while you can." Peg nodded wisely. "Once you rise to a position of responsibility, it won't be nearly so easy to get away."

Bob's flush now covered his entire face and was creeping down his neck. Aunt Peg looked at me and smiled. "There you are, dear. Are you ready to go?"

"Where?"

"We've been invited to Monica Freedman's house."

"We have?"

Peg nodded. "In my new position as all-purpose secretary, I've been asked to retrieve the club records Monica had in her possession. Mrs. Freedman is expecting us."

"You should have called," I said. "I'm not sure this is a good time. Bob is here, and I've got Davey—"

"It's all right," Bob said quickly, obviously eager to be rid of Aunt Peg. "We'll be fine."

"You see?" said Peg. "We're all set."

"Davey?"

"Go, Mom."

Well, that made me feel wanted.

"You'll look out for Faith?"

"Sure." Davey nodded importantly. "We both will. Right, Dad?"

"Right, son."

Dad? I hadn't heard that before. I swallowed the lump in my throat and went inside to get my purse.

Knowing Aunt Peg, she viewed this visit to Monica's as an opportunity to do some snooping around. My motivation was more selfish. At the moment, anything that took my mind off of Bob and Davey's growing relationship, seemed like a good idea.

Detective Shertz had apparently been busy over the last few days. On the way to Banksville, Peg and I compared notes on our respective visits from Greenwich's finest. It didn't take long. We'd been asked pretty much the same questions, and managed to ferret out only the same meager bits of information. All too quickly, Aunt Peg managed to work the conversation back around to the topic of my ex-husband.

"So that's the infamous Bob," she mused aloud. "I must say he doesn't look like much."

"That's the father of my child you're insulting."

"The absentee father." She slanted me a look. "If you ask me, it's not much of a bargain having him back."

"It's not as if I invited him."

"It's not as if you've thrown him out, either."

I didn't want to talk about Bob. I especially didn't want to hear the comparisons with Sam that would inevitably follow. Hoping to shock her into silence, I said, "Bob's thinking of seeking joint custody."

Peg never even missed a beat. "When pigs fly."

"That's why he's here."

"Oh, pish. He's here because coming seemed like a good idea at the time. He's found some money, and gotten himself engaged, and now he's decided to tie up loose ends. That boy hasn't a clue how to be a father to Davey."

We agreed on that, at least.

"He'll get over it," said Peg. "You'll see."

I could only hope she was right.

Banksville is a small village north of Greenwich, just over the state line in New York. There's a shopping center, a tennis facility, and several gas stations. Driving through town at moderate speed takes about thirty seconds. With Aunt Peg behind the wheel, if you blinked, you'd miss it.

The Freedmans lived in a raised ranch on an acre of land, about a mile beyond the village. The house looked like any one of thousands erected in the sixties, with economy and ease of construction taking precedence over style. Stockade fencing shielded most of the back yard from view. Melting snow had left puddles across much of the front; but the walk was shoveled and dry.

Monica's mother must have been looking for us, because the front door opened as we approached. Rhonda Freedman was a sturdily built woman who looked to be in her early sixties. She was wearing the sort of shapeless shift my mother would have called a house dress and had slippers on her feet. Behind glasses with bright blue frames, her eyes were red rimmed.

Aunt Peg introduced us both and told her how sorry we were for her loss.

Mrs. Freedman nodded wearily as if she'd heard the

same words many times recently. I'd lost both my parents and I knew how little the condolences helped.

Inside the door was a half flight of stairs, and we followed Mrs. Freedman up to the main floor. To the right, was a large open area, combination living and dining room. A waist-high baby gate blocked the entrance, and when we reached the landing, I saw why.

Behind the gate, there were Beagles everywhere: on the furniture, under the tables, spread out across the floor. Most were sleeping, but a few mustered the energy to stand up and bark. A talk show was playing on a large screen TV in the corner. I could have sworn some of the dogs were watching.

"Just ignore them," said Mrs. Freedman, turning left and heading down a hallway. "There's a lot of them, but they won't fuss at you, especially not when Oprah's on."

I glanced at Aunt Peg, but she was nodding as though that made sense, so I didn't say a word.

Mrs. Freedman led the way to a plainly furnished room that looked to be part guest room, part office. A twin size bed and dresser were on one side; a desk and credenza, complete with computer and printer, took up the other. It was the walls, however, that drew my gaze.

They were covered with sketches of Beagles, some charcoal, some pen and ink, all carefully matted and framed. The little hounds were pictured cavorting through fields, sitting beside a saddle, and playing with a tennis ball. The sketches were life-like; but more importantly, the artist seemed to have captured the essence of the dogs' personalities.

Mrs. Freedman saw where I was looking. "Monica's work. She was very talented." She stopped for a sigh, then gestured toward a cardboard file box beside the desk. "All the club records are in there. I found them as soon as I started tidying up. I figured the club would want them back."

"You did just the right thing calling Lydia," Aunt Peg assured her. "It will only take us a moment to gather everything up."

"No hurry. I'm going to go back and catch the end of Oprah. Take all the time you need."

"Since we're here, maybe we should take a quick look through the computer files," Aunt Peg suggested. "I'd hate to miss something and have to come back and bother you again."

I was appalled at her audacity, but Mrs. Freedman didn't seem to mind. "Go right ahead," she said, already turning away. "The police have already been here and had a look-through. I don't imagine it will make much difference to Monica now."

If Aunt Peg was disappointed to have been beaten to the punch, she didn't let it show. While I headed for the file box, she went immediately to Monica's desk. I lifted the top off the cardboard box, and she switched on the computer. The directory of files was tiny. Aunt Peg began scanning through them.

"Nothing," she said, closing the first. The second took her more time, but yielded similar results. "No wonder the police didn't find anything." she muttered. "There's nothing here."

I turned my attention back to the cardboard file box. Inside, it was divided into four partitions with headings lettered neatly on plastic covered tabs. The first said insurance receipts. It was followed by tax receipts, current bills, and finally, kennel club business.

The kennel club folder took up the most room as it was filled with papers. I lifted it out and carried it over to the bed. Apparently finished with the computer, Aunt Peg switched it off and came to sit beside me.

"Everything seems to be what you'd expect," she said, thumbing through the papers. "Membership lists, a copy of the by-laws, membership applications, sponsor forms, club stationery."

"What are those?" I asked, pointing.

"Club newsletters, past and present apparently. Monica really was a bit of a pack-rat, wasn't she?"

Aunt Peg lifted the top one out, which carried a mid-February date. The front page was set up in columns like a small newspaper and said "BELLE HAVEN HAPPENINGS" across the top.

"Between us, Monica and I wrote up most of the club news," Aunt Peg explained. "Once a month, she'd Xerox the newsletters and mail them out to all members. They also serve as notices for each upcoming meeting."

"There's another meeting in a week or two, isn't there?"

"That's right. Now that you mention it, the March newsletter is overdue. Monica must have been just about ready to mail them out when she died."

"So where are they?"

Aunt Peg closed the file and set it aside. "Let's check the desk. It would be a big help if we could find them. The sooner they get in the mail, the better."

We found the March newsletters in the bottom drawer; thirty-five envelopes with the Belle Haven return address, all stuffed and stamped, but not sealed. Aunt Peg gathered up the bundle and divided it in half. "We'll take these along to the post office right now. Here, help me lick."

Tagging along with Aunt Peg definitely has its better moments. This was not one of them. By the time I'd sealed the first ten, my whole mouth was sticky and tasted like paste. Toward the bottom of the pile, one envelope felt different when I picked it up. Heavier. I lifted the flap and looked inside.

"There's an extra piece of paper in this one. A letter, maybe."

Aunt Peg leaned over and read the address. "It's Lydia's. I wonder what Monica was sending her." She took the envelope and tipped its contents out onto the desk.

"That's tampering with the U.S. mail."

"Oh pish. It hasn't been sent. It can't be mail if it hasn't been mailed."

No use arguing with logic like that.

A folded sheet of plain white paper fell out beside the newsletter. Aunt Peg picked it up and unfolded it. Together, we read the short, handwritten message.

Dear Lydia,

A club president should be above reproach, don't you think? Too bad Belle Haven has something to hide.

⮑❁ *Sixteen* ❁⮐

Aunt Peg gasped softly. "Lydia?"

I continued to stare at the note. It wasn't signed. Instead, there was a small pencil sketch of a Beagle in one corner. I turned the paper over. Nothing was written on the back.

"What do you think it means?"

"That's perfectly obvious. It means that Lydia Applebaum had a motive for murder."

"Maybe." I put the note and the newsletter back in the envelope. "But what do you suppose Monica knew? What was Lydia hiding?"

"Only one way to find out." Aunt Peg walked over to the bed and picked up the kennel club file. She jammed the top back on the cardboard file box and nudged it back against the desk with her knee. "Bring those newsletters, would you?"

I gathered them up and hurried after her. Aunt Peg in high gear was a sight to behold. She had us out the door and back on the road without a single wasted motion.

"Do I dare ask where we're going?"

"Melanie," she sniffed. "Don't be dense."

Lydia's house. That's what I thought.

Lydia Applebaum's house was only a ten minute drive from the Freedmans'; but it was light years away in terms of location, style, and money spent. Like Aunt Peg, she lived in Greenwich, but Lydia's house was closer to town, located on a small, curving private road that looked as though it might once have been the driveway of a great estate.

Aunt Peg pulled in the circular driveway of the large white colonial and stopped before the front door. "Let me do the talking," she said.

As if I had a choice.

Ignoring the doorbell, Aunt Peg lifted a large brass knocker and let it drop. There was a flurry of high-pitched barking from within. A moment later, Lydia opened the door. A small herd of Miniature Dachshunds eddied around her feet. Yapping happily, they spilled out down the wide steps.

"Hello Peg, Melanie," she said, smiling uncertainly. "Was I expecting you?"

I could understand her confusion. Greenwich was not the sort of town where neighbors tended to drop by uninvited.

"No. I'm sorry there wasn't time to call." Stepping carefully around dozens of little paws, Aunt Peg led the way inside. "Something came up while we were at Monica's retrieving up the club records and I thought we should talk about it right away."

"Of course." Lydia counted noses—the Dachshunds,

not ours—then closed the door behind us. "Come right in."

Lydia's living room was furnished in muted shades of cream and gray, which set off the Dachshunds' red coats beautifully. As I sank deep into a plushly pillowed couch, the dogs draped themselves over the furniture around us. I wondered how she managed to keep everything so clean.

"We brought your newsletter." Peg dug the envelope out of her purse and handed it over. "Monica had them in her desk, all ready to be mailed out."

"Thank you." Lydia took the envelope and put it on the table without looking at it.

"I think you'd better open it. Monica put something extra inside that apparently she wanted you to see."

"I don't understand." Lydia's smile faltered. She opened the envelope, looked at the newsletter and set it aside, then read the note. "What is this about?"

"We were hoping you would tell us."

The note fell from her fingers and landed in her lap. One of the Mini Dachshunds reached out and batted the paper with its paw. "You know Monica," Lydia said, looking back and forth between us. "She was always joking around."

"Really?" Peg's brow rose. "I never noticed that."

"Surely you don't think . . . ?"

"That the note gives you a motive for murder?" I asked. "It did cross our minds."

"Don't be ridiculous!" Lydia snapped. "It does nothing of the sort."

"How would you know? You just said you had no idea what it was about."

The club president reached down and retrieved the paper. The dog in her lap had chewed off one of the corners.

"We didn't come here to accuse you of anything," Peg said gently, looking at her friend. "We're just trying to understand what was going on."

"There was nothing going on." Lydia's voice held just the slightest hint of a tremor. "Monica and I were acquaintances, at best. She knew nothing about me."

"Monica and I were acquaintances too," said Peg. "But she thought she knew something about me."

"She did?" Lydia and I both stared.

Aunt Peg nodded. "You know what Monica was like. She loved having information. She gathered other people's secrets. I think she felt it gave her some sort of power."

Lydia nodded. She looked as though she was beginning to relax. "What could Monica have known about you?"

"Do you remember when my dog, Beau, came down with SA last year?"

"Certainly," said Lydia. "You were very upset about it."

I remembered it, too. Beau was Champion Cedar Crest Chantain; and he had been Aunt Peg's prize stud dog. He'd been stolen the summer before and I'd spent three months looking for him.

"I made the announcement in the fall after I got him back," said Peg. "But a few weeks earlier I'd been talking to Monica. The subject of genetic diseases came up and we were commiserating about how hard it is to control them.

"I imagine I must have mentioned something about

Beau and SA. I certainly didn't come right out and say he had the disease. How could I? I'd only just found out myself and I hadn't yet had a chance to inform the breeders who had bred bitches to him. But somehow Monica put two and two together.

"She called a few days later and said what a shame it was that such an important dog had to be removed from the gene pool. Then she left this great dramatic pause, so that I had to pay attention to what was coming next."

"Which was?" I prompted.

"Monica said that since nobody else knew about Beau's disease, maybe it should just be our little secret."

"Not likely," Lydia said scornfully. It sounded as if she spoke from experience.

"I gather she knew one of your secrets, too?"

I had to give Aunt Peg credit. Her own confession had gone a long way toward softening Lydia's defenses.

"It really wasn't a big deal," the club president said.

Peg and I both remained silent.

"I bred a litter of puppies last fall. After they were born, the owner of the stud dog and I got into an argument. Of course, you know both parties have to sign an application for litter registration or the A.K.C. won't accept it. The stud dog owner threatened to withhold his signature."

"So you signed it for him," Aunt Peg guessed.

Lydia nodded.

Forgery. It sounded like a big deal to me. But then these were puppies we were talking about, not counterfeit currency.

"Didn't the owner of the stud dog protest?" asked Peg.

"No, you see by the time the papers were returned, we'd

kissed and made up. So there was no reason that the A.K.C. ever had to be the wiser. Unless Monica wrote and told them what had happened."

"They would have suspended your privileges," said Aunt Peg. "Probably for years."

"So Monica was blackmailing you," I said.

"Oh, no," Lydia said quickly. "It was nothing like that. She never asked for money. It was more that she just wanted me to be aware that she knew."

Of course Lydia would say that, I thought. Nobody but a fool would admit to being blackmailed by somebody who'd recently turned up murdered. And the president of the Belle Haven Kennel Club, didn't strike me as any sort of a fool.

"I think we should have the note back," I said.

"Oh dear!" Lydia held up her hand and several small scraps of paper fluttered to the floor. "Zipper seems to have destroyed it while we were talking."

Zipper, I took it, was the happy looking Dachshund in her lap. The one with bits of paper sticking to his jowls. Until that moment, I'd been inclined to believe Lydia. She didn't look like a murderer to me, and I wasn't at all certain that the information Monica knew about her was worth killing over. But now I had to wonder. I'd seen her retrieve the note from Zipper several minutes earlier. When had she fed it back to him?

Looking none too happy about the situation, Aunt Peg stood. "Did you tell the police about any of this?"

"Of course not. There was no reason to." Lydia set aside the Dachshund in her lap and rose as well. "We've known each other a long time, Peg. You must know I'm not capable of killing anyone, much less someone so unimportant as Monica Freedman."

"I must admit it would come as a bit of a shock," Peg said grimly. "But then yours is the only motive, isn't it?"

"Hardly." Walking us to the door, Lydia was once more very much in control. "You just told me Monica had something on you as well."

"Except that I went ahead and made it known that Beau had SA. I doubt you plan a similar announcement."

Lydia sighed. "Do you honestly believe you and I are the only ones Monica played her little games with?"

I stopped. "There were others?"

"Of course there were others." Lydia grasped the knob and drew the front door open. "If I were you, I'd talk to Cy Rubicov. He didn't think any more highly of Monica than the rest of us did."

"Monica had something on *Cy?*"

"That's for him to tell you, if he so chooses. All I'm saying is that Monica got around, and her position as club secretary gave her quite a lot of access. Where there's one secret, there are bound to be more. This month, the note was in my newsletter. Whose do you suppose it would have been in next?"

Leaving the question hanging in the air, Lydia Applebaum closed the door firmly behind us.

"I don't know," I said when we were back in the car. "It's hard to believe anyone would commit murder over a litter of puppies."

"It wasn't the puppies that were important, it was the document Lydia falsified. If the A.K.C. had known, they wouldn't have dealt with it lightly, I can assure you of that." Aunt Peg frowned, looking distracted. She never pays attention when she's driving, so I knew that wasn't what was on her mind.

"What?" I asked finally.

"I was thinking about what Lydia said about Cy Rubicov. Of all the members of the Belle Haven Club he's the one with the biggest financial stake in the dog game. If anyone really had something to lose, it would be him."

It wasn't hard to see where she was going with this. "Next on the list?"

Aunt Peg nodded.

I ran all that past Sam the next evening when he came by to see how Davey and I were doing. Monica's murder interested him peripherally, but it was Bob he really wanted to talk about.

I know he meant well. I know he was trying to help. But I had no desire to talk about Bob. Zero. None. He was a problem I currently had no way of solving, so why make myself feel worse by dwelling on it endlessly?

I wouldn't exactly say Sam and I argued all evening, but there were more long gaps in the conversation than we're used to having. Bob was off visiting other friends in the area, so at least I was spared the necessity of introducing the two of them. My ex-husband and my current lover. I could see how that would have gone over well.

Of course it was difficult to keep from talking about Bob when Davey kept bringing him up. After four days' acquaintance, he was sure that his father walked on water. By the end of the evening, I think even Sam was ready for a change of topic.

Sam stayed for dinner, but left soon after Davey went

to bed. Worse still, I wasn't entirely sorry to see him leave. I sat down at my desk, pulled out my briefcase, and got down to writing pupil evaluations with a vengeance.

This was all Bob's fault. He wasn't even here and my life was still turned upside down. It was too bad there wasn't some way I could pin Monica's murder on him.

∽❀✿ *Seventeen* ✿❀∽

Frank called early the following morning to invite Davey and me to dinner. When my brother offers to cook, I start looking for ulterior motives. Usually he's hoping to borrow money. This time, however, he pleaded innocence.

"Aunt Rose and Peter are coming," he said. "We haven't seen them in a while so I thought it would be nice."

Rose was our father's sister. For the last three decades, she'd also been known as Sister Anne Marie. To everyone's surprise, she'd left the convent the summer before to marry Peter Donovan, who'd put aside the priesthood at the same time. Peter was teaching college in New London now and by all accounts, they were very content.

Of course it would be nice to see them. Then again, if we were a *nice* family, we'd do things like this regularly.

"What's the catch?" I asked.

"What catch?"

"You're cooking? Rose and Peter are coming? And I'm getting less than a day's notice? What are you hoping I won't find out about until it's too late?"

"Why are you always so suspicious?" asked Frank.

Many years of experience. Anyone could have told him that.

"Is Aunt Peg coming?"

"I'm feeling sociable, Mel, not crazy."

He had a point. Anyone sitting down at the same table with Rose and Peg was more likely to feel like a referee than a dinner guest.

"So you just decided it would be fun to get Rose and Peter, and you and me and Davey together?"

"Sure," said Frank. "Why not?"

Right.

He told me that Davey and I were expected at six, and that we'd been volunteered to bring dessert. I guessed I'd find out what else he had in store for me when we got there.

Frank lives in Cos Cob, a quiet section of Greenwich not too far from the water. His three room apartment takes up the top floor of an old Victorian house, and he does upkeep and maintenance in return for a reduced rent. Frank's furniture, such as it is, would look right at home in a college dorm. He hadn't owned a dining table the last time we visited, and when Davey and I arrived I saw that nothing had changed.

"I'm doing the whole thing buffet style," Frank explained. He took the key lime pie I'd brought and stowed it in the refrigerator. Following him into the kitchen, I pretended not to notice the boxes from Hay Day Market, a local gourmet take-out, piled on the counter. "I don't think anyone will mind eating on their laps, do you?"

Certainly not my son. But an ex-nun and a former priest? That might be a different matter.

"We'll do fine," I said.

"Good." Frank looked me over carefully. So carefully, in fact, that I began to wonder what he was looking for. "You seem to be holding up pretty well."

Holding up from what? I wondered. Plague? Fire? Pestilence? Was there something going around I hadn't heard about?

"I called the other day. You and Peg were off somewhere, but I had a chance to talk to Bob."

Aha. Finally the light dawned.

"It was an interesting conversation. Of course, I felt a little stupid since I had no idea he was back."

"He's not back," I said carefully. "He's visiting. He and Davey are getting to know one another."

"So I heard."

The doorbell rang in the other room.

"I'll get it!" yelled Davey.

I heard him squeal with delight and Frank and I entered the living room to find Peter swinging him in a wide circle. I guessed that was one of the benefits of not owning much furniture.

"Again!" cried Davey, when Peter set him down.

"I don't think so," said Peter, sounding winded. He smoothed back his thinning gray-brown hair and unbuttoned his top coat. He was a pleasant looking man, medium height, with a waistline that had expanded several inches in the last year. "I'm much too old for that kind of behavior."

Rose was tall and slender, with impeccable posture. Her strong features softened when she looked at her husband.

"You're not old. Otherwise, what would that make me?"

"Well seasoned?" Peter teased.

Lord, they looked happy together. I knew they deserved it, these two people who had devoted the major portion of their lives to serving God, but still I couldn't help but feel a small twinge of jealousy. What would it be like to have a partner you could count on completely, a person you planned to spend the rest of your life with? At the rate I was going, it didn't look as though I'd ever find out.

"Let me take your coats," said Frank, stepping into the role of host with more aplomb than I'd have given him credit for. "What can I get everyone to drink?"

In no time at all we were settled around the living room. Rose and Peter were seated side by side on the couch; I had the only chair. Davey and Frank were on the floor. Davey had brought a supply of matchbox cars with him and he ran them up and down the legs of the coffee table. Every so often, I gave him a nudge and told him to pipe down on the sound effects.

"I'm so glad Frank was able to get us all together," said Rose. "I know you didn't get much notice, but I was so hoping he'd be able to pull it off."

"*You* were hoping . . . ?" I looked at my brother, then back to Rose.

"He didn't tell you this was my idea?"

"Actually, no."

"It doesn't matter." Aunt Rose smiled serenely. Turnbull women are strong—some might even say bossy—and three decades in the convent hadn't dulled Rose's ability to manipulate events to her own satisfaction. "I thought we should talk."

"Sure," I said. "About what?"

Her gaze flickered in Davey's direction. On the floor beside my son, Frank took his cue. "Come on, sport. Let's go out to the kitchen and see about dinner."

"No," Davey said firmly, cars all lined up in a row. "I want to stay here."

"There might be some ice cream in the freezer . . ."

That got my son's attention. "Before dinner?"

"Shhh," whispered Frank. "Don't tell your Mom."

Giggling together, they disappeared into the kitchen. I could just see it now. Another nutritionally balanced meal shot to hell.

Once Davey was gone, Aunt Rose didn't waste any time getting down to business. "Frank tells me your ex-husband has returned."

I nodded. "Bob's visiting from Texas. He's never really had a chance to get to know Davey—"

"Oh for Pete's sake, Melanie! We can all stop pretending. The way I understand it, Bob's had plenty of chances. He's just never availed himself of the opportunity."

"You could put it that way."

"I could and I have. I heard this Bob of yours told Frank he's getting married."

"He did?" Apparently their conversation had covered more ground than I'd imagined.

Peter leaned forward, resting his elbows on his legs. "He also mentioned he's thinking of seeking joint-custody."

"That may be what he said, but it's not going to happen. I'm not allowing Davey to travel halfway across the country to be cared for by a father he's never known, not to mention some child bride."

"Good for you," said Rose. "I never expected to hear any differently, but I just wanted to make sure. Have you spoken with a lawyer?"

I'd certainly thought about it, but it was a move I didn't want to make quite yet. Lawyers solved some problems, but they also created others. They thrived in an atmosphere of adversity. So far, Bob and I were getting along, with Davey benefiting from our mutual good-will. For my son's sake, I wanted to hold off any outside interference until I felt I had no choice.

"Not yet. At the moment, Bob's plans seem to be pretty vague. As soon as I retain a lawyer, matters will begin to escalate. I'm hoping it won't have to come to that, that I'll be able to make Bob see reason by myself."

"Just the same," said Peter. "I'll do some asking around and line up a few names. And if there's anything else you need, you just let us know."

"Thank you," I said, feeling unexpectedly touched. "I appreciate that."

"Do more than appreciate it. Use it, if you need to. You've got our number."

Aunt Rose reached out and patted my hand. "God never asks more of us than we're capable of handling. You do the best you can, dear, and everything will be all right."

I wished I had her faith, but I didn't. Even as a child, growing up in a strictly religious family, I never had. The most I could muster now toward the Catholic Church was ambivalence, which was why Davey had been baptized but mass wasn't part of our weekly ritual.

"I'll pray for you," Rose promised. "We both will."

Behind her, the kitchen door swung open. Davey threw

himself into our midst. His hands and face were clean, but his breath smelled suspiciously like chocolate.

"Dinner's ready!" he announced.

"Did you help?" asked Peter.

Davey nodded emphatically. "I helped a lot."

"I'll bet," I muttered. Unpacking all those boxes must have been arduous work. Not to mention positioning the food on the serving plates so that it looked home made.

Frank pushed open the kitchen door until it stuck. "Come on in and help yourselves. Everything's all set."

Davey led the way, with Rose and Peter following close behind. When Frank would have gone after them, I stopped him with a hand on his arm.

"Thanks," I said softly, leaning up to kiss his cheek.

He colored slightly and looked away. I wondered when was the last time I'd expressed any spontaneous affection toward my brother. It was so long ago, I couldn't remember.

"It was nothing," said Frank.

"It was very nice of you."

He smiled. "Then you're welcome."

He draped an arm around my shoulders—a gesture as unexpected as the kiss I'd given him—and we went in to dinner.

Maybe there was hope for this family yet.

∽❀ *Eighteen* ❀∽

When Aunt Peg is trying to poke her nose into my life, which she does with annoying regularity, her persistence can be a real pain. When applied in other directions, however, it's actually quite a useful trait. Which is why I wasn't terribly surprised to have her call on Friday and tell me we were due at the Rubicovs' that evening at nine o'clock for dessert and coffee.

Of course she seemed to have forgotten that I have a five year old son.

"Bring him along," said Aunt Peg.

"He's supposed to be in bed by then."

"So he'll be a little tired tomorrow. It's Saturday. He can sleep late."

Another objection disposed of with Aunt Peg's usual dispatch. Obviously she'd never dealt with a young child who'd been kept up past his bedtime. I supposed I could have called around and tried to find a sitter, but I really didn't want to. Davey had spent so much time with his father lately that I welcomed the thought of having him with me, even if it wasn't under the best of circumstances.

Since Cy and Barbara lived in Greenwich, Davey and I met Aunt Peg at her house and we all went over together. The Volvo was making noises that didn't sound promising and the heater had recently given out, but application of foot to gas pedal was still producing forward motion. These days, that seemed to be about as much as I could hope for. I offered to drive and Aunt Peg accepted.

Davey was in the back seat bouncing up and down with excitement. He'd passed over-tired half an hour ago. Now he was getting his second wind. He was telling Aunt Peg dinosaur jokes, and she interspersed listening with giving me directions.

Cy and Barbara lived only minutes away in a development on North Street called Conyers Farm. Housing developments in back country Greenwich have little in common with those in other parts of the country. This one had been fashioned from the estate of a former business tycoon and consisted of thirteen hundred acres, much of it retained by the developer as open land. The minimum lot size was ten acres and the houses ranged from baronial manors to mini horse farms. There were wide streets, lots of trees, and an abundance of white fencing. Anywhere else, Conyers Farm would have been the pinnacle. In Greenwich it was just another good address.

The Rubicovs' house was set high on a hill and surrounded by enough lawn to keep a crew of landscapers busy full-time. It was constructed of stone and looked as though it had been designed to withstand the advances of an invading army. The castle—that was the only word for it—was three stories high, with turrets at either end, leaded glass windows, and a massive oak front door. All that was missing was the moat.

It wasn't the way I'd have chosen to spend my money, but it certainly was eye-catching.

I parked the battered Volvo in front of the stone steps. A pair of statues—snarling lions, only slightly under life size—guarded the wide oak door.

"Wow," said Davey, climbing from the car. "A real castle. Does a king live here?"

"No, honey." I looped a reassuring arm around his shoulders. If he tipped his head back any farther, he was going to fall over. "Just normal people, with lots of money."

"Maybe they'll give us some," he said hopefully.

"I don't think so." I stooped low and whispered in his ear. "And don't ask, okay?"

Aunt Peg had gone ahead up the steps. There was no need to knock; the door was already being drawn open by a middle-aged man in black pants and a crisp white shirt. "Good evening," he said formally. "Mr. and Mrs. Rubicov are expecting you. May I take your coats?"

The front hall was as wide as my driveway, and softly lit by a cut glass chandelier. We unbundled ourselves in the shadow of a curving staircase. In keeping with the castle motif, tapestries hung on the walls. There was a thick Persian carpet beneath our feet. It was all very beautiful, and very quiet.

It took me a moment to figure out why that seemed odd. Then I realized that all the houses we'd been to had one thing in common—the noisy, joyous presence of dogs. We'd been greeted by oodles of Poodles, droves of Dachshunds, and bunches of Beagles. Here there was only silence, without so much as a muddy paw print or Milkbone out of place.

The houseman took our coats and led the way to a set of double doors on the right. He knocked, then opened them to reveal a spacious library. Books lined two walls, windows a third, and the fourth held a fireplace, where a blazing fire had been lit. Despite the grandeur of the house, this room had been decorated with comfort in mind. The overstuffed furniture was covered in chintz and scattered with pillows. Cy and Barbara were seated near the fireplace.

Cy rose as we entered. "Peg, Melanie, how nice of you to join us." He walked toward us, arms extended in greeting. "And who's this fine young man?"

"I'm Davey," my son announced before I could introduce him. "You live in a castle."

"Yes, I suppose I do." Cy smiled.

"Do you have a dungeon?"

"No, but we have two towers. That's almost as good."

"No, it's not—"

I poked my son, hard.

Davey quickly changed tacks. "Can I see them?"

"Maybe some other time," I said, the classic mother's response. I angled Davey until he was standing behind me. "Cy, it's nice to see you again."

"My pleasure," said the gracious host. "Please, come in and make yourselves comfortable. Peg, how are things going these days in the world of Poodles?"

I've never been good at small talk. Luckily, Aunt Peg could chat the ears off a Basset Hound if she put her mind to it. She and Cy kept each other entertained while Barbara supervised the pouring of coffee and I kept an eye on my son. The next tray that appeared held a bowl of plump, red strawberries, another with real whipped cream, and a glass of milk for Davey.

I could get used to living like this.

As we helped ourselves to the strawberries, Aunt Peg steered the conversation around to the reason for our visit. When she mentioned Monica Freedman, Cy looked surprised. Barbara, on the other hand, seemed blandly disinterested. She sat back on the couch and stirred her coffee with a dainty silver spoon. There were only two strawberries in her bowl and no whipped cream. I supposed she believed that maxim about nobody being too rich or too thin.

"Monica?" said Cy. "What about her?"

"I've always had the impression that you're the kind of man who appreciates honesty, so I'm going to lay this right on the line," said Peg. "In all likelihood, Monica was murdered by a member of the Belle Haven Club. Melanie and I suspect that it had something to do with information she possessed about one of the members."

Barbara Rubicov glanced at Davey. I did, too. Absorbed in piling whipped cream on his spoon, he didn't seem to be paying any attention to the conversation.

"What does that have to do with us?" asked Cy.

"We've been to see Lydia," I told him. "She recommended we talk to you."

"She told you I had something to hide?" Cy sat up straight, his chest puffing out indignantly.

"You are a big-money player in the dog game," Peg pointed out. "You might have more to lose than most if Monica knew something she shouldn't."

"Let me get this straight." Cy's thick, white eyebrows lowered over his eyes as he scowled. "Did you come here tonight to accuse me of murder?"

I looked over at Barbara. To my surprise, she seemed faintly amused. Nevertheless, I could see that the chances of our being invited back any time soon were growing more remote by the moment. Leaving Aunt Peg to fend for herself, I loaded up on another helping of strawberries.

"Of course not," said Peg. "We just want to talk. Look around, Cy. Look at all you've accomplished. These are the achievements of a smart man, the type of man who might have noticed something that other people didn't. What's your take on this whole situation?"

Cy paused for a long sip of coffee before answering. "We're in the dark, just like everybody else. We hardly knew Monica, did we, Babs?" He looked to his wife for confirmation.

"We only saw her at club functions," said Barbara. "Even then, we really had nothing to talk about."

Much as I'd hoped there was more to learn, it was easy to see how that would have been true. Financially, socially, Banksville was a long way from back country Greenwich.

"If Monica was digging around in other people's private lives, I wouldn't have known anything about it," said Cy. "There certainly weren't any secrets for her to discover around here."

Barbara lifted her napkin and delicately patted her lips. "How interesting. You said Monica Freedman knew something dire about Lydia?"

"No." Aunt Peg smiled, but her tone was frosty. "I don't believe I said anything of the sort."

The two women eyed each other, like terriers with a particularly juicy bone between them. It was Barbara who backed down first. "My mistake," she murmured.

I turned back to Cy. "So you never received any messages from Monica?"

"Messages? Certainly not. As I just said, we barely knew the woman."

That seemed to be the end of that. I took Davey's empty bowl and set it on the tray.

Barbara reached over and patted my son's knee. "Perhaps you'd like to go see the tower now?"

"Sure!" cried Davey, leaping up. Strawberries and whipped cream are fine, but adult conversation bores him silly. His gaze darted my way. "Can I?"

"I don't see why not."

"Why don't you come, too?" said Barbara.

"Thanks, I'd like that."

Besides, maybe Aunt Peg could get Cy to open up if the two of them were alone.

The towers were located at either end of the house and we started by walking up the grand stairway in the hallway outside.

"Cool," said Davey, dashing on ahead. His hand slipped along the wide, polished banister. "I bet you could slide on this."

"That's what my boys used to do," Barbara told him. "When they crash landed at the bottom, I thought they were going to kill themselves."

"You have children?"

I probably shouldn't have been so surprised. It was just that most of the mothers I knew were like me, going in eight directions at once and struggling to keep all the different facets of their lives integrated and running smoothly. Barbara looked much too polished, too pulled together, to be part of that sorority.

"Two sons," she said. "Miles and Kevin. They're all grown up now. Kevin's working in Chicago and Miles is finishing his last year at Dartmouth." Her eyes followed Davey as he scooted ahead of us down the wide, second floor hallway. "It's nice to hear a child in the house again."

I could see why she would think that. Her home was beautifully decorated but it lacked warmth. It was perfection carried to the point of sterility. Children would have made a big difference. So would a dog. Like any one of the half dozen that she and Cy campaigned. Those dogs were living with their handlers now, but I wondered what happened to them when they were finished being shown. Why didn't they ever come home?

"It's the last door on the end," Barbara called ahead to Davey. "Go ahead and open it."

He did, but he didn't go in. The room was dark, and it wasn't until we caught up and Barbara flipped on the light switch that he gasped with pleasure. The room wasn't large but it was perfectly round, with a high ceiling and wide windows looking out into the inky night.

"Wow," said Davey. "This is cool."

"This was Kevin's room," Barbara told him. "We moved into this house when he was just about your age. He thought having a round bedroom was pretty special."

Judging by the look on my son's face, Davey agreed. Too bad the only way he was going to duplicate the experience was if I let him take his pillow and sleep in the clothes dryer.

Barbara crossed the room and stood in front of a door. "What do you think this is?"

"A closet?" Davey guessed.

"Even better. Look!" Clearly enjoying herself, she opened the door to reveal a steep, spiral staircase winding up to the floor above. "Kevin had his own private observatory. Do you want to go see?"

Davey scrambled up the stairway and disappeared. "Don't worry," said Barbara when I walked over to stand beside her. "There's nothing up there that can hurt him."

Either her children had been abnormally well behaved, or they'd been five years old so long ago that she'd forgotten what it was like. Usually I worried about things the other way around.

The sound of Davey's delighted laughter floated down the stairwell. I was thinking of following him, when Barbara said, "I'm glad we have a moment to chat. I didn't want to say anything in front of Cy. He hates it when he thinks women are gossiping, but I was thinking about what Peg said downstairs, about somebody in the club having a secret. Have you spoken with Joanne Pinkus?"

"No."

"You might give it a try. I don't know her well myself, but she called here once to get my input on some trophy decisions. In the course of the conversation, she told me about something she'd done. She was very righteous about it, but at the same time kind of defensive."

"Did it have to do with the trophies?" I asked.

"No, it was something else entirely. I think she was looking for my support. Maybe she told Monica about it, hoping for the same thing and then came to regret it later."

With a loud whoop, Davey came barreling down the spiral stairway. If I hadn't held out my arms, he'd have gone flying at the bottom. As it was, we both staggered backward into the bedroom. Nothing like a five-year-old up past his bed time and cruising along on a sugar high.

"That was great!" he said. "Want to go up, Mom?"

"No, I think we've taken up enough of Mrs. Rubicov's time. Will you say thank-you for showing you around?"

"Thanks!" Davey cried. "Can I have some more strawberries?"

I wanted to kick him, but Barbara only laughed. "I'm afraid the strawberries will be put away by the time we get back downstairs. Maybe another time."

As we ascended the wide stairway—Davey walking, not sliding—the door to the library opened and Peg and Cy emerged. They were talking dogs and dog shows. That was certainly Aunt Peg's favorite topic and Cy looked as though he was enjoying himself, too. Apparently we'd been forgiven for starting off the evening by accusing him of murder.

Back in the car, with Davey struggling to keep his eyes open, Aunt Peg admitted that she'd learned nothing further from Cy, if you didn't count the fact that he considered his Dalmatian to be a prime contender for that year's top ten. As Davey began to snore softly in the back seat, I told her what Barbara had had to say about Joanne.

"I've never paid too much attention to Joanne," she said. "She's basically a pet owner, using the club as a social life. She does a good job with the club's rescue work, but beyond that I've never really given her any thought. She's just part of the background."

From what little I'd seen of Joanne, I had to agree with

Aunt Peg's assessment. And that made me wonder about the conversation she'd supposedly had with Barbara. Somehow I couldn't imagine the two of them exchanging confidences.

I thought of the carefully orchestrated way in which I'd been drawn aside and fed just enough information about Joanne to make me curious. Had Barbara really been trying to point me in the right direction, or had she simple wanted to divert attention away from herself and Cy?

ᗡᘛ✳ *Nineteen* ✳ᘛᗡ

After the week I'd had, I was really looking forward to a calm, relaxing weekend. Davey, Sam, and I could use some quality time together. I pictured us strolling with the puppy in the park; or maybe seeing an afternoon movie. And after Davey went to sleep . . . I had that covered, too.

I'm no Cinderella. I have modest dreams. I figure that way they stand a halfway decent chance of coming true. That Saturday, however, my fairy godmother must have been out to lunch. And maybe dinner, too.

Instead of the quietly blissful weekend I'd planned, I ended up with a phone message from Sam saying he'd gone off to show in Massachusetts; six inches of snow from a last-gasp-of-winter snowstorm; and an ex-husband who seemed to have forgotten that I was no longer responsible for doing his laundry.

Times like this, I wish life was better at imitating art. Even a wicked stepmother wouldn't have treated me this badly.

Davey, who by all rights, should have slept late Satur-

day morning, was up at dawn celebrating the newly fallen
snow at the top of his lungs. After he'd let Faith outside
and the puppy had taken two quick turns around the back
yard, she joined in. For some reason, the two of them
seemed to think this celebration should be taking place on
my bed. That's how I discovered just how much powdery
snow can stick to a Standard Poodle puppy's legs. Enough
to wet a queen size quilt clear through, apparently.

While Davey dressed, I stripped the bed, threw everything in the washing machine, and started a batch of
French toast. Bob arrived while we were eating breakfast.

"Great," he said, going directly to the cupboard for a
plate. "French toast, my favorite."

There were two pieces cooking in the pan. _My_ two
pieces. I slapped a cover over them before he could help
himself. "I don't recall issuing an invitation," I said.

Bob stopped and stared. Then he began to laugh. After
a minute, I joined in. It's hard to stand on ceremony when
you're wearing flannel pajamas.

We split the pieces in the frying pan between us and I
started three more. Sitting at the table, Bob cocked his
head toward the basement door. "Do I hear the washing
machine?"

"Could be. It's running."

"You don't suppose . . . ?"

"You could run a load? I don't see why not."

"I only have a few things. I was thinking I could throw
them in with yours."

"Sorry," I said, grinning. "Mine's done."

Four and a half years and he still hadn't mastered laundry. He'd just met Jennifer. I wondered who'd been taking up the slack in the meantime.

"Come on, Mel. Don't be like that."

I took a big bite of French toast and chewed slowly. "Like what?"

"Obstinate. You always did have to have everything your own way."

"I did not." That was unfair. Also untrue.

Davey stopped eating and looked at us. The French toast on the stove began to smoke. I hopped up, grabbed a spatula, and turned the pieces over.

I was not going to fight with Bob in front of my son. "I'll make you a deal. I'll do your laundry."

"And?"

"You shovel the driveway." Of all the chores that came with owning a house, shoveling snow was the one I liked the least. I could mow, I could plant, I could even paint and plaster if I had to, but I hated shoveling snow.

"You're kidding." From the look on his face, you'd have thought I'd suggested he climb Mount McKinley and get back to me by noon.

"Why would I be kidding?"

"Why would *I* want to shovel snow?"

"Nobody wants to shovel snow. That's the whole point." The new batch of French toast was done. I slipped a hot piece on each plate, then dipped and started three more.

"It's March," said Bob. "The stuff will be melting in a week or two anyway."

"In the meantime, I'll have to live with it."

"I don't have any gloves, or the right kind of boots."

I shrugged and sat back down to breakfast. Faith pushed her muzzle hopefully into my lap. I scratched behind her ear, but didn't offer to give up any French toast. "That's the deal. Take it or leave it."

He took it.

After breakfast, Bob went back to the hotel and picked up his laundry. While I was sorting lights and darks, he and Davey went out in the backyard where they managed to build a snowman that was all of two feet high and bore a striking resemblance to E.T.

As they worked, Faith ran around in circles, barking like a lunatic. Every so often she'd stop and tentatively sniff the snowman. Dogs are creatures of habit. If something's going to change in their space, they'd like to be consulted. Faith was not amused by this small intruder in her yard. Even fashioning features out of dog biscuits didn't help, although I thought they added to the snow creature's otherworldly appeal.

By lunch time, I had my driveway shoveled and Bob had a basket filled with fresh laundry. Supplies being a bit low, we opted for peanut butter and jelly all around, then sat down to a family game of Scrabble. With Davey sitting between us, Bob and I were on our best behavior. Neither one said a thing when our son passed off the word "zfig" as a new kind of Newton.

It wasn't exactly the family grouping I had in mind but, all in all, things didn't turn out too badly. We did manage to get to the park; with Bob insisting we take his car until he found out that Faith was coming along, then arguing with equal vehemence that we take mine.

The Volvo stuttered all the way there, but only part of the way back. I saw that as a good sign. Where my car is concerned, I'm an optimist. I can't afford to be anything else.

Back home in the late afternoon, Bob was ready to sit down in front of the TV with a cold beer and a plate of nachos. Wives have to put up with stuff like that. Exes definitely don't. I thought about kicking him out, but decided it might be more productive to let him hang around.

Davey had gotten up early and had a busy day. By four-thirty, he was just tired enough to be really cranky. Any mother with young children knows that stage. They're bored with their games. All their toys are stupid. There's nothing good to do in the *whole* world.

Davey wanted to cling. He also wanted to whine. I handed him another cold beer for Daddy and sent him into the living room in the sincere hope that he'd continue to do both.

Sneaky? Self-serving? Maybe. But Bob had told me that he wanted to experience fatherhood. The way I saw it, all I was doing was helping him experience it to the fullest.

Left to my own devices in the kitchen, I unfolded Faith's portable grooming table and got out her supplies. Accustomed to the routine, she lay quietly while I line brushed the hair on her body, then slickered through her legs. I took out her topknot and reset all the bands, then unwrapped and rewrapped her ears. Faith doesn't much like having her nails clipped, but by now she's resigned to it. The same goes for plucking the hair inside her ears.

With a Standard Poodle, this is a long process. Doing a good job takes more than an hour. I did a great job. Probably the most thorough brushing I've ever done. Aunt Peg would have been proud. And when I was finished, the puppy looked great. Faith took the piece of cheese I gave her as a reward, then ran into the living room to see what Davey was up to.

When everything was put away, I followed. Father and son were seated together on the couch. Bob had one eye on a boxing match and the other on the Go Fish cards in his hand. Davey still looked sulky.

"I said go fish!" he shouted, slapping the pile of cards on the cushion between them. "That means you're supposed to *go fish!*"

No need to intervene there.

Quietly I withdrew, and spent the next half hour browsing through take-out menus before settling on ribs. Usually that's one of Davey's favorite meals. They come with curly fries and nobody says a word when you eat with your fingers. At five, that's enough to bump a meal straight to the top of the list.

Compared to some kids I've seen, Davey's usually pretty easy. But that night, nothing pleased him. The ribs didn't taste right. The fries were too salty. Even Faith's begging at the table—which he usually encourages shamelessly—got on his nerves.

After dinner, I sent him upstairs for an early bath. Bob got the job of reading him to sleep and didn't reappear for an hour.

Ah, the joys of fatherhood.

By that time, I had my feet up and was reading Nancy Pickard's latest. Bob came and stood in the doorway. "That dog . . . um, Faith, is on the bed with him. Is that okay?"

"Sure. That's where she sleeps."

"She won't wake him up?"

"She hasn't yet."

"Good." Relief evident, Bob came in and sat down on the couch.

"Nice day," I commented, setting my book aside.

"*Long* day."

I kept my smile to myself. "That's what it's like when they're Davey's age. They go and go and you can barely keep up, then suddenly boom, they're tired and it all shuts down."

"Do you know he made me play eighteen games of Go Fish?"

"Better than hide-and-seek. That's another favorite. At least you were sitting down."

"Great," Bob muttered. "When do they begin to amuse themselves?"

"When they get older, I guess."

"Jeez, eighteen games. And I only won one."

"Be glad you weren't playing for money."

Bob looked up. "He does that?"

"No. Just kidding."

"I should hope so."

His tone irritated me. If he'd wanted to have input into the way his son was raised, then he should have been around to provide it.

"I guess fatherhood isn't that easy, is it?"

"I never said it was." Bob frowned. "But it doesn't change the fact that Davey's my son."

"Of course he's your son. He loves spending time with you. And I'm delighted to have him spend time with you, whenever you want to come and see him. But we can't share him, Bob. Texas is just too far away. And who knows anything about this girl, Jennifer—"

"I do," Bob said. There was an edge to his tone. "I know plenty about her. She's going to make a great mother."

"How can you say that? How can you know? She's barely past childhood herself."

"She may be young, but she's a good person. She comes from a good family. You have no right to judge her, especially when . . ."

Bob stopped suddenly and looked away. An alarm went off deep in my subconscious. Bob and I were old hands at fighting. But we'd always done it face to face. It wasn't like him to turn away.

"When what?" I demanded.

"It's not like your own family is perfect, Mel."

A cool shiver raised the hairs on my arms and the back of my neck. "What are you talking about?"

"I've been to see Frank."

That was news to me. I waited in silence for what would come next.

"You didn't know that, did you?"

"My brother and I don't talk every day," I said quietly.

"From what I can tell, you hardly talk at all. But he talked to me. Actually we had an interesting chat about old times. I didn't know your father was an alcoholic."

When I'd been married to Bob, I hadn't known it either. My parents had made a conscious effort to shelter me from anything unpleasant, anything that might hurt. And their efforts had worked, up to a point. How could they have known that finding out everything later, after their deaths, when it was too late for me to do anything but mourn all over again, would only hurt more?

"I remember when your parents died," he said.

Of course, he'd remember. I was pregnant with Davey, and we'd gone to the funeral together.

"Your father was driving when their car went off the road. Maybe he'd been drinking then."

Bob was guessing. I knew the truth. But the scab over

that particular wound was still too fresh. I wasn't about to discuss it with him.

I glared at him. "What does this have to do with anything?"

"It has everything to do with it. What makes you think you have any right to question my suitability as a parent? Or Jennifer's either, for that matter?" Bob stood, waving an arm angrily to encompass the room. "From what I can see around here, you're not necessarily doing such a great job yourself."

"I'm a terrific mother—"

"You drive a car that sounds like a death trap, feed my son french fries for dinner, and let a dog the size of Rhode Island sleep on his bed. He keeps mentioning some guy named Sam, and now I find out about your father. Talk about instability. This is one hell of a way for my kid to be growing up."

I wanted to fight back. I wanted to scream so loud the windows rattled. But much as I hated to hear it, there were elements of truth to what he'd said.

I'd tried my damnedest for Davey, but there were times when I felt that I had to be everywhere at once. No matter how carefully I tried to set my priorities, sometimes Davey's needs got lost in the shuffle. All working moms had moments of doubt, I knew that. But it didn't make them any easier to overcome.

When I looked up, I was almost surprised to see Bob still standing there. "I think you'd better go."

"You think about what I said." He walked over to the closet, yanked on his coat, then let himself out the front door.

Upstairs, Faith woofed quietly when she heard the door

open. My son slept in his bedroom, blissfully unaware of the turmoil that swirled around him. Downstairs, I curled myself up into a tiny ball, pulled my knees up under my chin, and wondered if Bob was right.

✺ *Twenty* ✺

I spent a restless night in bed and got up early, eager to do anything that would take my mind off Bob and what he'd said. Alice Brickman called after breakfast and invited Davey over to play with Joey. And like Sam, Aunt Peg was away showing in Massachusetts. That left me and Faith.

I thought about washing the kitchen floor. I thought about bathing Faith. Both would make me feel virtuous, but both were essentially mindless physical activity which would leave me plenty of time to think. Right now, that was the last thing I needed.

Instead, I got on the phone and called Joanne Pinkus. She was home, and seemed more delighted than I would have been by the prospect of a visit from someone she barely knew. Maybe she was hoping I wanted to talk insurance.

Joanne lived in Norwalk in a small frame house that had the look and feel of the fifties. It was set on almost an acre of land, however, with mature trees and plantings that afforded plenty of privacy. A post and rail fence lined with wire mesh, circled the property.

As I drove up, two black and tan Norwich Terriers, presumably Rupert and Camille, raced along the fence barking a welcome. Faith pressed her nose against the window and stared. She's been to handling class and shows, so she's seen lots of other dogs; but for some reason, the little ones always seem to surprise her. I cracked the windows and left her lying on the seat with a new rawhide bone nestled between her front paws.

I'd barely rung the bell before the door was flung open. "This is great!" said Joanne. "I'm glad you're here. Come on in."

The yard had been muddy and I would have wiped my feet, but Joanne grabbed my arm and was already pulling me inside. Her mass of hair was casually messy; her plump body shoe-horned into leggings and a long pullover sweater.

I wondered if she owned a full-length mirror. If so, I wondered if she ever used it. In their brown stretch casings, her legs looked like two sausages ready to burst at the seams. The bulky sweater she'd topped them with had settled into a broad crease over her hips.

"Coffee?" she offered.

I fell in behind her as we headed toward the kitchen. "I'd love some."

Joanne filled two ceramic mugs from a pot on the counter. There was a pitcher of milk and a bowl filled with little pink packets of Sweet 'n Low on the table. As I helped myself, Joanne opened the back door and the two Norwiches came scrambling inside.

Racing side by side, they were going so fast that they were halfway across the kitchen before they saw me. Both skidded to a stop, stiff-legged, and began to bark. I leaned down and held out a hand.

"That's Rupert," Joanne said as the first one came and sniffed my fingers. "He loves everybody. Camille will take a little longer."

Approximately thirty seconds, by my count. By the time we'd carried our coffee into the living room and were settled on the couch, Camille was already trying to nudge her way onto my lap. On the other side, Rupert lay down on the cushion and stretched out along my leg.

"Dogs are a great barometer," said Joanne, looking on approvingly. "They always know whether visitors really like them or are just full of bullshit."

I smiled at her vehemence. "Do you get many visitors who are full of bull?"

"Probably most of them, I'd say. Are you married?"

"Not now. I used to be."

"Dating?"

"Only when I have to."

"Then you know what I mean. Luckily, I've got a good job that keeps me busy and I'm really involved with the work I do for the club. Otherwise, I'd probably have stooped to taking out an ad in the personals by now. This being single in the nineties jazz is a real drag."

The last thing I needed was a reminder of the problems I'd left at home. I quickly changed the subject. "I came to ask you a few questions about Monica, if you don't mind."

"Monica? Why?"

"I've been looking into some of the circumstances surrounding her death, and one thing I've discovered is that

Monica was very good at ferreting out other people's secrets."

I paused, but Joanne didn't seem inclined to fill in the silence. As she sipped at her coffee, I continued, "She was also apparently in the habit of sending people notes about what she knew."

"Notes?" Joanne tried to look surprised. It didn't quite come off.

"In their newsletters."

"Oh." She stared down at her mug.

"She sent one to you, didn't she?"

"Two, actually," Joanne said finally. "The bitch. I don't know what she thought she was trying to prove." She stopped and frowned. "I guess that's why you're here, isn't it? Well you don't have to worry. What Monica knew was no big deal. Certainly not worth killing anyone over, if that's what you're implying."

Joanne was fidgeting in her seat. It wasn't hard to see why she'd confided in Barbara and Monica. Joanne wanted to talk; whatever her secret was, she seemed almost anxious to share. Either what she was hiding wasn't serious enough to do real damage; or her social life was empty enough to leave her sadly lacking in confidantes.

"You have dogs, don't you?"

"One," I said. "A Standard Poodle puppy."

"I'll bet you take pretty good care of her."

"I do."

"Why?"

The question was unexpected, and I had to stop and think. "Because she depends on me. Because she can't take care of herself. I own her, which makes her my responsibility. She's smart and she's funny, not quite human, certainly . . ." I smiled, glad Aunt Peg wasn't here to correct me. "But close enough that her well-being is important to me. It's my duty to keep her comfortable and happy."

"Precisely." Joanne nodded, looking satisfied. "That's the way I feel about Camille and Rupert. Actually, I guess I'd have to say that's the way I feel about all dogs. We bred them, that makes them our responsibility. That's why I do rescue work. That's why I had to report Paul and Darla. I didn't have any choice."

"Wait a minute," I said. "Back up. You didn't have any choice about what? Who did you report them to?"

"The ASPCA. The one over in Westport, that's where they live."

"You reported Paul and Darla Heins to the 'SPCA? What for?"

"Well . . ." Joanne flushed slightly. "Both of them are getting on, you know. Paul's still pretty much okay, but Darla—I'm not sure the woman even knows what day it is. And their house! Have you ever seen it?"

I shook my head.

"It was filled top to bottom with Pugs. They've been breeding them for years. I swear they must have had thirty or more, some of them not entirely housebroken, if you know what I mean."

I could guess.

"The situation was out of control," said Joanne. "I tried talking to Paul about it. I told him I'd start trying to help him find homes for some of the younger dogs, but he just brushed me off. He said that he and Darla loved the Pugs and he wouldn't dream of changing a thing."

"So you reported them to the authorities?"

"I had to. There wasn't anything else I could do. It

wasn't healthy for all those dogs to be living like that, nor for Paul and Darla, either."

Barbara had been right. Joanne did sound self-righteous. I wondered what made her think these decisions had been hers to make. "Then what happened?"

"They sent someone over to have a look. A report was filed, and the Heinses were cited for neglect." Joanne's voice dropped. "Some of the very old dogs were in pretty bad shape. I believe they were put to sleep. A number of the younger dogs were taken away and placed."

I tried to imagine how Paul and Darla must have felt. Violated. Humiliated. As if they'd lost control over their own lives. Whether or not Joanne had been justified in terms of the dogs' welfare, what she'd done had to have been devastating for the Heinses.

"And you told Monica about all this?"

"Of course I told Monica. She was the club secretary. Besides, she was a dog lover, too. I knew she'd see that I had done the right thing."

"And did she?"

"Not exactly." Rupert jumped off the couch and went to join his mistress. Joanne stroked his back absently. "She seemed to think the matter was something the club should have handled privately." Her chin lifted. "Monica accused me of being on some sort of ego trip. But I wasn't. It was the dogs I was concerned about."

Yeah, right.

"How long ago did all this happen?"

"Over the winter," said Joanne, suddenly looking vague. "Maybe in December."

Right around Christmas. Perfect.

"And then Monica sent a note in your newsletter?"

"Yes. It said something stupid and melodramatic about what I'd done. I tore it up and threw it away."

"You said earlier that there were two notes. When did the second one come?"

Joanne thought back. "Probably a couple weeks later."

"In the next newsletter?"

"No, that one was mailed by itself."

"You're sure it was from Monica, though."

"Of course. She signed it."

I remembered the note intended for Lydia. Instead of a signature, there'd been a small sketch in one corner. "So your first note was signed as well."

"Now that you mention it, no. There was some sort of little drawing . . ."

"A Beagle?"

"Yes. It was jumping up and down in the corner."

Just like Lydia's. "Did both notes say the same thing?"

"More or less." Joanne shrugged, trying to look casual. "The second one might have mentioned something about the Board."

The Board of Directors of the kennel club. "Are you a member?" I asked.

"No, but I should be. Head of the rescue service ought to be a board position. It's more work than any other job." Her words held the conviction of often repeated sentiment.

"I take it the club doesn't agree?"

"They've taken the idea under advisement. Monica said it was a good thing the rest of the Board didn't know what I'd done. You know, like she wanted me to wonder whether she was going to tell them or not. Monica enjoyed manipulating people that way."

I finished my coffee and stood. "By the way, where were you that night when Monica's Beagles began to howl?"

Joanne's gaze was level and direct. "When Monica was murdered, you mean?"

I nodded.

"Not standing over her with a rock in my hands. That's for damn sure."

On the way home I stopped off at the Brickmans' to pick up Davey. Alice was up to her elbows in spring cleaning. Carly was dozing in her swing. The two boys were angling for a trip to the Stamford Nature Center to check and see if any new baby animals had been born.

What the hell. It wasn't as if I had plans. I piled them into the car and off we went.

Then I second-guessed myself all the way there. Was this the kind of thing I would have done before Bob had called me a bad mother? Or was I only trying to prove how wrong he'd been?

We saw otters and geese and two new baby lambs. Davey and Joey had a great time. And I spent the whole day wondering.

❧✿ *Twenty-one* ✿❧

March had come in like a lion. Now, in keeping with tra-
dition, it was going out like a lamb. A warm front settled
over the Connecticut coast, and spring was in the air. For
the first time in months, windows in the school classrooms
were open. The air was fresh and sweet with the smell of
budding and rebirth. Birds were back in the trees.

It was hard to tell the children to sit down and open their
books when I wanted to be outside just as much as they
did. Attention spans, already short, seemed to vanish.
With spring vacation due to start at the end of the week, I
wasn't the only teacher who felt as though she was swim-
ming upstream.

Before Friday, however, I had plenty to keep me busy.
Faith was entered in a dog show that weekend, which
meant that I had to find time to clip her face, feet, and the
base of her tail. The clipping would be followed by a bath
and blow-dry, after which I was going to try my hand at
scissoring in the lines of her trim.

Scissoring is an exacting job, and I usually counted on

Aunt Peg's help. But Peg had a litter of puppies due over the weekend and was staying home to dog-sit. For the first time, I'd be on my own.

I might have been nervous about that, but with so many other things going on, there was hardly time. Early in the week, I had a long talk with Sam on the phone. We discussed the dog show in Massachusetts where his bitch had won two points; and the fact that a new client was interested in some of his software designs. He also mentioned that a tree had fallen during the weekend storm, knocking out the power lines to his house.

It was all mundane stuff, the sort of things that up until recently, we'd have chatted about over a casual dinner. But with Bob around so much, talking on the phone had begun to seem easier than trying to juggle everybody's schedules. Sam was giving me some space, and I was grateful for the understanding. I just hoped I could get things back to normal before the gap between us widened too far.

Bob, meanwhile, was underfoot so much of the time, I was beginning to think I saw more of him now than I had when we were married. At least then, he'd had a job. Now, presumably, his only goal was to spend time with his son. And who was I to stand in the way of such a noble aim?

Monday, I had him take Davey down to sign up for spring soccer. Tuesday, I let him handle the dentist appointment. Wednesday, they took Faith and went to the beach. It took me an hour to get the sand out of Faith's coat, but seeing the condition she'd left Bob's Trans-Am in, made it all feel worthwhile.

Thursday, Bob was there when we got home after school. Perfect timing, as far as I was concerned. I had an appointment in Westport.

"I won't be too late," I told Bob, after I'd fixed Davey a snack, rewrapped Faith's ears, and pumped some air into Davey's soccer ball. "I'm sure you can find plenty to do."

"Too late for what?" asked Bob. He was reading the newspaper—*my* newspaper—while Davey danced around the kitchen in stocking feet and shared his string cheese with Faith.

"I'm going out. I have an errand to run in Westport."

"You're not taking Davey?"

"No, why would I? You're here, and I'm sure he'd rather stay home." As I spoke, I was already heading toward the front door.

Bob hopped up and followed. "I'm meeting some friends after they get off work."

"Good for you."

"I told them I'd be there at five."

I smiled sweetly. "Maybe you'd better call and change that."

"Mel . . . !"

"Yes?" I drew the door open.

Davey had followed us into the hallway. Bob looked at him, then back at me. "Nothing."

His teeth were gritted when he spoke. I liked that. I gathered Davey into a quick hug. "See you later, sweetie."

"Bye, Mom."

As I closed the door, I heard Davey say, "How about a game of Go Fish? No, make that Monopoly!"

Sometimes it's the little things in life that make you smile.

I took my time getting to Westport. When I'd spoken to Paul Heins on the phone, he'd told me that he was retired and that he and Darla were usually at home. I wondered how many Pugs they had left now. Bad as Joanne's description of their living condition had been, the idea of an empty house seemed even more depressing.

It turned out I needn't have worried. The overflow of Pugs was gone, but by my quick count at least six or seven remained. The Beagles had howled when guests arrived; the Dachshunds had yapped. Pugs snuffled. They massed around me, their sharp nails digging into my legs as they all sought attention at once.

"That's enough now!" Paul said sharply. He shooed the dogs aside long enough for me to get in, then shut the door behind me.

"Dear, is somebody here?" Darla's voice floated out from the living room.

"It's Melanie Travis," Paul called back. "You know, I told you. The young lady from the kennel club."

Darla appeared in the doorway. She was wearing a silk dress with sneakers, and had a cardigan sweater draped over her shoulders. Her wispy white hair was neatly combed and her lipstick freshly applied. She was carrying a poker from the fireplace in her hands.

"A visitor," she said, beaming. "Isn't that nice?"

Paul stepped over, took the poker from his wife and leaned it against the wall. Then he grasped Darla's elbow gently. "Let's all go in the living room, shall we?"

The room we entered wasn't large. A couch and love seat faced each other in front of a window; two wing back chairs flanked the fireplace. The Pugs ran on ahead of us and quickly made themselves at home. It was easy to see why the upholstered cushions were worn in places, and the legs of the coffee table were covered with scratches.

"Now shoo!" said Paul, waving ineffectually at a trio of Pugs that had hopped up to take over the couch.

Two ignored him. One rolled over on her back, wiggled her fanny, and kicked her legs in the air. Paul sat down carefully between the three dogs and began to rub the bitch's stomach. I found myself a place on the love seat.

"How about tea?" asked Darla. She looked to her husband for approval. "Shall I serve some tea?"

"That would be lovely," said Paul. "Do you need any help?"

"Of course not." Darla's smile wavered slightly. "I'll be right back."

As she left the room, one of the Pugs on the floor launched itself up into my lap. It felt as though somebody had dropped a twenty pound sack of flour onto my legs. Startled, I gave a small yelp.

"Oh, dear," said Paul. "Shall I—"

"No, I'm fine. I like dogs." Even small, heavy, snuffling ones. I shifted my weight and maneuvered the Pug into a more comfortable position.

"You said on the phone that you wanted to talk to us about Monica. Darla and I have already spoken with the police. We're happy to help in any way that we can, but I'm afraid there probably isn't anything we can tell you that you don't already know."

"I was wondering about something that might have happened before Monica died," I said. "Did she ever send you a note enclosed in one of your club newsletters? Maybe sometime over the winter?"

Paul sighed and looked away. "Yes, as it happens, she did."

"Monica knew you had a secret, didn't she? Something

you didn't want the rest of the Belle Haven Club to know."

"I see word has gotten out," Paul said sadly. "Is that why you've come? Has the club decided they don't want us as members anymore?"

"No, not at all." Obviously he'd forgotten that I wasn't even a member of Belle Haven, much less an emissary they would send on their behalf. "My visit has nothing to do with club business."

"Club business." Paul shook his head. "That's the trouble with the world today. Everybody's too concerned with everyone else's business. Darla and I were doing fine. There was no need for anyone to come into our house. No need at all. And to take our dogs away . . ."

He paused, swallowing heavily. I could see the effort it cost him to continue. "It was humiliating, that's what it was. Absolutely the lowest point in our lives."

"I'm very sorry about what happened," I said quietly.

Paul didn't acknowledge that I had spoken. He seemed lost in thoughts of his own. After a moment, he glanced toward the doorway and said, "If you'll excuse me, I think I'll go see what's keeping Darla."

"Of course."

Some of the Pugs followed when he left. The others stayed behind with me. Five minutes passed. Finally I got up and headed in the direction Paul had gone. A swinging door took me into the kitchen, and I found him there by himself. Water was running in the sink and he was filling a tea kettle from the faucet.

The back door stood open. As I entered the room, I could see Darla standing outside on the terrace, holding a tennis racquet.

Seeing me, Paul put the kettle down and went to the

back door. "Darla," he called. "Please come inside now and see to our guest."

"It's really not necessary," I told him. "It was kind of you to offer me tea, but I really should be going."

"So soon?" asked Darla, coming in to join us. "You just got here." She turned to check with Paul. "She just got here, didn't she?"

"Only a few minutes ago," Paul confirmed. He took the tennis racquet and put it on the table. "But I'm afraid she has to go."

I looked at the two of them, both frail and elderly, both using every bit of will they had to cling tenuously to the life they'd built together over the years. I didn't care what the circumstances had been. How could Joanne ever have justified hurting these two fragile souls?

"There's just one more question, if you don't mind?"

"Of course not dear." Darla smiled happily. "We don't mind at all."

"The night that Monica was killed. Where were the two of you when the Beagles began to bark?"

Paul and Darla looked at each other. "Why, we were just outside the restaurant, weren't we?" asked Paul.

Darla nodded in agreement.

"We started down with everyone else. But as you can see, we don't move as fast as we once did."

"Were any of the other club members still around?" I asked. "Or had everyone gone on ahead?"

"There was somebody . . ."

"Mark Romano," Darla said. Her filmy blue eyes seemed to swim into focus. "He was there. Remember, dear? He held the door for us."

"He certainly did." Paul patted his wife's shoulder fondly. "Such a nice young man."

"A nice young man," Darla echoed. "He caught one of the Beagles."

"Did you see Penny, too?" I asked.

"No." Darla's slender shoulders rose and fell in a shrug. "No Penny. She wasn't there." She looked around the kitchen. "Where's the tea? Didn't you tell me we were having tea?"

"In just a minute," Paul said soothingly. "Just let me see our guest to the door."

Flanked by an honor guard of Pugs, Paul led the way back out. "Now I have a question for you," he said, when we were alone. "You knew about the note that Monica sent, and that terrible business with the humane society. But here's what I've always wondered. Who was it that turned us in? Was it Monica?"

I looked at him, surprised. It hadn't occurred to me that he wouldn't know. Apparently Joanne's burst of self-righteous zeal hadn't extended to putting her name on what she'd done.

I wondered if Monica had known that by sending a note, she'd shifted the blame toward herself. I wondered if Paul Heins would consider the humiliation he and Darla had been through grounds enough to commit murder. I looked at his scrawny shoulders and forearms. It didn't take much strength to bash a rock down on someone's head.

"It wasn't Monica," I said.

He shook his head unhappily. "Then I guess we'll never know."

I could have told him, but I didn't. I couldn't see how it would help. Now that Joanne knew she'd jeopardized her chances of gaining her coveted board position, she'd be inclined to keep quiet. There was no reason for this to go any further.

"What happened is over," I said. "Monica can't tell. And nobody else will. Your secret is safe." It was small consolation, but all I had to offer.

"I hope so," said Paul.

He didn't sound convinced.

❧❦ *Twenty-two* ❦❧

Saturday's dog show was in Elizabeth, New Jersey.

By Aunt Peg's reckoning it was a local show, meaning that although I would have to drive through three states to get there, I wasn't going to spend the night. Like most of the exhibitors I've met, Peg travels all over the east coast in search of good judges to show her Poodles to. She doesn't think anything of hopping down to Delaware for the day, or signing up for a circuit in Maine. I enjoy showing my puppy, but I'm not a fanatic. Elizabeth seemed like enough of a hike to me.

Bob stopped by at eight o'clock Saturday morning and picked up Davey. He'd planned a trip to Mystic Seaport and wanted to get an early start. I was just finishing loading the Volvo when he arrived.

Bob peered in through the window and saw my folded table, the metal tack box that held grooming supplies, Faith's big crate, and a stack of towels, all piled on the back seat. "What's going on?" he asked. "It looks like Gypsies have been camping in your car."

"I'm taking Faith to a dog show. I told you that."

Bob has a convenient way of forgetting things that don't seem important to him. "Oh yeah." He laughed. "You all get your dogs duded up in ribbons and bows and parade around in a circle, right?"

"Wrong."

My tone was enough to make him reconsider his next jibe. Instead he asked, "You win anything at these shows?"

"A ribbon. Maybe some points toward Faith's championship, if we're lucky."

"No money?"

"No money."

"Hardly seems worth it to me."

How could I explain, when I was only beginning to find out for myself how engaging the sport of showing dogs could be? There were many things I enjoyed about going to the shows and sometimes, the few minutes Faith and I spent in actual competition was the least of it. I liked the camaraderie of exhibitors as we all got ready to go in the ring; the challenge of learning how to groom a Poodle so that my puppy could compete on equal footing with the pros; and I really enjoyed the time spent working directly with Faith.

While I was trying to figure out how to condense that all into a short, easy to digest answer, Bob moved on. "Where is the show?"

"New Jersey."

He stared. "You're driving all the way to New Jersey in *that* car?"

"Do I have a choice?" Deliberately, I glanced over at the Trans-Am. I wondered if he'd gotten all the sand out of the seats yet.

"Sorry," Bob said quickly. "I promised Davey we'd see the ships. You know how it is."

I did know. Besides, keeping my son happy at a dog show was hard enough. The notion of having to entertain child and man-child both, was more than I wanted to get involved with.

Still, it felt a little odd ten minutes later when I finally got on the road, with only Faith for company. In the last five years, Davey and I had spent so much time together that I had come to take his companionship for granted. Now I wasn't sure whether to feel free, or bereft.

The New Brunswick Kennel Club holds their spring show indoors at the Dunn Sports Arena. It's a small venue, so the entry is limited. The rings take up the center of the room and preparation of the dogs goes on around the sides. Even though it was early when I arrived, the grooming area was already just about full. I saw a small space over near Bertie's set-up and dragged my dolly that way.

She had a gold and white Lhasa Apso out on a table and looked up as I approached.

"What do you think?" I asked. "Can I fit?"

"How much stuff have you got?"

"One dog, with a table and crate."

"Sure." Bertie was already moving to rearrange her things into tighter formation. "I think I can squeeze you in."

"Thanks," I said gratefully. This was the first time I'd been to a dog show as an exhibitor without Aunt Peg. I'd been half afraid I'd find myself tucked off in some dark corner, all alone.

I finished unloading, parked my car, then walked Faith back into the building and hopped her up on the table.

Bertie and the dog had vanished. Presumably Lhasas were being judged. I laid Faith down on her side and began line brushing through her hair. Bertie reappeared ten minutes later.

"Did you win?"

She shook her head as she opened the door to a wooden crate and placed the Lhasa inside. "Best Op."

That was shorthand for Best of Opposite Sex. The top award for most breeds is Best of Breed. Other breeds have divisions based on size, or coat color, or texture. Poodles, for example, come in three sizes; and for them, the top award is Best of Variety. If Best of Breed or Best of Variety is won by a dog, then Best of Opposite Sex must be awarded to a bitch. If a bitch is chosen to win the breed, then BOS goes to the best dog.

For me, winning Best of Opposite Sex would have been cause for celebration. But for the professional handlers who entered hoping to win the breed and then go on to compete in the group, it meant coming up second best.

"Too bad. Did you get beaten by something pretty?"

"Pretty enough." Bertie grimaced. She opened another crate, took out a Tibetan Terrier and dropped him lightly onto the table. "Actually, I shouldn't say that. The dog that beat me *was* a nice Lhasa. Probably better than mine. Doesn't mean I didn't want to beat him though."

In showing dogs, as in any sport, it takes drive and determination to succeed. From what I could see, Bertie had plenty of both. In time, with hard work and practice, she could probably overcome a lack of innate talent.

Unless something got in her way.

Or someone. Like a nosy club secretary with a penchant

for finding out other people's secrets. I wondered what sort of juicy tidbits someone like Bertie might have tucked away in her background.

"Do you mind if I ask a few questions while we brush?"

Bertie rolled her eyes. "Are you still snooping around trying to figure out what happened to Monica?"

"Yes."

"Are you getting anywhere?"

"Yes." In a manner of speaking.

"So who did it?"

"I don't know."

Bertie turned away to fish through her tack box before coming up with the leash she wanted. "Doesn't sound to me like you've learned too much."

"I've learned that Monica was good at finding out things people didn't want her to know."

"That's no surprise. Monica was always poking her nose in where it didn't belong. What else did she have to do with her life? She was still living at home with her mother, for Pete's sake. If I was stuck doing that, you can bet I'd be looking for a little excitement, too."

"Is that what you think she was doing, looking for excitement?"

"Maybe." Bertie thought for a moment. "That, and power. She liked playing head games with people."

"People like you?"

"People like anybody." Bertie's tone was casual, but she didn't meet my gaze.

"I've heard she was in the habit of sending messages to club members. She enclosed notes in their monthly newsletters."

Bertie developed a sudden interest in the catalogue. She opened it up and flipped through the pages to the judging schedule in the front. "What?"

I knew perfectly well she'd heard what I said. "Did Monica ever send you any notes? Maybe something signed with a sketch of a Beagle?"

"No." Bertie looked up and snapped the catalogue shut. "Of course not."

"You're sure?"

She picked up the Tibetan Terrier and tucked him under her arm. "Sorry, gotta go. I'm late."

She scooted between two crates and disappeared into the crowds surrounding the rings. I stared after her for a moment, then reached over and picked up the catalogue she'd left on the table. The Tibetan Terrier judging was coming up all right, but it wasn't due to start for fifteen minutes.

Maybe Bertie wasn't as smart as I'd thought.

Without Aunt Peg's guidance, getting Faith ready to go in the ring seemed to proceed at a snail's pace. I had shown the puppy before. I knew all the mechanics of preparation, but somehow the fine details eluded me.

I was prepared for my scissoring to lack Aunt Peg's polish. What I hadn't expected was that the top-knot would go in crooked on the first two attempts. Or that I'd be putting hair spray in the neck hair before I remembered I hadn't put on Faith's collar. It was the little things. In the end, they added up to a huge difference.

I was so nervous about being late that I got up to the ring early. Then I had to wait while the winners in the breeds scheduled before us had their pictures taken. Ten minutes passed before the other Standard Poodles even began to assemble outside the gate.

In the classes, dogs are judged first, followed by bitches. As the Poodle judging started with the Puppy Dog class, Crawford arrived ringside with a stunning black bitch. He came over and stood beside me.

"Nervous?" he asked.

"Does it show that much?"

"You look like a deer caught in oncoming headlights."

"Great. That will really impress the judge."

"What's your number?"

I glanced down at my arm where the numbered arm-band should have been. It wasn't there. All that extra time and I'd forgotten to pick up my number. Crawford, whose Open class entry went in after Faith's puppy class, was of course already wearing his.

"I don't know," I said, panic rising. "I forgot—"

"Don't worry, the steward will know. Stand right here. And for God's sake, take some deep breaths."

I did. While Crawford went and consulted with the ring steward I held Faith's leash and concentrated on breathing in and out. It didn't seem to help.

Crawford returned with the cardboard number and a rubber band to hold it in place. I held out my left arm and he slipped it on.

"Good thing you're so nervous," he said casually.

"Why?"

"It makes my job easier. Aside from my bitch and your puppy, there's not much else here, is there?"

As we were standing in the middle of a decent sized entry of Standard Poodles, I assumed he wasn't talking numbers. That meant he was talking quality. By ranking her as his chief competition, he was paying her a compliment.

"Really?" I said. "Do you think so?"

"I'm certain of it," he said, as the dog judging ended. "Now get in there and make sure the judge sees what a nice puppy you have."

Without his urging I probably would have slunk into the ring and gone to the end of the line. But Crawford wasn't having any of it. Every time I was tempted to let down, he leaned over the partition and glared at me. With him glowering like that, I didn't have any choice but to forget about my fears, get down to business, and show the puppy.

It helped that Faith was a natural ham. It also helped that, thanks to Aunt Peg's fine breeding program, she was indeed a very pretty Poodle. There were only two other puppies in the class, but I was delighted to win it.

"Don't go anywhere," said Crawford, as he passed me on his way into the ring. "You have to go back in."

There were six bitches in the Open class, but Crawford's black took the blue ribbon easily. The steward called my number and I led Faith back into the ring to try for the title of Winners Bitch and the points. It was over quickly, with Crawford's bitch prevailing. But when the judge motioned Faith over to the marker for Reserve Winners, I found I couldn't stop smiling.

"See?" said Crawford. "I told you so."

"Congratulations. And thank you."

"Don't thank me," Crawford said briskly. "It was the puppy. She gave you all the help you needed."

Not quite, but he was gone before I could argue the point.

I took Faith back to the set-up and put her back on the table. Bertie was away again, probably either showing a dog or trying to drum up more business. I laid Faith down, sprayed conditioner into her neck hair to break up the hair spray and was about to wrap her ears when somebody tapped me on the shoulder.

I turned and saw Paul Heins, looking very dapper in khaki pants and a cashmere sweater. Beside him, Darla was covered in flowers; the motif repeated in the pattern of her dress, the embroidery on her cardigan, and the clasp of her wicker purse.

"Hello," I said. "It's nice to see you again." They both looked well. I hoped that meant that my visit hadn't caused them any distress.

"We watched you show your puppy, dear," said Darla. "You did a very nice job."

"Thank you."

"Yesterday you had some questions for us," said Paul. "But overnight I got to thinking, and I was wondering if I might ask something of you."

"Of course." I smoothed Faith's plastic wrap and wound it around the long hair on her ear.

"How did you know that Monica had sent a note enclosed in our newsletter? I hadn't mentioned that to anyone."

"From what I've been able to determine, Monica sent notes to a number of the Belle Haven Club members."

"She did?" Paul sounded shocked.

"Yes. At least three that I know about. I suspect there were probably more."

"Then we weren't the only ones . . ."

"Who had something you didn't want the rest of the club to know about? No, you weren't."

Paul was silent for a moment, thinking about that. I walked around to Faith's other side, to get to her other ear. I thought I'd put my pin brush on the table, but now I didn't see it. I was reaching around to check in my tack box when I realized that Darla had it.

She held up the brush and looked at it like she'd never seen one before. Short haired breeds, like Pugs, don't require nearly as much preparation for the ring as Poodles do. Still, I couldn't imagine she hadn't run across a pin brush somewhere.

On the table, Faith shifted restlessly. I knew she was wondering what was holding me up. I reached over and gently took the brush out of Darla's hands. She smiled at me as I went back to work.

"You know, it's funny," said Paul. His voice was so low that for a moment I wondered if he was talking to himself. "You spend your whole life trying to build a history of achievement, of accomplishment. You know you're going to grow old someday, but you can only think about it in abstract terms. You see the broad picture, but not the day to day indignities, the loss of rights and abilities that you once took completely for granted."

He looked up, his gray lashed eyes finding mine. "Darla and I don't have much left anymore. But we have each other, we have our dogs, and we have our membership in the kennel club to keep us going.

"For whatever reason of her own, Monica tried to make us feel bad about that. I never thought I'd say this about another human being, but I'm glad she's gone. Does that make me a terrible person?"

"No," I said softly. "I think Monica was the one who must have been a terrible person. Terrible enough that somebody wanted her dead."

"Dear?" said Darla. "Isn't it time to go? Didn't you tell me we were going to watch the groups?"

"Yes, I did." Paul gripped his wife's fragile arm. "We'll go right now."

I watched them walk away. I hoped when I was that age, I had someone to hold my arm and take such good care of me.

∽❋ *Twenty-three* ❋∽

After the Heinses left, Bertie came hurrying back. She stowed a Finnish Spitz in a crate and got out the black and white Tibetan Terrier she'd shown earlier. A brush was tucked inside the waistband of her skirt. She pulled it out and ran it hurriedly through the TT's coat.

"You must have won," I said.

"Best of Breed." Bertie nodded. "The Non-Sporting group's about to go in. Crawford's Dalmatian pretty much has a lock on it, but I might get a piece."

I'd done all I could for Faith without benefit of either tub or hair dryer. I opened her crate and put her inside with a rawhide chew.

"Shall I come and clap?" I asked.

"Sure." Bertie smiled, as she whisked the dog off the table. "That would be great."

In a perfect world, judges aren't supposed to be influenced by applause from ringside. In theory, the only guide they should use in placing the dogs is their own expertise. Reality, however, is sometimes quite different.

For one thing, by the time group judging rolls around most of the day's casual spectators have usually left. The hard-core dog fanciers sitting ringside are often just as knowledgeable as the judge inside the ring. They have opinions, they have favorites; and they're not shy about making their preferences known.

While it's doubtful that a mediocre dog could parlay any amount of applause into a blue ribbon, it's also true that ringside approval can be used to draw the judge's attention to an up-and-comer that he otherwise might have overlooked.

I had no idea whether the Tibetan Bertie was showing was any good or not. But so far, she'd dodged every inquiry I'd made with the agility of a Saluki coursing over open ground. I needed to find a way to get her to open up. Maybe cheering enough to demonstrate that I was standing in her corner would do the trick.

Bertie ran on ahead. By the time I got to the group ring, the Non-Sporting dogs were already lined up in size order. Crawford's Dalmatian was first, followed by a cream colored Standard Poodle. Bringing up the rear were the slower moving Boston Terrier and Bulldog. Bertie and her TT had found a place in the middle.

The ranks of spectators had thinned considerably, and I found an empty chair and sat down. As the judge gaited the entire line of dogs around the ring for the first time, there was already a smattering of applause. Looking around, I followed the sound to its source. Cy and Barbara Rubicov were beaming at their Dalmatian like a pair of proud parents.

Even to my uneducated eye, he looked like a winner: cleanly built, well muscled, and beautifully marked, with dozens of well delineated black spots covering his body, legs, and head. The Dalmatian moved with speed and grace; and Crawford was enough of an expert to showcase his exhibit, while letting himself fade into the background.

The judge began the individual examinations by bringing the Dalmatian out into the middle of the ring. Some officials judge primarily with their eyes; others rely on their hands as a final guide. I watched as this judge lifted the Dalmatian's head and cradled it briefly in her palms. She gathered a quick impression of head and expression, then moved her fingers to lift the dog's lips and look at the bite.

Standards vary from breed to breed. Some require that teeth be counted. Others, like Chow Chows, demand a visual inspection of the tongue. But with a Dalmatian, checking for correct bite is usually routine, over in only a matter of seconds.

That's why I was surprised to see the judge pause for an extra moment. She didn't frown, exactly, but neither did she look pleased. Crawford's expression was calm, but that wasn't unexpected. He was the consummate professional. If the dog's tail fell off, he'd find a way to make you believe that's what he'd intended all along.

Curious, I glanced over to where the Rubicovs were standing. Cy was talking to the person beside him and when he finished, all three laughed. But the set of his shoulders was stiff and the hand that hung at his side was balled into a fist.

Nor did the tension leave him as the judge completed the rest of her examination. The Dalmatian was clearly a ringside favorite. When the dog was gaited, the applause that accompanied his trip to the other end of the ring and back was long and sustained. Crawford brought the Dalmatian back into line with a flourish. He was grinning, but Cy's smile was tight.

By the time Bertie's turn came to show her Tibetan Terrier, the spectators had already rallied behind the Dal, the Standard Poodle, and the Bichon Frisé. I clapped like mad, but only induced a handful of others to accompany me. The judge made her placements, pulling out the Dalmatian on top. Whatever it was she'd seen, she'd obviously decided it wasn't important. Looking enormously pleased, Cy and Barbara accepted congratulations from those around them.

Bertie's Tibetan Terrier had made the cut, but didn't get a ribbon. Since I knew she'd been hoping for a better result, I figured I could pretty much give up on the idea that she'd be in a good enough mood to talk. Instead of heading back to the set-up, I skirted around the ring to where Cy and Barbara were standing. I might as well congratulate the winners, and rack up a few brownie points there.

But before I could reach them, I saw Cy turn and stride quickly away, heading toward the other side of the building. Immediately I changed direction and went after him. After a moment it became obvious we were both following Crawford, who was leading the Dalmatian back to his section of the grooming area.

Cy looked distinctly irritated. And although Crawford must have had an inkling that his biggest client was behind him, he never stopped or even slowed his stride. All at once I wanted very much to hear what these two had to say to each other.

Reaching the first aisle of crates and tables, I veered off

to the left before either man noticed me. Crawford's set-up was tucked away in an alcove off the main room. I circled around, looped behind a concession stand, and ended up around the corner hidden from view—hopefully close enough to hear what they were saying.

If they'd been whispering, it wouldn't have worked; but they weren't. Cy was too angry.

"What was that about?" he demanded.

"They're shifting again. I told you that might happen." Crawford's voice was pitched a good deal lower. I had to strain to hear what he was saying.

"You also told me you could fix it."

"I can. I have an appointment with Dr. Rimkowsky on Tuesday. By next week, everything will be fine."

"Next week? What about this afternoon? You told me the dog had a good shot at Best in Show!"

"He does," Crawford said soothingly. "Anna Peabody is judging and you know she's too vain to wear her glasses. She'll never notice a thing."

"She'd better not."

I shrank back just in time to avoid Cy as he came striding out of the alcove. I killed a minute or two by looking over the selection of dog toys at the concession, then followed him back across the room. Cy had rejoined Barbara at ringside. Obviously the fireworks were over.

I was thinking of heading home when I noticed Mark and Penny Romano, also by the group ring. With the Non-Sporting group over, the Working dogs were in. The Romanos cheered loudly as the Doberman Pinscher was moved.

"Yours?" I asked, walking over to stand beside them.

"No, unfortunately." Mark turned and smiled. "He's an awfully nice dog."

"I was wondering if I could ask you two a question?"

"Sure," said Mark while Penny nodded.

"I've found out that Monica was sending extra notes along with some of the club newsletters. I was wondering if she ever sent one to you?"

"No—" Mark began, but Penny interrupted him.

"Yes, she did. Remember?" She crooked a finger at me and I leaned closer. "Monica," Penny confided in a low tone, "thought I was a lush."

I straightened and took a deep breath of fresh air. Some secret. Of course Penny was a lush. Anyone with a brain or a nose could figure that out.

"Bitch," Penny muttered.

Mark looked as though he fervently hoped his wife was talking about one of the entries in the ring. She wasn't.

"Monica Freedman was a bitch," she repeated, just in case there'd been any misunderstanding the first time around.

Mark slipped an arm around his wife's shoulders. It looked as though he gave her a warning squeeze. Penny refocused her attention on the ring.

"I'm afraid Monica wasn't our most popular club member," Mark said apologetically.

"So I hear."

I waited, hoping Penny might have something more to add, but she didn't. In the ring, the judge made his selections. The Doberman Mark and Penny had been cheering for went second. They drifted away and I went back to the set-up and packed up. I brought my car over from the parking lot, loaded up, and went home.

Bob and Davey weren't back yet, so I used the free time to sit down with a cup of coffee and call Aunt Peg.

"Any puppies yet?" I asked when she picked up.

"Not a one. The bitch's temperature has dropped and she's spent the entire day either trying to hide under the bed where she's much too big to fit, or else digging up the whelping box and tearing everything to shreds. It won't be long now. How did you do at the show?"

I told her about Faith's Reserve, and Aunt Peg was suitably pleased.

"I've seen that bitch of Crawford's," she said. "She's very pretty. There's no shame in being beaten by one like that."

"I stayed and watched the Non-Sporting group."

"Did Crawford's Dalmatian win it?"

"Yup."

"That figures. Cy thinks he has a shot at top ten this year and I don't blame him."

"Maybe," I said. "Maybe not. Who is Dr. Rimkowsky?"

"A veterinarian in Bridgeport. His specialty is canine orthodontia, and he's probably the best on the east coast. Why?"

"Spot has an appointment with him on Tuesday. When the judge was examining his bite, she seemed to see something she didn't like. Later I heard Crawford tell Cy that they—presumably his teeth—were slipping again."

"So Crawford's had some work done on the dog's bite, has he?" Peg sounded amused, but not necessarily surprised.

"Isn't that unusual?"

"Not really. Technology's advancing in all areas. Why should dogs be any different? It used to be that when you bred a litter of puppies, what the bitch produced was what you had to work with. But not any more.

"Now, all sorts of subtle alterations are possible. Not legal, mind you; but possible. Terriers have their tails fixed. With Shelties, it's ears. And of course, any dog that comes up with a bad bite can simply get braces."

"They actually do that?"

"They most certainly do. From what I hear, Dr. Rimkowsky's business is thriving. The dogs wear the braces for several months until the correction is made. After they come off, some dogs are fine. Others wear rubber bands at home to hold everything in place."

"Have you ever had a dog's bite fixed?" I asked curiously.

"Only once. And I did it for health reasons, not so he could be shown. The dog was neutered and placed in a pet home. Regardless of appearances to the contrary, there are still some of us who think of showing dogs as a sport, you know."

"I'm sure there are," I said demurely.

In the living room, Faith began to bark. A moment later, the front door flew open and bounced off the wall.

"Hey Mom!" yelled Davey. "We're home!"

"I think I have to go," I said.

"Are you free tomorrow? I'll probably be stuck here waiting for something to happen. Why don't you come over and we'll talk some more?"

We made a date for early afternoon and I hung up the phone just as Davey came barreling into the kitchen. He tossed a bag filled with souvenirs onto the table.

"It was awesome!" he cried.

Behind him, Bob followed more slowly.

"Awesome?" I asked, cocking a brow in Bob's direction.

"Awesomely tiring." He sank into a chair. "I thought there were just a few ships or something. It's a whole village."

"With a newspaper and a barrel shop and a boatyard," Davey said excitedly. "Did you know there's an aquarium, too?"

"I seem to remember hearing something like that. Did you have fun?"

"We had a great time." To my surprise, Davey walked over and wrapped his arms around me. "I wish you could have come, too."

"So do I. Next time, okay?"

"Okay." He took Faith and went running out of the kitchen.

Davey had left his bag on the table. I opened it and found a poster, a mug, a tee shirt, two candles, and a ship in a bottle. "Do you think you bought enough?" I asked.

Bob had his head down on the table, cradled in his arms. He opened one eye. "Davey asked for all that stuff," he said. As if that was a perfectly good reason.

"Didn't it ever occur to you to say no?"

"I thought I wouldn't have to. I thought after he got a few things he'd figure that would be enough."

Such naiveté. It was touching, really.

"What a day." Bob sighed. "I feel like I'm a hundred years old. Doesn't he ever wind down?"

"Not that I've seen," I said cheerfully. "Want to stay for dinner?"

"I'm too tired to eat. I'm going to go back to the hotel, take a shower, and fall into bed."

He couldn't wait to get away. It was written all over his face.

"By the way," I said. "I'm going to be out all tomorrow afternoon. You'll take Davey, won't you?"

The only answer he could manage was a groan.

☙❀ *Twenty-four* ❀❧

Sunday morning, I called Frank early enough to get him out of bed. Nine o'clock. By then, Davey and I had been up for hours. Then again, we hadn't been working half the night, as I knew Frank had.

All right, so maybe I thought the jolt would be good for him, okay?

I'd spent the last week stewing over the fact that it was Frank, my own brother, who'd given Bob the information he needed to feel justified in trying to take away my son. Frank and I didn't have the best of relationships, but I'd never have expected him to betray me like that.

I knew his machine would come on after the fifth ring. I let the phone ring four times, then hung up and dialed again. On my third attempt, Frank picked up.

"Shit," he said. "This better be an emergency."

"It's Melanie. And good morning to you, too."

"Is it morning already? It feels like the middle of the night."

"Rise and shine. I want to talk to you."

"Can't it wait until a more civilized hour?"

I'd been waiting seven days already. At first I had been too upset to call. By mid-week, pain had softened to hurt. But sometime in the last few days, my resolve had hardened. Now I was angry.

That seemed to me to be the perfect time for Frank and me to talk.

"Wake up," I said. "I have something to say to you."

"I'm awake," Frank grumbled. "A constantly ringing phone has that effect."

I knew how my brother felt. I can be grouchy in the morning too. I pictured him sitting up in bed, trying ineffectually to rub the sleep from his eyes. But I refused to feel sorry for him.

"I hear you and Bob got together last week."

"Is that what this is about? God, Mel. Get a grip. We used to be family, remember? Just because you and he are enemies now—"

"We're not enemies," I said firmly. "Bob and I get along fine." Especially when we had two-thirds of the country between us and he wasn't trying to take my son away. "I understand you told him some things he didn't know about the family."

"Yeah." Frank's tone was guarded. "I guess I did."

"Why?"

The silence lingered for an extra few seconds. Then Frank said, "I thought it might help."

"You *what*?"

"Damn it Mel, deafening me isn't going to accomplish anything. I thought it might help if he knew a few things."

"How could that possibly help?"

"I'll tell you if you promise not to yell again."

He sounded like a four year old. Seething, I promised.

"We were just talking, you know? Bob mentioned something about taking Davey back to Texas. I knew how you felt about that so I said, you can't take Davey away from my sister He's all she has. You know how broken up she was when we lost our parents. Then one thing just sort of led to another. I thought it might make him more sympathetic if he heard the whole story."

I sighed softly. Frank had botched things up big-time, but at least he hadn't done it intentionally. I supposed that was something.

"I take it it didn't work?" he asked.

"No, it didn't."

"Sorry about that."

"Apology accepted. Just don't try to help anymore, okay?"

"If that's what you want, sure."

I'd started to hang up the phone, when Frank said, "Listen, since I'm up anyway, there's one more thing. I was talking to one of the other bartenders at Francisco's. A girl named Beth."

If Beth was old enough to tend bar, she was old enough to be called a woman. I thought about correcting him, as I had Bob, but decided against it. Sometimes Frank and I get along better if I keep most of what I'm thinking to myself.

"Anyway, she and I were talking about that lady who got murdered in the parking lot."

I sat up and paid attention. "Did Beth see something?"

"No. She was inside the restaurant the whole time. She didn't even know anything had happened until the police showed up."

"Oh."

"But she had plenty to say about those kennel club people. I think you ought to reconsider getting involved with them. Beth works most Tuesdays so she gets to see them come and go, and according to her, half of them are nuts. The way they carry on, she said it's less surprising that one of them is dead, than that more aren't."

I chuckled at that. Beth sounded pretty astute for someone watching from the sidelines. "Did she mention anything in particular?"

"She saw a couple of them get into a fight. In February, I think. Two women came into the bar after the meeting, and both of them were pretty steamed."

"Was one of them Monica?" I asked eagerly.

"The lady that got murdered? No. The police showed Beth her picture, and she said it wasn't. One of these women was a knockout of a redhead."

It had to be Bertie. "What about the other?"

"Beth didn't know. Just some middle-aged lady with her glasses hanging around her neck. She ordered a Piña Colada."

That rang a bell. I had to stop and think for a moment, but then I remembered. Sharon LaPlante wore her glasses on a string around her neck. I'd noticed that because Louis had said she was always losing things. Just before he'd served her a drink that was white and frothy.

"Is Beth on this week?" I asked.

"I guess so."

The April meeting of the Belle Haven Kennel Club was scheduled for Tuesday night. I hadn't decided if I was going to attend, but the extra bonus of being able to talk to Beth tipped the scales in that direction.

"Take some advice from your little brother," said Frank. "Stay away from these people. They're a bunch of kooks."

Tell me something I don't know.

Bob arrived at noon, no surprise there. Meal times seemed to activate his homing instincts. I fixed sandwiches for the three of us, and let Davey have two double-fudge brownies for dessert. Why should I be the parent who is always the mean one?

Besides, by the time the sugar hit his blood stream, I'd be long gone.

Usually Aunt Peg likes me to bring Faith along when I visit. But today the puppy was staying home. With a brand new litter coming, Peg wasn't taking any chances with germs.

I didn't bother to ring the doorbell. As I climbed the steps, I could hear the Poodles barking up a storm and figured that was probably notice enough of my arrival. A few moments later, Aunt Peg opened the door and quickly drew me inside.

"Come on," she said, sprinting back up the stairs with amazing speed for someone her age. "Hurry up. I think we're about to have another one."

"Another puppy?" My eyes widened. "She's having them now?"

"Since eight o'clock this morning. I was up all night watching and wouldn't you know, Chloe waited until it got light to get started. Six so far, three boys and three girls. Hurry *up*."

Striding down the second floor hallway, Aunt Peg opened the door to a guest room just wide enough for me to slip inside. Shooing away the curious Standard Poodles milling about outside, she came in too, then shut the door behind her.

The black Standard Poodle bitch was lying in a large, low-sided wooden box. She rose a bit as we came in, dislodging the small black babies nursing at her side.

"There's a good girl," Aunt Peg crooned. "You're doing a fine job. You remember Melanie."

Peg took my hand and extended it so the bitch could sniff. Chloe did indeed remember me and she settled back down among her new brood with a groan.

"What's the matter with her?" I asked. "Why does she sound like that?"

"She's having contractions. It won't be long."

I was wearing a jacket and I took it off and threw it on the bed. A minute later, my sweater followed. Chloe was lying on her side, still moaning softly.

"Maybe she's hot. It's awfully hot in here. Why don't you turn the heat down?"

"It has to be hot," said Aunt Peg. "Puppies are born without the ability to regulate their own body temperatures. The worst thing you can do to a newborn puppy is allow it to get chilled. They can live without food for a certain period of time, but they can't live without warmth. Ohh, here we go . . ."

Moving quickly, Aunt Peg reached into the whelping box and began to gather up the puppies. There was another, much smaller box sitting off to one side. It was made of cardboard and had a heating pad in the bottom. Hurriedly, Peg transferred the puppies into the small box and out of the way as Chloe began to have the hard, pushing contractions that would soon produce another puppy.

"Good girl," Peg whispered, stroking the bitch's side. "You're doing great."

Three good pushes and the job was done. The puppy arrived head-first and curled in a fetal position. Aunt Peg broke the sac and cleaned off the puppy's nose and mouth. As soon as she was sure that the baby was breathing, she took her hands away and let the bitch take over.

Chloe dried the puppy and severed the umbilical cord. Moving blindly, the puppy crawled around the floor of the box, seeking food and warmth. Aunt Peg lifted Chloe's hindquarter, replaced the soiled pads beneath her with fresh ones, then guided the newborn to a teat. It latched on and began to suck contentedly.

"What about the others?" I asked. "Shouldn't we put them back?"

"Not yet. Puppies very often arrive in pairs. You get a long time off in between, then two come almost together. Let's wait a few minutes and see."

As usual when it came to dogs, Aunt Peg was right. In what seemed like no time at all, Chloe's contractions started again. This time I knew what to expect. As Peg encouraged the dam along, I picked up the new puppy and placed her on the heating pad with her litter mates. They'd all piled together into a small heap and were sleeping soundly.

Ten minutes later, another girl puppy had arrived. Aunt Peg changed the bedding once more, then Chloe lay back down in the whelping box and we moved her litter back in with her. The puppies awoke, cheeping like little birds. They scrambled around, then began to nurse.

"That may be it," said Aunt Peg. "Eight is a good size

litter for a Standard. But there could also be one or two more."

"How do we know?"

"We don't. So we wait and see. If any more are coming now, it will be a while. How about some tea?"

I followed her down to the kitchen. The herd of house Poodles was waiting outside the bedroom door and milled around us as we walked. I recognized Beau, the dog I'd spent the previous summer searching for, and gave him an extra pat. His tail came up, wagging happily, and he trotted along at my side.

If Aunt Peg noticed the defection of her favorite, she didn't mention it. She put the pot on for tea and plunked a jar of instant coffee down on the counter for me. No wonder Belle Haven hadn't asked her to run hospitality for their show.

"There are sticky buns in the bread bin," she said. "How many shall I heat up?"

"I just had lunch."

"I haven't eaten since last night. I'd better warm the dozen."

She did. And got out the butter, too. When I'm with Aunt Peg, I need all the willpower I can muster. She eats like a longshoreman. And she keeps enough sweets around to stock a bakery.

She got out a tray and we carried our supplies back upstairs so that we could eat and keep an eye on things at the same time.

"I had an interesting conversation with Frank this morning," I told her, when we were settled once more beside the whelping box. "According to another bartender at

Francisco's, Bertie and Sharon LaPlante had a fight in the bar after the February meeting."

"Bertie and Sharon? That's an unlikely pair."

"That's what I thought."

"Let's go back for a minute," said Peg. "I know you've been doing some asking around. How many club members have admitted to getting notes from Monica?"

"Nearly every one I spoke to. First of all, Lydia. You know about her."

Aunt Peg nodded. "She sent us on to Cy, who was adamant that he had nothing to hide."

"Nothing except the braces on his top winning dog's teeth," I said around a bite of sticky bun.

All right, so I'd caved in. Aunt Peg was on her third.

"And then Barbara sent you on to Joanne."

"I saw her last Sunday. She got two notes."

"Two? What had she done?"

"Reported Paul and Darla Heins to the ASPCA for animal neglect."

"She didn't!"

"She did."

Aunt Peg's frown was ferocious. "What an appalling thing to do to those dear old people. If Joanne knew there was a problem, she should have spoken to the Board. Good Lord, Paul and Darla have been members of Belle Haven for thirty years. We'd have all pitched in and solved the problem. Joanne must have known that."

"Maybe she did. But she took her complaint to the authorities, and she feels pretty self-righteous about it, too."

"Joanne's been angling for a Board position," Aunt Peg muttered. "But although we wouldn't dream of telling her, nobody feels she has the knowledge or experience. Maybe this was her way of paying us back."

I slathered my second sticky bun with butter. It tasted even better that way. "Joanne told Monica what she'd done, and the Heinses got a note in their January newsletter."

Aunt Peg lifted a hand and ticked the names off on her fingers. "Lydia, Joanne, Paul and Darla. Possibly Cy. There certainly seems to have been no shortage of motives."

"You may as well sit back and get comfortable," I told her. "There are more."

ᗱ❋ *Twenty-five* ❋ᗱ

In the whelping box beside us, Chloe stirred. Aunt Peg offered her a drink of cool water and a few strips of boiled
chicken. When she was satisfied the Standard Poodle was
comfortable, Aunt Peg turned back to me.

"Who else?"

"Mark and Penny Romano. Penny told me about the
note they got yesterday at the show. Apparently, Monica
called her a lush."

"I'd fault her for bad manners." Aunt Peg chuckled.
"But Monica wasn't revealing anything the rest of us
hadn't already guessed."

"And then there's Bertie."

"Did she receive a note, too?"

"She says she didn't. But every time I try to talk to her
about Monica, she sidesteps my questions."

"Do you think she's hiding something?"

"Maybe." I shrugged. "Maybe not. Bertie's smart, she's
ambitious, and she's trying to make a name for herself in

a tough profession. Under the circumstances, I can see how she might be wary."

"I wonder what she would have to argue about with Sharon."

"Maybe Louis."

Aunt Peg looked up, surprised. "Louis?"

"Bertie was hanging all over him after the March meeting. Maybe there's something going on."

"Bertie and Louis?" Aunt Peg was skeptical. "I'm not sure I see that. Louis has always struck me as a very proper man."

"Maybe he felt it was time to break out of his shell. And if Bertie were involved with Louis, that might explain why she's been so defensive with me. Do you think Monica knew?"

"She's known about everything else. Incredible as it seems, when you run through the list of club members who were present that night, it looks as though every single one of them had a reason for wanting to keep Monica quiet."

My thoughts, exactly.

"Maybe we should try looking at this from another angle," said Aunt Peg. "Most of us were in the parking lot when the Beagles got loose. You and I were together. I'll bet other people were, too. Now if we could just figure out who was missing . . ."

I was already shaking my head. "Unfortunately, it's not that simple. The club members I've spoken to were scattered all over the place. And with all the confusion, if anybody was lying about where they were, we'd never know."

"This is getting us nowhere," Aunt Peg said grumpily. Usually she likes puzzles. Maybe it was lack of sleep. "And don't forget about the other mystery. What ever happened to those missing dinner checks?"

"They still haven't turned up?"

"No. I talked to Lydia yesterday."

"Do you think they're connected to the murder?"

"I don't see how. But that's exactly the point, isn't it? This whole thing is baffling."

Peg and I don't always come to the same conclusions. For once we were in perfect agreement, so I decided to let the subject rest.

I reached into the whelping box and ran my fingers down the back of a sleeping puppy. Only hours old, its hair was already long enough to hold the beginning of a curl. Chloe lifted her head and sniffed my hand. She didn't push me away exactly, but she did decide she had a sudden need to tend to the puppy in question. I watched as she licked him from one end to the other with her long, pink tongue.

"They're wonderful, aren't they?"

"Absolutely amazing." Peg's voice, like mine, was hushed. "I've been doing this for longer than I care to think about, and each time a new litter is born it feels like a miracle."

We sat in silence and watched some more. The puppies' eyes and ears were still closed, but their noses were working fine. They sought each other out and nestled together for warmth, with Chloe curled around the whole brood protectively.

Just observing made me feel oddly content. It brought back memories of Davey's birth. Back then, so new to motherhood, I'd spent hours simply staring at him while he slept, trying to figure out how such a miraculous baby had come to be mine.

And yet in eight short weeks, Aunt Peg would be placing most of these puppies in their new homes. After all the time and effort she'd put into these babies, she would have to trust someone else to continue to do their best for them. I thought of Davey and wondered how she could bear to let them go.

"They're so small and defenseless," I said. "Don't you worry about them when they leave?"

Aunt Peg chuckled softly. "By the time these puppies go to their new homes, they'll be running the entire house and eating everything in sight. Caring for them will be a full time job."

"But still . . ."

She must have guessed the direction of my thoughts, because Peg stopped to consider her answer carefully. "When it's the right time to let go, you'll know. A mother has to learn to trust her instincts."

I sighed softly, thinking about what Bob had said. The decisions I made now would effect Davey for the rest of his life. I knew what I wanted, but that didn't necessarily make it right. Bob was Davey's father. Was I justified in denying him equal time in his son's life, or was I only being selfish?

"Even a mother who isn't perfect?"

That earned me a hard look. "I've known a lot of mothers in my day," Peg said sternly. "Canine *and* human. Some were mediocre by my standards, some were really quite excellent. But not a single one was perfect. Whatever gave you the idea that you needed to be?"

"Davey."

"He's complained about the job you've done?"

"No, of course not. How could he? He's never known anything else. He's totally dependent on me. That's why I have to make sure I get everything right."

"Nobody gets everything right. It's impossible. All you can do is try. From what I've seen, you're doing a wonderful job."

"Really?"

Aunt Peg nodded. "Do you think I would have allowed you to have a puppy of mine if you weren't? How many families with young children do you think I sell to? Not very many. Children aren't easy, you know."

The voice of authority, if not experience. Still, I was glad to have her vote of confidence.

Ten minutes later, Aunt Peg walked me out to my car. Chloe was resting comfortably, with no sign of any more puppies to come. The house Poodles followed us down. Clearly they were miffed at being excluded from what was happening in the bedroom. Aunt Peg opened the front door and let them race out.

The pack circled the yard, diving on a trio of soggy tennis balls under the limbs of the big Japanese maple tree. Three Poodles emerged victorious. The others gave chase.

"There's something I've been wondering about," I said, watching them run. "At nearly every house we visited, we were inundated by dogs. At the Rubicovs', there wasn't a single one. What happens to their dogs when they're finished showing them?"

"That's no great mystery. Most of their dogs are probably leased."

I turned and stared. "Like rented?"

"More or less. Say a breeder has a very good dog, but lacks the resources to give it the career it deserves. Someone like Cy has the money, but no need to use the dog in a breeding program. Through the lease arrangement, he gets the glory of the big wins, and in the end, the dog returns home to be a part of the breeder's kennel."

"Oh." I'd been hoping for something juicy, but that sounded pretty straightforward.

"The person you have *me* wondering about is Louis," said Aunt Peg. "I can't picture him and Bertie together, and yet . . ."

"Bertie and Sharon were arguing about something."

"Precisely. I'm stuck here with Chloe, but you could go talk to him. Maybe tomorrow in his office. It's in downtown Greenwich, and you can catch him there without Sharon. Maybe he'll have something interesting to say."

"Do you suppose I should make an appointment?"

"Drop in," said Peg. "Catch him by surprise. And call me when you're finished. I want to hear everything."

Was there ever a time when she hadn't?

When I got home, Bob and Davey were both asleep in front of the TV. On a beautiful spring day, no less. A stock car race was droning around a track and I switched off the set. Faith's barking upon my arrival hadn't awakened them; but for some reason, that did.

"Hey," said Bob, struggling back to consciousness. "Is the race over?"

"Yes," I lied. "The white car won."

I'd stopped at the supermarket on the way home and

my arms were filled with groceries. Bob didn't leap up and offer to help, but he did eye the bags speculatively.

"Am I invited to dinner?" he asked.

"If you want to be. Meatloaf, mashed potatoes, and carrots. It'll be ready in about an hour."

"Great."

Faith hopped up and snuggled next to them on the couch. Everybody was warm and safe. In a little while, they'd be well fed. It wasn't up to Ozzie and Harriet's standards, but it made me feel good.

The law offices of Stickney, LaPlante, and Goldblum were located in a beautifully restored frame house on Mason Avenue in downtown Greenwich. I hadn't been sure about dropping by unexpectedly and, judging by the look on the receptionist's face, she didn't think much of the idea either. Her gaze slid from me to Davey and back again, before she inquired about the nature of my business.

I gave her my name and told her the visit was in reference to Belle Haven Kennel Club business. She pursed her lips and disappeared into the inner sanctum. Davey and I had a seat. The appointments in the waiting room were sumptuous: leather furniture, wooden tables, and a profusion of healthy potted plants.

I'd brought *The Cat in the Hat* for Davey, and he opened the book eagerly. He can't read yet, but he's heard most of his favorite rhymes so often that he knows them by heart. Tuning the pages as he says them aloud, gives him the illusion being very grown up.

After the chilly reception, I was prepared to be kept waiting. To my surprise, Louis came out personally only a few moments later. I introduced him to Davey and they shook hands solemnly. After instructing the receptionist to keep an eye on my son, he ushered me back to his office.

It was a large room with a high ceiling, framed by antique molding. Louis waved me to a chair, then sat behind his desk. A wide expanse of polished teak separated us. The leather bound blotter was empty; the gold pen set beside it, neatly aligned. His pipe was in a holder beside the phone and the sweet aroma of his tobacco hung in the air.

Louis folded his hands and assumed a solicitous pose. "Ms. Greeley said you had Belle Haven business to discuss. I do hope nothing's wrong."

"Nothing new. I don't suppose the missing checks have turned up?"

"No, I'm afraid not. It's beginning to look like we'll have to make the money up."

"That's too bad," I murmured. Louis wasn't the only one who could make concerned noises. "Would you mind if I asked you a few questions about Monica Freedman?"

"Not at all. From what I hear around town, the police investigation is all but stalled. It's in the club's best interests to have Monica's killer found and brought to justice. I'm happy to help in any way I can."

It was an impressive speech. Convincing, too. I wondered if his firm handled litigation. No doubt Louis would be great in front of a jury.

"Were you aware that Monica was practicing a kind of emotional extortion on a number of the club members?"

"No," Louis said, frowning. "This is the first I've heard of such a thing. Are you sure?"

"Quite sure. So you never received any extra notes from her, maybe something that was included with your club newsletter?"

"Not that I saw. My wife usually opens the mail, but I'm sure she'd have mentioned something like that."

"Speaking of your wife," I said slowly. "She and Bertie were observed arguing loudly after the February meeting. Do you know what that was about?"

Louis's brow creased. "Sharon and Bertie, arguing? I can't imagine what they would have to disagree about at all, much less loudly enough to make a scene."

"Maybe about the fact that Bertie is a very beautiful younger woman . . . ?" I let the thought dangle. "A woman who's a little more affectionate than she needs to be with some of the male club members?"

"Is she?"

Surely that didn't come as a surprise to him. "I saw her after the meeting last month. You and she seemed very friendly."

"That's just Bertie's way," said Louis. "It doesn't mean anything."

"Then you and she aren't involved?"

"Involved in what way . . . ?" His voice trailed off as he realized what I was asking. "Certainly not! The very idea is preposterous!"

"Is it?"

"It most certainly is. Not that Bertie isn't an attractive woman. But a man in my position weighs his priorities. The last thing I need is a complication like that."

"Because you've applied to judge, you mean?"

"That's part of it. I also have a position in the community, not to mention a lovely wife."

Ah yes, the lovely wife. The one who'd been seen arguing with the beautiful complication in the bar.

One thing about lawyers, they could defend either side of an argument with equal fervor. Prosecution or defense, it all depended who was paying. Or where their loyalties lay.

I left Louis's office a few minutes later, feeling distinctly unsatisfied. The only thing I knew for sure was that Monica Freedman had had too many enemies. And that I wasn't a whole lot closer to figuring out who'd killed her than I'd been before.

ᕦ⁕ *Twenty-six* ⁕ᕥ

After leaving the law office, Davey and I drove down to Bruce Park and ate lunch outside at a picnic table. The weather was sunny and pleasantly warm for April. Buds were beginning to appear on the trees, and even though it was a weekday afternoon, the tennis courts were full. I'd packed peanut butter and jelly—my son's perennial favorite—and Davey scarfed down two sandwiches before even coming up for air.

"So," I said, leaning back and tilting my face up to the warmth of the sun. "Is it fun having your Dad around?"

"Yeah, sure." Davey folded his napkin into a paper airplane and sent it sailing off into the bushes.

"I guess it's going to be hard for you when he goes back."

"Why can't he stay here?"

"Because his job, and the rest of his life are in Texas now. That's where he belongs." I waited as Davey scooted off the bench, retrieved his plane and sailed it, looping, over the table. "What if you could go to Texas sometime and stay with him. Would you like that?"

Davey squinched up his face, thinking hard. "On an airplane?"

I nodded.

"Would you come, too?"

"Probably not. Just as your Daddy's life is there, mine is here. But we both love you very much, so we both want to spend as much time with you as we can."

"Then Daddy should move back to Connecticut," Davey said firmly.

"I don't think he can do that."

"If he wanted to, he could. Grown-ups can do anything."

The implacable logic of a five-year-old. I beckoned him to me and gave him a hug. His hands were dirty, but his hair smelled like sunshine. I buried my face in his neck and blew out a stream of cold air. Davey squirmed away, giggling with delight.

"I'll tell you what this grown-up wants to do," I said. "This grown-up wants to go catch that Good Humor truck. What do you think?"

"Yea!" cried Davey. "Beat you there!"

We didn't solve the world's problems that afternoon; or even, as it happened, our own. But we did sit in the sun, giggle a lot, and eat toasted almond bars. It seemed like a good deal to me.

I called Aunt Peg when we got home and told her about my visit to Louis's office. "Do you think he was lying?" she asked when I was done.

"He was very convincing," I said, hedging.

"He's a lawyer. He's paid to be convincing."

"He did admit he thought that Bertie was a beautiful woman, but said she'd be too much of a complication."

"Oh pish!" Aunt Peg snorted indelicately. "Where beautiful women are concerned, men have been dealing with complications for generations. And if he'd lie to us about Bertie, do you suppose that means he'd lie about the dinner checks, as well? He *was* the last person to see them."

"I know, but what could he possibly have had to gain by taking them?"

"What would anyone have had to gain?"

She had me there. I hate it when Aunt Peg has more questions than I have answers, and it happens all the time.

"I've got to go," I said. "Sam's coming to dinner."

"It's about time."

I knew I shouldn't, but I had to ask. Like the impulse that makes you poke a sore tooth with your tongue.

"What is?"

"Don't think I haven't noticed. It's shameful the way you've been neglecting Sam since that ex-husband of yours arrived on the scene."

Me neglecting Sam? I thought I could make just as good a case in the other direction. Tonight, hopefully, we'd both have a chance to rectify that. It was time to reaffirm what we both knew inside—that our relationship was solid enough to weather a few bumps.

Even major ones, like an ex-husband who'd all but taken up residence in my house.

With daylight saving time newly in effect, it was still

light outside when Sam pulled into the driveway just after six o'clock. I had chicken marinating on the counter and wine chilling in the refrigerator. While Davey and Faith waylaid our guest by the front door, I slipped into the powder room, combed my hair and put on some lipstick.

"Wow," said Sam, holding open his arms.

I'm probably several years and a skein of stretch marks past my last legitimate wow, but I was too pleased to argue. "Nice to see you, too," I murmured, cuddling in close.

"Hey Sam!" said Davey, wedging his small body between us. "Want to play Nintendo with me? I've got a whole bunch of new games."

"Maybe later." Sam released me and we both gave ground. "First I want to spend some time with your mom."

"All right," Davey conceded ungraciously. "I guess that means I have to play with Faith." Boy and puppy ran back to the living room.

Sam helped himself to a beer and opened one for me. "He hasn't actually taught that puppy how to play Nintendo, has he?"

"Not yet." I grinned. "But it's probably only a matter of time. You know what Aunt Peg says, Poodles can learn to do anything."

"I'm a Poodle fan myself, but somehow I think this is one learning curve they won't surmount."

"Probably only because they don't see the point of moving a blip across a screen."

Sam pulled out a kitchen chair and sat down. "Where'd all the new games come from?"

"Bob. Where else? His theory of child-raising seems to be, when in doubt, spend money."

"Not a particularly healthy attitude."

"In the short run, Davey's fine with it. A few new toys won't change his values. And in the long run . . ." I looked at him and smiled, "I'd rather not ruin a great evening by talking about it."

"Fine by me."

Sam reached out a hand and pulled me down onto his lap. His legs were hard with muscle. I wiggled just enough to make him grin, then braced a hand on his shirt and felt the warm skin underneath. Sam's breath smelled like beer and his kiss tasted like heaven.

Two weeks apart had definitely been too long.

His fingers slipped inside my sweater, then up the bare skin of my back. "No bra. You must be one of those wicked women I've heard about."

"I hope so. Later, you can find out for yourself."

"No time like the present." Sam grasped the hem of the sweater and raised it, lowering his mouth to my breast. My back arched and I gasped aloud.

In the living room, Faith began to bark. Dimly I was aware of the front door opening.

"Hey!" Bob yelled cheerfully. "What's for dinner?"

Sam raised his head and lowered my sweater. "That isn't . . . ?"

Heaven disappeared in an instant. I dropped back down to earth with a thud. "It is."

"You invited him, too?"

"Of course not." Hurriedly, I stood and rearranged my clothes. "He must have invited himself."

"Does he do that often?"

"You'd be surprised," I grumbled, heading out to see my new guest. "Hi Bob. We're having chicken. Sorry you can't stay." Pointedly I opened the door he'd just shut behind him.

"No problem." Bob moved past me and into the living room. He took the Nintendo controller Davey held out to him and sat down on the couch. "I like chicken."

"I'm very happy for you. But you can't stay."

"Mommy, please?" Davey turned an imploring gaze upward. And why not? Now he had someone to play with, too.

"Another time. Tomorrow. No, that's the Belle Haven meeting. Wednesday? Perfect. Okay, guys?"

I felt, rather than saw, Sam come up behind me. He stood in the doorway and looked at Bob, who was leaning forward in his seat, grinning like a fool as he vanquished a small ape with a barrel. Expression intentionally bland, Sam cocked a brow in my direction.

"I was very young," I muttered unhappily. "So sue me."

"Sue who?" asked Bob. "Do I know her?" He turned to look and his monkey fell off a cliff. "Damn!"

"Daddy!" Davey cried.

"Sorry, darn." His gaze slid back to Sam. "Who the hell are you?"

"Daddy!"

"Sam Driver." He held out a hand. "You must be Bob."

"I must be." Bob stood and the two of them sized each other up with all the intensity of ten-year-olds about to butt heads over a football. "You're the one I've been hearing about."

"I am?"

Bob nodded. "Davey talks about you all the time."

"That's good." Sam looked pleased.

"Maybe. Maybe not." Bob looked less pleased. "What's your relationship with my son?"

Davey gave a frustrated squeal as his monkey got eaten by a bee. "Your turn, Daddy."

"Not now, Davey."

"We're good friends," said Sam. He looked past Bob and smiled at Davey. "Aren't we?"

My son returned his smile. "The best."

"Are you sure that's wise?" Bob asked me.

"Perfectly. I'm also sure that it's none of your business."

"Daddy, it's *your turn*. I can't play again until you go."

"Honey, play with Faith for a minute, okay?" I took both men by the arm and led them out to the kitchen. "If we're going to fight, I'd just as soon we do it out here. Davey doesn't have to hear this."

"Fight?" Bob said innocently. "I don't want to fight."

"Good." I spun on my heel and headed toward the front door. "Then you can go back to your hotel."

"Wait," said Sam. "I think he should stay. It's probably a good idea for us to have a chance to get to know one another."

What was the matter with him? Was he nuts?

"Stop talking around me," said Bob. "Don't I get any say in the matter?"

"Why not?" I snapped. Everybody else was having one.

"Good. Then I'll stay." He went to the refrigerator and took out a beer. "Got any chips?"

I threw up my hands. They were both crazy. "Cabinet over the dishwasher. Help yourself."

I'd thought childbirth seemed endless, but that evening set new records. Sam and Bob spent the first hour scoping each other out, and the second engaged in a subtle duel of one-upmanship. By the beginning of the third hour, I was ready to throw them both out.

I know women who think it's flattering to have two men battle for their attention. Not me. I ended up feeling like a pawn being manipulated on the game board of male supremacy. And of course, both men were feeling too macho to help me cook, much less clean up afterward.

Davey didn't fare much better. I'm sure he wondered why questions directed at Sam were often usurped by his father, and vice versa. Being the center of that much attention is wearing on a five-year-old. And while most of the tension seemed to go over his head, there were times when he did look torn between Sam and Bob, and more than a little confused.

By the time dinner was over, however, my son had obviously figured out how to work the situation to his advantage. He suggested a game of hide-and-seek, and grinned with delight when both men suddenly avowed an abiding love for the game. At least that was something I could encourage wholeheartedly, especially as it got them all out of my hair for a while.

I finished doing the dishes and sat down in the living room with a second cup of coffee. Faith was lying on the floor, eating the toe out of an old slipper. Aunt Peg would have frowned mightily at the sight, and with good reason.

If the puppy ate my new slippers, I'd have no one but my-self to blame. But Faith was having so much fun, I didn't have the heart to play the disciplinarian.

Sam came sauntering in.

"Game over?" I asked.

"No, I'm supposed to be counting to one hundred while they hide."

"Davey almost always goes to the same places. Want a clue?"

"What? And ruin the suspense?" He went to the door-way and had a listen up the stairs, then came over and sat down. "Bob doesn't seem too bad."

"My thoughts exactly, the first evening I met him."

"He tries very hard with Davey."

"He has to," I said, feeling exasperated. "Fatherhood doesn't seem to come naturally."

"Maybe you're being too tough on him."

"Maybe you're in no position to judge."

This was going well.

The last thing I'd wanted to do that evening with Sam was argue. Of course it was beginning to look like all the *good* ideas I'd had in mind were out of the question.

"Ready!" yelled Davey. "Come and find us!"

Sam rose. He glanced down at Faith. "You know you shouldn't let her chew on a slipper like that."

"I know," I said complacently.

He shrugged and headed upstairs.

Bob and Sam left within a few minutes of each other after I put Davey to bed. Despite my pointed hints, Bob had been determined to hang around as long as Sam re-mained; and there was definitely something distracting about an ex-husband hovering in the background. I'm sure

I wasn't the only one who cheered when the evening was finally over.

I went upstairs and checked on Davey. He was sleeping soundly, his arm curved around Faith who was resting her head on his pillow. She saw me, thumped her tail up and down a few times, then went back to sleep.

Mothers should have it so easy.

❧❦ *Twenty-seven* ❦❧

After a disastrous evening like that, I spent the next day making things up to my son. Joey Brickman came over and I took both boys to an early afternoon movie. It felt liberating to be out running around town during the week. Of course, the only reason we were doing so was because we'd been too broke to go away during the school vacation like everyone else.

That evening, I had Joanie, the neighborhood babysitter coming to watch Davey, while I went to the Belle Haven Kennel Club meeting. I'd also arranged to meet Aunt Peg there. That was a big plus, because it meant I could cut out early if things got too boring.

I arrived a few minutes late, but didn't hurry inside. Instead, I walked down to the end of the row, to the spot where Monica's van had been parked two and a half weeks earlier. Then it had been dark; now it was light enough to see the area clearly. For a moment, I simply stood, scuffing the toe of my shoe back and forth over some loose gravel.

The spot was empty now; there was nothing to mark it as one where a young woman had lost her life. That seemed kind of sad to me, but then I didn't have to worry about business in the restaurant. I was sure Francisco's was happy with things just the way they were.

Inside the door, I ran into Mark and Penny Romano and we went up the stairs together. "I've been telling Penny how very lucky you are to have such a delightful son," said Mark.

"Thank you." Delightful wasn't the way I'd have characterized Davey's behavior on the day they'd met, but like any mother, I never turn down a compliment. "He's home tonight with a sitter."

"Baby sitters, just think." Penny sighed. "Soon we'll have to worry about things like that, too."

"Maybe," said Mark. "Or maybe we just won't go out." I glanced at Penny's slender figure. "Are you . . . ?"

"Working on it," said Mark. "And the sooner, the better. We're not getting any younger."

We walked into the meeting room, and the Romanos went off to flag down a waitress. I headed over to Aunt Peg, who was saving me a seat.

"It's about time," she said. "They're about to start serving."

What could they do to punish me for tardiness? Refuse to let me join the club? Grinning, I sat.

Since this was the last meeting before Belle Haven's show, attendance was high. The two legs of the horseshoe shaped table extended the entire length of the room. I looked around and recognized a fair number of faces.

Lydia was seated at the head of the table. I hadn't seen the club president since Peg and I had visited her at home. Tonight, she looked tired and drawn, as if the job of leading Belle Haven was weighing heavily on her shoulders.

Seated to one side of Lydia were Cy and Barbara Rubicov. In contrast to the club president, Barbara was smiling and vibrant, her yellow silk suit setting off a new tan. If I hadn't just seen her at a dog show, I'd have guessed she'd been on vacation.

On Barbara's other side, Cy was sitting next to Louis LaPlante. The two men had their heads together and were talking in low tones. In the next seat, Sharon had her purse in her lap. She was searching through it, and muttering under her breath. I wondered what she'd lost now.

The Heinses were sitting at the end of one leg of the horseshoe, next to a couple I didn't know. Directly across from them was Bertie. As always, she looked striking, but tonight there seemed to be a stillness, a wariness about her. When the meal was served, she dedicated herself to eating it with quiet intensity, not joining in any of the conversations around the room.

I wondered if Louis had spoken to her about my visit, maybe warning her that they had to keep a lower profile. Though I watched, I couldn't detect any interaction between them. I wondered if that, in itself, might be significant.

Once again, Joanne Pinkus was seated beside me. She had new pictures of Rupert and Camille to share, and chattered all through dinner like an over-eager puppy, desperate to find something that pleases. At least she wasn't wearing leggings. That pleased me right off the bat.

Predictably, Joanne wanted to discuss whether I'd made

any progress in finding out who'd killed Monica. Using the excuse of a full mouth, I shook my head. It was kind of depressing, actually. Chewing or not, I wouldn't have had much to say.

"I think the whole thing's ghoulish," she said, giving her shoulders a little shake. "Imagine being murdered like that. One minute you're there, and the next . . ."

I stared at my plate with more fascination than it deserved and kept eating.

"At least it was fast. If Monica had lingered in the hospital, her mother could have lost everything."

I looked up. "What do you mean?"

"She didn't have any insurance. None."

"No health insurance?"

Joanne shook her head. "None. I talked to her once about buying some, and she wasn't covered at all. Not life, not health, not even car insurance. She said she couldn't afford it."

"What about the van?" I asked, interested in spite of myself. "Monica must have had insurance on that."

"It was in her mother's name," Joanne said, looking superior. "Can you believe that? For a thirty-three-year-old woman, Monica was still tied pretty close to home."

The sign-up sheet came around, and we both dutifully recorded our names. Dessert was served and Lydia called the meeting to order. During the president's report, she announced that the dinner checks were still missing, and there was general grumbling all around.

When the room quieted, Cy spoke up. "It seems a shame for everyone to have to pay twice for the same meal. I know those checks are going to turn up eventually. In the meantime, if there's a shortfall, I'd be happy to cover it."

"Thank you, Cy." Lydia favored him with a smile. "I'm sure the club members appreciate your offer." Not only that, but more than a few looked like they'd leap at the chance to take him up on it. "Let's give it until the end of April. Then we'll make a decision about our next move."

The meeting ambled on through officer reports, committee head reports, unfinished and new business. When it looked like just about everything had been covered, Lydia took the floor again.

She reminded everyone of the reception she was hosting on Sunday for former club member, Thelma Gooding, who was judging at the Riverhead show. I gathered Thelma must have been pretty popular, because nearly everyone was planning to go.

"Now we come to one of the pleasant duties of my job," Lydia continued. "I'm delighted to announce some recent achievements by our club members. Since our last meeting, Cy and Barbara's Dalmatian, Ch. Sunnyside's Spot On, has won three groups and a Best in Show."

There was a murmur of appreciation, followed by a burst of spontaneous applause. By anyone's standards, the Rubicovs' Dalmatian had had a terrific month.

"Thank you very much." Cy rose to his feet. "Of course, you all know I didn't do any of the work."

I joined in the laughter at Cy's charming self-deprecation. Beside him, Barbara looked enormously pleased.

"I'm lucky to have a dog as good as Spot to show and a handler as talented as Crawford Langley on my team. But that doesn't stop me from being proud as a peacock over the whole business. So who wants to see pictures?"

He reached down and came up with several white cardboard envelopes, filled with eight-by-ten glossies. Cy handed the win photos out in both directions and we passed them around.

"And that's not the end of our good news," Lydia said when Cy had sat back down. "We have another pair of club members with a group win to celebrate. It happened in Maine two months ago, and nobody even told us. Talk about hiding your light under a bushel!" She directed a coy glance at Louis. "I read about it in the *Gazette*. What makes this win even more exciting is that it came from the classes."

There was another round of pleased applause.

"Of course we're all envious, but that doesn't mean we don't want to share your good fortune. Louis and Sharon, wouldn't one of you like to tell us all about it?"

Not Sharon, apparently. Unaccustomed to being in the spotlight, she was flushing a dull shade of red.

"We didn't want to make a fuss," Louis said modestly. "To tell the truth, the win came as quite a surprise. We only sent that bitch up to Maine to try and finish her. We never thought she was that good."

"Hmmph," Aunt Peg muttered under her breath. "I should be so lucky."

"It really wasn't a big deal," Sharon said softly. "It was a very small show."

Cy's pictures finished circling the table and he gathered them up. "Every group win's a big deal," he said, poking Louis in the arm. "Come on. Let's see a picture."

"Come to think of it," Louis said, frowning. "I don't believe I've seen one. I wasn't at the show myself, but I'm sure Sharon had one taken, didn't you dear?"

His wife nodded. She was still looking uncomfortable, as though she wished the attention would focus on anyone but her.

"Call the photographer," Mark advised. "They're always getting mixed up. Once I got back a picture of a Bearded Collie."

Louis made a note on the pad in front of him. "I'll do that."

After that, Lydia wrapped up the meeting with dispatch. I checked my watch and was delighted to find that it was only just after nine o'clock. There would be plenty of time to stop in the bar and talk to Beth, the bartender.

When everyone began to gather up their things, I told Aunt Peg where I was going and ran on ahead. The bar was through an open doorway at the foot of the stairs. The room was of medium size and dimly lit. On a Tuesday night, there wasn't much of a crowd; one couple at a table in the back, and three men at the bar, nursing beers and cheering over a hockey game they were watching on TV.

The bartender was a woman in her early twenties. She had delicate features and glossy, dark brown hair that was parted in the middle and fell halfway down her back. She smiled when I came in and her face took on a quiet radiance. I could easily see how Frank might have been interested.

"You must be Beth," I said, slipping up onto a stool.

"That's right."

I held out a hand. "My name is Melanie Travis. My

brother, Frank, works with you on weekends." Behind me I could hear the low rumble of footsteps on the stairs. "I wonder if you could do something for me?"

"Maybe. Depends what it is."

"My brother told me that you saw a couple of the kennel club people having an argument. Would you mind looking out that door and pointing out which ones they were as they walk by?"

"I guess I could do that." Beth had been rubbing down the bar with a white cloth. She tucked it over the rail and stared at the entrance.

Bertie was easy. Beth picked her out as soon as she came into view. Sharon, on the other hand, was almost past before Beth decided she was the one.

"Did you overhear what they were fighting about?"

"I'm a bartender," said Beth. "All I do is serve the drinks. It's not my job to overhear things."

"No, but I'll bet sometimes you can't help yourself."

Beth smiled. "That's the truth. But with these two, I didn't have any reason to pay attention. I mean, the group is from a kennel club. Does that sound flaky, or what?"

"It sounds pretty flaky," I agreed.

"Besides, it happened a couple of months ago. If it hadn't have been for that other lady being murdered, I never would have given it a second thought."

"Maybe they were talking about dogs?" I prodded to see if that might jog anything loose.

Beth shrugged.

"A man named Louis?"

"Not that I remember." She frowned, thinking back. "There was one thing. Actually it was pretty funny. The older lady called the younger one stupid. Said it was a good thing she had big tits because her brain was the size of a pea."

"Really?" I laughed. That didn't sound like mild-mannered Sharon at all. "She must have really been mad."

"Believe me, she was. They both were."

Beth reached up a hand, looped a long strand of hair around her finger and tucked it behind her ear. "I think your brother's kind of cute. Is he seeing anyone?"

"Not that I know of."

"He's not gay, is he?"

"No." I laughed again. Frank had had a long string of girlfriends, most of them not nearly as appealing as Beth seemed to be.

"How do you think he'd feel if I gave him a call sometime? I don't want him to think I'm too pushy."

"I think he'd be flattered." I reached across the bar, picked up a cocktail napkin and wrote down Frank's telephone number. "Go ahead and try it. My brother's not the most mature person in the world, but he's a pretty nice guy."

"When it comes right down to it, they're all immature, aren't they?" Suddenly looking awfully world weary for one so young, Beth picked up the napkin and pocketed it. "Listen, can I get you something to drink?"

"Sure, a draft would be good."

"Make that two," said Aunt Peg, coming up behind me. "Let's move over to a table, shall we?"

She waited until Beth had served the beers, then said, "Now, tell me everything you found out."

It was a big order for a very small amount of information. I repeated what Beth had told me. "I don't know," I said at the end. "If I was accusing another woman of having an affair with my husband, I can think of a lot of things I might call her, but stupid isn't necessarily one of them."

"What if Bertie believes Louis is going to divorce Sharon and marry her?"

I shrugged and took a swallow of beer. The mug was cold, the beer colder still, and it went down very easily. "Bertie doesn't strike me as the kind of woman who's in any hurry to get married. At the moment, she's too interested in building her career."

That reminded me of something else I'd heard. "Speaking of putting things off until later, did you know Penny Romano is trying to get pregnant?"

"At her age?" Aunt Peg sniffed. "I doubt it. That woman's at least forty, and I'm being generous."

When it came to dogs, Aunt Peg kept up with all the latest medical developments. Her magazine rack was filled with newsletters from Cornell and the University of Pennsylvania. But where human fertility was concerned, recent advances had obviously passed by unnoticed.

"She's not too old. Not these days. Anyway, they said they'd been working on it. They're probably seeing a fertility specialist."

"If the doctor has any sense, he'll enroll her in A.A. first thing," Aunt Peg said briskly. "Now enough about that." She'd never had any children of her own, and couldn't be bothered faking an interest in anyone else's.

"I'll have you know I'm finding this whole situation extremely irritating. We've done nothing but go around in circles. The problem with trying to find Monica's killer is not that we don't have enough clues, we have too many."

I nodded in agreement. "Everybody had a secret. What we need to figure out is who thought their secret was worth killing over."

☙❋ *Twenty-eight* ❋☙

"Who had the most to lose?" asked Aunt Peg.

"Cy," I said. The answer seemed obvious. "He's put a lot of money into Spot's career. If word got out that the dog had had his bite fixed, Cy might as well have poured it down the drain."

"That's true," Aunt Peg agreed. "But Cy and Barbara are very well off. I imagine they could take a loss like that in stride. Besides, I happen to believe that there are plenty of things more valuable than money."

Only because you have enough, I was tempted to retort. Wisely, I kept those thoughts to myself.

"You mean like Lydia's good name?"

"Precisely. She *is* president of Belle Haven. We may not be the largest club, but in certain circles, we're very well regarded. Lydia can be quite forceful when she wants to be, and the fact that she cut a corner or two doesn't necessarily surprise me."

"But is she capable of murder?"

"I imagine almost anyone is capable of committing murder if they feel they have no choice. If the A.K.C. were to have proof that a signature had been falsified on the litter registration, they would revoke all showing and breeding privileges. For someone like Lydia, that would be a tremendous blow."

All right," I said, sipping at my beer. "So Lydia had a pretty solid motive. And I still think Cy did, too. What about the Heinses?"

"I suppose they stood to lose their dignity," Aunt Peg said slowly. "What little Joanne hadn't robbed them of already. Do you see them killing over that?"

"No." In truth, I couldn't imagine either Paul or Darla hurting a fly.

"Which brings us to Joanne, herself."

"She's young and strong enough to have done it fairly easily. And based upon what she did to the Heinses, I'd have to say that she seems to be lacking in basic human compassion." I stopped and shook my head. "But think about motive for a minute. Her secret was pretty much out of the bag already. We know she told Monica and Barbara, and she discussed it with me quite readily."

"She was justifying again." Aunt Peg frowned mightily. It was obvious Joanne wasn't one of her favorite people. "If that girl isn't stopped, she'll justify her way right onto the Board."

On TV, a hockey player scored. The trio of patrons at the bar erupted into cheers.

"We haven't talked about Mark and Penny yet," said Peg.

"Unless I'm missing something, they didn't have much of a motive either. Like Joanne, their secret was out in the open. Almost everyone seems aware of Penny's drinking problem. I can't possibly see how killing Monica would help."

"Which brings us around to perhaps where we should have started: Louis and Sharon."

"And Bertie, don't forget about her."

"Hardly," Aunt Peg said drily. "Of all the club members who were there that night, she's the newest, and probably the one I know least. What's your take on her?"

"I doubt I've learned anything that you don't already know. Everyone else I've spoken to has at least professed to want to help. Not Bertie. Whenever I try to ask her anything, she immediately goes on the defensive. She says she never received anything from Monica."

"Nor did Louis, if we're inclined to believe the two of them."

"If they are having an affair," I said, "how much would they stand to lose?"

"In Louis's case, maybe his marriage."

"Except that we're supposing Sharon already knows what's going on. Otherwise, what would she and Bertie have been fighting about?"

"Good question." Aunt Peg drained the last of her beer. "Monica really did manage to tie this club up in knots, didn't she? Maybe it's like that Agatha Christie book and they all acted together."

I had to laugh. "The only person who would buy that theory is someone who's never been to a meeting. The members of the Belle Haven Club can't even agree on how much they should charge for an entry fee. The thought of them acting together to plot a murder is ludicrous."

I fished a couple of dollar bills out of my purse and left them on the table as a tip, then followed Aunt Peg out. We didn't seem to be much closer to finding Monica's murderer, but on the other hand, there was a whole month before the next Belle Haven Kennel Club meeting.

That alone was something to smile about.

Wednesday, I awoke to the sound of birds singing in the trees. The sky was a clear, cerulean blue and the forecast promised a temperature in the seventies. I told Davey he could wear shorts, then had to scoot around under his bed pulling out storage boxes to find a pair.

Dressed like summer was just around the corner, my son took Faith out into the back yard for a game of catch. I was busy pushing up storm windows and pulling down screens when Bob arrived. He let himself in and trooped upstairs to my bedroom.

"Here, let me help."

He strode across the room, reached arms around me to grasp a screen that was sticking, and forced it down where it belonged. There was an awkward moment when he realized he was standing with his arms around me, then we both retreated quickly. Bob sat down on the bed; I went to work on the next window.

"Do you ever wonder what it would have been like if I hadn't left?" he asked.

"No."

"Never?"

"I used to," I said quietly. "But not anymore. There was a time when I'd have given anything to have you back. I guess I was just that desperate."

"Maybe you loved me that much."

"Maybe I did." I turned to face him. "That was a long time ago."

"I don't want us to be adversaries, Mel."

"We're not—"

"Don't argue, okay? Let me say what I came here to say. Davey's a great kid, and I know I have you to thank. Maybe I could have made things easier on you. No, strike that. I *know* I could have made things easier.

"But I was young and I had a lot of growing up to do. I thought just because I had a job, and a house, and a family, I was an adult. But I wasn't. I guess the way I acted proved that. I know you won't believe this, but meeting Jennifer has made a tremendous difference in my life. For the first time, I'm learning how to be the grown-up in a relationship, how to take responsibility. It isn't easy."

As if this was news to me.

"I'm very happy for you, Bob." And I was, truly. But after two and a half weeks in my ex-husband's company, I was ready for him to pack up his newfound maturity and take it back to Texas.

"You've been here for a while now," I said, finishing off the last window. "I guess Jennifer must be missing you."

"So she says." Bob tried not to look too pleased, but didn't succeed. "We talk on the phone."

I walked out into the hall and started down the stairs. Bob followed along behind. "I bet she's wondering when you're coming home—"

"Daddy!" Davey shrieked from the foot of the stairs. Faith leapt up, waved her front paws in the air and barked in accompaniment. "When did you get here?"

"Just a little while ago. Guess what?"

"What?" Davey grinned delightedly.

"I've got a surprise."

"For me?"

"For you and Mommy. It's a secret."

I continued past them and went into the kitchen. The last thing I needed was to hear any more secrets. There was a bag of groceries sitting on the counter that hadn't been there earlier.

I opened it up and found cold cuts, onion rolls, a jar of my favorite sweet pickles, and a rubber chew toy for Faith. Our surprise, unless I missed my guess. I got out plates, napkins, mayo, and mustard and went to work.

Lunch was an odd meal. It started with the three of us sitting around the kitchen table, and Faith lying next to Davey's chair where hand-outs were most likely to come her way. Five minutes into the meal, Davey got up and ran to the front door.

I hadn't heard anything, and neither had Faith. She got up and went along anyway. Davey was back thirty seconds later. He looked at Bob, and shook his head.

"What?" I asked.

"You'll see!" cried Davey, laughing.

Bob merely grinned.

The first time that happened, I was mildly curious. The second, I was beginning to get annoyed. Especially as whatever was going on, had Davey too excited to eat. He dropped half his sandwich on the third trip and I watched as Faith gobbled it up.

"That's it," I said. "Sit at the table until you're finished."

"I can't!" Davey wailed. "I might miss it."

"What?"

Outside, a horn gave two sharp toots. In an instant, Davey was up and running again. Faith went flying after him.

I looked at Bob. "Who's here?"

"Let's go see."

There was an unfamiliar car in the driveway: a top of the line Volvo station wagon, with silver metallic paint and wrap-around lights. The driver was barely visible behind the tinted windshield. He was wearing a sports jacket and sunglasses and didn't look like anyone I knew.

"So," Bob said grandly. "What do you think?"

"Who is he?" I hissed under my breath.

"Not him," Bob said, as the man climbed out. "The car. What do you think?"

"It's very nice. Bob, what's going on?"

"Surprise!"

I frowned, feeling very confused. "Surprise what?"

"Mommy, look!"

I turned in time to see Davey open the station wagon's door and scoot inside. Faith quickly followed. "Davey, wait!"

The sound of the horn cut me off. Davey leaned out the open window and waved.

"I'm sorry," I told the driver of the car, as I hurried past him. "I'll have my son out of there in just a second." I didn't even dare mention the dog. Faith had hopped over the seat and was exploring the back of the station wagon. I hoped her feet weren't too dirty.

The man grinned and shrugged, like he wasn't bothered in the slightest. Was the whole world crazy, or was it just me?

"Mel, wait!" said Bob. "You don't get it."

"Of course I don't get it." I stopped next to the Volvo's shiny new hood and blew out an exasperated breath. "What's going on?"

"This is your new car."

"Oh, good." Then I realized what he'd said. "My *what?*"

"Your new car. I bought it for you yesterday."

I sagged back against the fender. The metal felt smooth and unblemished beneath my hands. New paint, no dings, no rust. The engine probably worked, too. Holy moly, a new car. My new car.

"Are you kidding?"

Bob shook his head.

I ran my fingers over the side-view mirror. Remote control. When my old Volvo had been manufactured they hadn't even invented that. The windshield was gleaming, and so was everything else. I stuck my head inside where Davey and Faith were tumbling around on the leather seats. Damn, it even smelled good.

Reluctantly I pulled back out and straightened. "I can't accept it."

It killed me to say it, but it had to be done. Bob had spent the last two weeks trying to buy Davey's affection and compliance, now he was trying to buy mine. There was no way I was going to let him bribe me into negotiating custody rights for my son.

"Sure you can," Bob said easily. "Besides, you pretty much have to. I traded in your old car."

"You did *what?*"

Bob reached in his pocket and produced a Volvo key. He must have slipped it off my key chain earlier. "Mr. Krupnick here was kind enough to offer to drive out and make the trade."

"Bob," I said quickly, "we need to talk."

"Okay. We'll talk while we drive. Let's take her out for a spin."

"Yea!" cried Davey.

He'd gotten out of the new car and was turning cart-wheels in the yard. Faith ran circles around all of us, barking like a fool. A neighbor, driving by on the road, slowed to see what was happening. I felt like Alice, spinning down into Wonderland. Any minute now, the red queen was going to show up and yell "Off with her head!"

"No, now," I said firmly. "We need to talk now."

"What's the matter?" Bob reached out and took my hand. "This is a present. I want you to have it."

"I can't. It's too much."

"So what? I have the money."

"I know that. You've been throwing it around ever since you got here."

"Maybe things got a little out of hand," Bob said, looking sheepish. "But this is different. You need this car, and you know it as well as I do."

"I need a lot of things, but that doesn't mean—"

"The car is yours. It's a gift, plain and simple. No strings. No conditions. Just take it and say thank-you."

I gazed at the shiny new Volvo, feeling unexpectedly teary. It was silver, like a freshly minted coin. I wondered how it would feel to sit in the leather seats. To turn the key and hear the engine turn over on the first try.

"No conditions?" I repeated.

"None."

He'd let my hand drop. I reached out, took his, and squeezed it hard. "Thank-you."

We spent the rest of the day driving around Fairfield County; bumping over dirt roads, speeding down the parkway, and generally comporting ourselves like people who'd never been exposed to automated transportation before. We had the windows and sun roof open, and the radio on full blast. The Volvo purred when I turned it on, and handled like a dream. According to the sticker, I was even getting good gas mileage.

I asked Bob to stay for dinner that evening, but he said he was having dinner at Frank's. That bothered me some. The last time the two of them had gotten together, I'd had good reason to regret it. But Bob seemed happy about the invitation and frankly, I was in too good a mood to worry.

Left by ourselves, Davey and I drove down to the Bull's Head Diner and had dinner. Then we opened the sun roof so we could see the stars, and took the long way home.

༒ ❧ *Twenty-nine* ❧ ༒

Davey had a play-date with Joey the next morning. I dropped him off, then drove into downtown Stamford. According to the phone book, Cy Rubicov's company headquarters were located in Landmark Square, a tall, brick and glass complex on the corner of Broad and Atlantic. Considering what I'd learned since, I was reasonably certain that Cy had lied when we'd spoken before. It was time to confront him with what I knew and see how much more he might admit.

The offices for Rubicon Freight ("We'll take you anywhere you want to go, and beyond") took up half the fifth floor, with a reception area that was wide and spacious. Floor to ceiling windows filled the wall at the far end and sunlight spilled in from outside. The decor was high-tech; lots of chrome and glass, with a minimum of clutter. In the background, I heard the gentle hum of computers and muffled conversation.

All at once, the paltry excuse I'd come up with for my visit—that I'd decided to volunteer my services to work on the hospitality committee for the Belle Haven show—seemed just this side of absurd. I gave the receptionist my name, and told her I didn't have an appointment. I thought that might earn me the bum's rush right then and there, but she asked me to have a seat and picked up her phone. Only moments later, I found myself being ushered in.

Cy was talking on the phone, but he grinned and waved when I entered. The receptionist withdrew, closing the door behind her, and Cy quickly concluded his call. He came out from behind his desk, hand outstretched.

"Melanie, what a nice surprise. What can I do for you?" He motioned toward a grouping of chairs around a small table, and we both sat.

"I was in the neighborhood, and I decided to drop in and offer to help on your committee for the show."

"Offer accepted. Now tell me why you really came."

Away from Barbara, in his own milieu, he was brasher, and rougher around the edges than he'd seemed before. This was a man who had amassed a fortune in the interstate trucking business, and though I'd never doubted his intelligence or ability, now I could see the energy and the enterprise that had taken him so far.

When I hesitated, Cy looked me straight in the eye. "I didn't get where I am today by letting people bullshit me. You want to work on my committee, I'm happy to have you. Now tell me the real reason you're here."

"Okay." I straightened in my seat. He wasn't the only one who could be blunt. "I want to talk to you about your Dalmatian."

"What about him?"

"Did Monica know that he'd had his teeth fixed?"

Cy swore softly under his breath. "What is it, common knowledge? If Crawford's been blabbing—"

"He hasn't."

"Then how'd you find out?"

"I'm nosy."

"I guess you are. But that doesn't answer my question."

"I watched the judge examine his bite at the New Brunswick show. Then I overheard a reference to Dr. Rimkowsky. It was pretty easy to put two and two together. Did Monica Freedman do the same?"

"Yeah." Cy frowned. "I guess she did."

"I assume she sent you a note about it. Probably something enclosed with your newsletter?"

"What are you, reading my mail now?" His voice rose.

"Monica sent out a number of notes. She'd found out some secrets, and apparently she wasn't above gloating about what she knew."

"You mean I wasn't the only one?"

"Not by a long shot."

Cy swore again. "Imagine that. And here I thought she had it in for me."

"Did she try to blackmail you?"

"No, although after I got the note, I figured that was coming next. Then she got killed, and it never did."

"You must have been relieved."

Cy gave me a hard look. "Monica Freedman was small time. She was nothing to me one way or another. I ignored the first note she sent me. I wouldn't even have bothered to read a second."

"Even if she threatened to have your top winning dog disqualified?"

"First she'd have to prove to me that she could do that," Cy said complacently. "It would have been her word against mine and Crawford's. Monica was a nobody, she'd have been crazy to take us on."

"Still, she could have made a lot of trouble for you."

"All right, worst case. She gets Spot ousted. You think I would commit murder over something like that? Think again. Spot's a good dog and he's going to win his share. But if he doesn't?"

Cy's shoulders rose and fell in an eloquent shrug. "In terms of everything else I've got going on, it's no big deal. And believe me, I know from big deals. If I don't win with Spot, then I'll win with another dog. It's the way the game is played."

I had to admit that what he said made sense. Cy wasn't Spot's breeder. He had no emotional ties either to that particular dog, or to the Dalmatian breed. To him, Spot was a commodity, an investment no different from others he might have made over the years.

Not that I was willing to absolve Cy completely. He'd lied to me once, and was perfectly capable of doing so again. He was also a man of driving force and ambition. In his climb to the top, no doubt he'd had to push some people out of the way. He'd referred to Monica earlier as a nobody. Maybe for him, disposing of the club secretary had been no more than a minor annoyance.

"The night Monica was murdered," I said. "Where were you when it happened?"

Cy eyed me shrewdly. "How would you expect me to know when that was?"

"All right then, when the Beagles began to bark."

"Babs and I were in the car. We had the windows up and

the motor running. We didn't hear a thing. When I started to back out, I saw everyone running around. That's the first time we knew something was wrong."

By then, Monica was already dead. *If* Cy was telling the truth.

"One last question?"

"No point in stopping you now."

"Are you going to use Bertie as a handler?"

"What does that have to do with Monica's death?"

"Maybe nothing. Let's just say I'm curious."

"Hell, we passed curious a long time ago. We're heading straight for damn annoying now. Not that it's any of your business, but no, at the present time, I'm not planning to send any of my dogs to Bertie."

"Do you mind telling me why?"

"That part's easy." Cy rose from his chair, signaling the conversation was over. "She's not good enough."

"She's pretty enough."

"Lots of pretty women in the world. The kind of money I'm laying out, I'm looking for talent, and results. What Bertie's got, that only works for some judges."

I wondered if he was referring to Louis, but Cy was already striding across the room to open the door. I guessed that meant I wasn't going to find out.

"Glad you could stop by," he said, as I gathered up my things. "I could use a few more people on my committee working breakfast. Think you can make it to the show by six?"

Six, right. The show ground was in Purchase, New York. And I had to get Davey up and ready, too. I could see I wasn't going to be getting much sleep the night before the show.

Cy grinned happily. I imagined he was thinking the same thing.

"No problem," I told him breezily. "See you there."

Friday was the last day of school vacation and I wanted to spend it with Davey. The dog shows that weekend were only an hour away on Long Island; and both Sam and Aunt Peg had agreed that Saturday's Poodle judge was worth an entry. The problem was, if I showed Faith, I'd have to spend most of Friday getting her ready. The choice was pretty easy. While Sam and Aunt Peg were busy clipping and bathing and blowing dry, Davey and I took the train into New York and went to the Museum of Natural History.

Davey's so wrapped up in his love of cars that the whole dinosaur fetish has just about passed him by. Even so, his mouth dropped open when he saw the first massive skeleton, and for the next five hours, I don't think he even took time out to blink. As motherly achievements go, it was pretty gratifying.

Saturday was Davey's monthly day with Frank. My brother let himself get talked into taking Faith, too, and I dropped child and puppy off first thing in the morning. Then I continued down I95 to the Whitestone Bridge.

Last time I'd crossed this bridge onto Long Island, the old Volvo had overheated while waiting in line at the toll booth. This time, in my spiffy new station wagon, I flew across in the fast lane. Only the thought that I was breaking in a new engine kept me from really opening it up and seeing what the car could do.

When I got to the show, I headed first to the grooming area. Sam and Aunt Peg were set up next to each other.

Each had a black Standard Poodle on the table, and both were busy brushing.

I greeted them both, then paused uncertainly. Sam and I hadn't parted on the best of terms the other evening; and while I wanted to smooth things over, I had no desire to try and to do so with Aunt Peg hovering in the background like an over-anxious school mother.

"Oh go on," she said impatiently, after a moment had passed. "Kiss and make up, and get it over with."

"Aunt Peg!"

"You think I don't have eyes?" she demanded.

"Everything's fine," I lied. "Really."

"I can tell." Aunt Peg looked back and forth between us. "The happy look on your faces gives it away. I guess that means Bob's still around. Honestly, Melanie, that man's been nothing but trouble. Why you don't just pack his bags for him and send him home to Texas?"

Sam was looking down, pretending to concentrate on his brushing, but he was also biting back a grin. It wasn't the first time the two of them had ganged up on me.

"Bob is Davey's father. I can't just tell him to get lost."

"Of course you can. Just open your mouth." Aunt Peg demonstrated proper technique. "Hold it right next to his ear, and say "Get lost!" Believe me, that'll do the trick."

For a moment, I was half tempted to invite her over to give it a try. That's when I decided I needed to escape. "I'm going for coffee," I said. "Anybody want anything?"

Both declined the offer, which was good because what I really wanted to do was find Bertie. I didn't doubt for a minute that she'd deny having an affair with Louis La-Plante. But it would be interesting to watch the expression on her face when I asked the question.

I canvassed the grooming area, then set off to look around the rings. I was so busy scanning faces, that when Lydia Applebaum stepped out of a doorway right in front of me, I didn't see her until I'd nearly barreled right into her.

"Oh," I said, sidestepping quickly. "Sorry."

The door to the ladies' room was just swinging shut. Lydia looked at me and wrinkled her nose. "Are you looking for the bathroom? I'd wait a moment, if I were you. Penny Romano's in there, throwing up."

Retching sounds were clearly audible from within. "Is she okay?"

Lydia's lips thinned into a disapproving line, and I knew what she had to be thinking. I'd smelled liquor on Penny's breath at this hour of the day, too. But she had also told me she was trying to get pregnant. I remembered my first several months well. Morning sickness had gripped me pretty hard.

"Don't worry about Penny," Lydia said snidely. "It's nothing she hasn't brought upon herself."

"Maybe not. She might be pregnant."

"I don't see how." Lydia walked away. The absolute assurance in her tone made me turn and follow.

"What do you mean?"

"Penny can't have children. That's why she babies those Dobermans of hers so terribly."

I shook my head. "But she told me she was trying to get pregnant."

"You must have misunderstood." Lydia turned into the superintendent's office. "Now if you'll excuse me, I have some entries to fill out."

By the time I got back to the ladies' room, Penny was gone. Only the unpleasant aroma lingered.

Was Lydia right? I wondered. It wouldn't be the first time I was mistaken about something. Still, the thought irked me.

If I couldn't even keep the simple facts straight, how did I ever expect to figure out who was responsible for Monica's murder?

⊶ ❋ *Thirty* ❋ ⊷

When I finally found Bertie, she was hurrying from the Chihuahua ring with a little tan dog and a third place ribbon in her arms, and an unhappy expression on her face.

"Not you again," she said. Without breaking stride, she headed back to the grooming area.

I fell into step beside her. "Last time we talked, you asked if I was learning anything interesting."

"Don't tell me." Bertie dodged between two tables and around a stack of crates. Her set-up was the end of the aisle. "You found the killer."

"No."

"Too bad." She opened a small crate and popped the Chihuahua inside, then tossed the ribbon in the direction of her tack box. "Given up yet?"

"No."

"Perseverance," she said sarcastically. "I like that." Bertie opened another small crate and drew out a Pug. "Sorry, gotta go."

Last time she'd walked out on me, I'd had to stay with

Faith. This time, I simply followed. Halfway to the ring, she glanced back, saw me, and gave me a disgusted look.

I caught up again at ringside. Pugs were scheduled next, but the Maltese winners were having their pictures taken. "Look," said Bertie, sounding exasperated. "I didn't do it, okay?"

"Okay."

"You can stop following me around now."

"I just have a couple more questions."

"You always have a couple more questions. Why don't you go bother somebody else?"

"I have been. Now it's your turn again."

She looked resigned. "All right. After Pugs, I'll have a break. Come and see me then."

I nodded and didn't follow when she went to see the ring steward about her armband. But I didn't leave the area either. Bertie had proven too adept at escaping for me to trust her completely. I found an empty chair ringside and sat down.

Bertie's Pug was in the Open Dog class, so his turn came quickly. She and the dog looked good together, and I'm sure the wide smile she gave the elderly male judge didn't hurt. Her Pug took the points, and Bertie waited with him near the gate to go back in for Best of Breed.

A chair scraped beside me and I looked up as Joanne Pinkus sat down. "I can't believe she won again," she muttered.

"Who?"

"Bertie, who else?"

"I thought she did a nice job," I said, feeling my way. I didn't know enough about Pugs to have any idea whether Bertie's dog had deserved to win or not.

"Let's just say she sold what she had to sell."

I wondered if I should warn Joanne to keep her voice down. Ringside observers tend to have notoriously sharp ears. "You think her Pug shouldn't have won?"

"Who knows? I have Norwiches. All I'm saying is, that's one lady who gets more than she deserves. I'm a feminist," Joanne said defiantly. "And I hate to see her coasting by on her looks."

It seemed to me that a real feminist would have been pleased to see another woman striving hard, and succeeding, in a tough profession. Not Joanne. I wondered how much of what she was saying was idealism, and how much good old-fashioned jealousy.

Bertie had the kind of looks that would intimidate any woman, much less one with Joanne's plain features and frizzy brown hair. As the handler walked the Pug back into the ring, Joanne scowled and crossed her arms over her chest.

"Did Bertie ever handle any of your dogs?" I asked.

"Not me," Joanne snapped. "I don't need that kind of edge. Not that she didn't make sure I knew her services were available. I'm sure the only reason she joined the Belle Haven Club was to try and drum up new clients."

"Did it work?"

"I guess so. I think Paul and Darla had her finish a dog or two. And maybe the LaPlantes. Now she's set her sights on Cy. At least he seems to have the sense to stick with a real pro."

In the ring, Bertie's Pug was awarded Best of Winners. The handler got her ribbon and left immediately for the grooming area. I jumped up and went after her.

When I arrived at Bertie's set-up only seconds behind her, she didn't seem surprised to see me. She sighed, then hopped up and sat on a grooming table. "Okay, get it over with. What do you want to know now?"

I probably wasn't going to get a lot of chances, so I decided to lead with my best. "Did Monica know about what's going on between you and Louis LaPlante?"

I'd hoped her expression might give something away; and it did. Confusion.

"I don't know," she said carefully. "What is going on between me and Louis?"

"I think you're having an affair."

Two bright spots of red appeared in her cheeks. "You're out of your mind!"

I let the silence stand.

"You're crazy," she said again. "What on earth would make you think something like that?"

"I've seen the way you act around Louis. I also know that you and Sharon were overheard having a fight in Francisco's."

"Not about Louis."

"What then?"

"That's none of your business."

I shrugged and leaned back against the wall of stacked crates behind me.

Bertie considered things for a moment. "Look," she said finally. "I like Louis. He's a nice man, and someday soon he'll be a judge. But he and I are not having an affair. In the first place, he's married."

"That would stop you?"

"Yes, it would." She reached around behind her and

plucked a large soda in a plastic cup off the top of a crate. Bertie fitted the straw to her mouth a took a long sip.

"All right," she said. "We're going to be honest for a minute, and you're not going to repeat anything I say, right?"

"Right."

Not unless she confessed to killing Monica. And I didn't think promises made to a murderer counted, anyway.

"Maybe I do play up to Louis a bit. Like I said, he's going to be a judge and that kind of connection can be useful. But I'm thinking in terms of my career. An affair would end. Then where would I be as far as showing to Louis or any of his friends? Nowhere. And who needs that?

"Besides, if you've made such a point of watching me you probably know that the way I treat Louis isn't any different than the way I am with most men." Bertie looked at me, her eyes hard. "They look at me and they see an attractive package. I know what they want, and I give it to them. In return, maybe I get a few extra wins. Use what you've got, baby. That's my motto."

Mine too, although in my case that had meant studying hard in school and getting a graduate degree that would help me support my son. Maybe Bertie and I weren't so different. We were both just trying to get the job done.

"Why does Joanne dislike you?" I asked, changing the subject.

"Joanne's a bitch," Bertie said. "Next question."

Ooo-kay.

"Who do you think killed Monica Freedman?"

"I don't think about it."

"If you did?"

"Maybe Joanne. She's . . ." She stopped, then frowned. "You know, there was one thing."

"What?"

"I remember noticing Paul and Darla Heins. They were acting kind of strange that night."

"Strange how?"

"I was one of the last people to leave. I think Lydia was the only one still in the meeting room. When I passed Paul and Darla on the stairs, they were walking down. Then they stopped and turned back. Next thing, they changed their minds and started walking down again."

"Maybe they forgot something."

"Maybe." Bertie shrugged. "I went into the ladies' room for a minute and I think I still beat them out of the restaurant."

She glanced down and checked her watch. "Time's up. I've got Finnish Spitz in ten minutes."

I straightened and looked around her set-up. It was several crates bigger than it had been two weeks earlier. "It looks like business is booming."

"I'm doing okay." Bertie reached down, opened a wire crate and caught a mid-sized foxy looking dog as he shot out into the aisle. Easily, she hefted him up onto a table. "Don't forget what I said earlier, about not repeating what I told you. I'm working damn hard to build a good reputation. The last thing I need is someone like you screwing things up for me."

"Got it."

"I mean it," Bertie said firmly. "Stay out of my business. I was honest before, and I'll be honest now. I don't make a good enemy."

As I walked away, I felt her eyes boring into my back the entire length of the aisle.

When I got back to where Sam and Aunt Peg were set up, they were discussing taxes. April fifteenth was a week away and neither had filed yet. I tend to do my income taxes early. They're pretty straightforward and I usually get a little money back, so I hate to let the government hang onto it for any longer than necessary. I'd filed over a month ago.

"Done?" said Sam. "What do you mean you're done? I'm still trying to line up all my receipts."

"I did that in February."

"There's something wrong with that girl," Aunt Peg commented in a loud whisper. "Doesn't she know it's un-American not to have to run around in a frazzle at the last minute?"

Obviously, I did my last minute frazzling when I was showing Faith. By comparison, even with the Poodle judging fast approaching, both Sam and Aunt Peg looked calm and competent. Sam was spraying up his bitch's top-knot; while Hope, who was already sprayed, was having a final scissoring.

"I'm organized," I said smugly. "That's the key."

"I'm organized, too," said Sam. "I keep receipts for everything. But when you're self-employed, the paperwork alone can kill you."

What he said jiggled something in the back of my mind. Something about tax receipts. Not mine, necessarily. I knew my taxes were done and gone. Where would I have run across someone else's financial records recently?

Before I could come up with an answer, Aunt Peg put

me to work. She sent me to the ring to pick up armbands, where I discovered that the judge was running fast. I got the two numbers, and hurried back to pass along the news.

Aunt Peg lifted Hope off the grooming table and set her gently down on the floor. The big black puppy looked beautiful, and she knew it. She shook out, then stood and posed, the pom pon on her tail high in the air and wagging back and forth.

Poodle puppies are allowed to show with a thick coat of hair all over their bodies. Once they reach one year of age, however, they must be put into one of the two adult trims required by the breed standard. After this show, with their first birthday fast approaching, both Faith and Hope would have their hindquarters and front legs clipped into the continental trim. With a different set of lines and a whole new profusion of hair required, both bitches would sit out of competition at least six months to mature.

When Sam was ready, we set out for the ring in a procession. It never ceases to amaze me how many people want to reach out and touch a Poodle, especially one whose owner has just devoted hours to getting it ready to be shown. I walked in front, carrying a can of hair-spray and an extra comb, and running interference through the crowds of spectators.

The entry in Standard Poodles wasn't large and the dog classes were over quickly. Even though Hope was eligible for the Puppy class, Aunt Peg had entered her in Open as a subtle way of signaling to the judge that she felt her puppy was ready to take on all competition and, with luck, go home with the points. Sam's bitch was older by at least a year and she, too, was entered in the Open class.

Standing by the gate, awaiting their turn, the two Poodles made a beautiful pair. I was glad I wasn't the judge who would have to choose between them.

Apparently the judge agreed with me about their quality, because although there were four entries in the class, he quickly narrowed his selection down to Sam's and Aunt Peg's bitches. I'm still trying to train my eye to pick up the subtle differences between dogs that Aunt Peg sees so easily, but it seemed to me that Hope had Sam's bitch beaten on head and showmanship, while his Poodle was the better mover.

Playing no favorites, I cheered for both and was delighted when the judge awarded Hope her first two points. Sam was gracious in defeat; Aunt Peg, magnanimous in victory. After she'd had Hope's picture taken, and she and Sam had wrapped their bitches' ears and taken apart their top-knots, she invited us both back to her house for an early dinner.

Sam glanced at me before answering. I knew what he was thinking. Our last dinner together hadn't been a great success. In fact, since Bob had arrived on the scene, it seemed like nothing we'd done together had turned out right.

"I don't know—" I started to say.

"Is Davey covered?" Aunt Peg asked.

"He's with Frank. I'll be lucky if the two of them roll in before Davey's bedtime."

"Good. That's settled then. As for you . . ." Aunt Peg turned to Sam. "I've tendered a perfectly decent invitation and I don't see any reason why I should have to take no for an answer."

She was meddling again, and judging by the look on

Sam's face, he knew it, too. Not only that, but it seemed that nothing short of taping Aunt Peg's mouth shut would induce her to stop.

Sam crossed his arms over his chest stubbornly. In a way, I almost felt sorry for him. It wasn't his fault he didn't know Aunt Peg as well as I did.

"I was thinking of calling ahead for Chinese," she said. "General Tso's chicken, Shrimp Lo Mein, maybe some steamed dumplings."

Sam loved Chinese food. Since none of us had cared enough for dog show food to bother having lunch, I bet his mouth was watering already. I knew mine was.

Looking very pleased with herself, Aunt Peg began to pack up her things as if the matter was already settled.

I looked at Sam and lifted a brow.

He grinned in return.

General Tso's chicken it was.

∽❀ *Thirty-one* ❀∽

I called Frank from Aunt Peg's house and discovered that he had to work that evening. The bartending job. I'd forgotten all about it.

"No problem," said Frank. "Bob says he can take Davey home and stay until you get back."

"Bob? I didn't know he was with you."

"Sure, we had a great day. They can tell you all about it when you get home."

He hung up before I could ask any more questions. It was probably just as well. As long as I didn't know too much, I could put the whole thing out of my mind and concentrate instead on enjoying the opportunity to spend time with Sam. No ex-husband, no five-year-old angling for equal attention, no outside distractions.

If you didn't count Aunt Peg, that is.

But for once, Peg was on her best behavior. We'd stopped on the way home and picked up take-out; then Sam and I set the table while she tended to her Poodles. Hungry as we were, we'd still ordered too much food. We all had seconds, and then thirds, while we talked about the show and Peg's new litter of puppies. Briefly the conversation touched on Monica's murder when I told Aunt Peg about my conversations with Lydia and Bertie. Sam listened politely, but since he didn't know most of the people involved, the conversation soon moved on.

In keeping with the upbeat tenor of the evening, Bob's name wasn't even mentioned until it was time to go and Sam walked me out to my car. It was hard to avoid talking about him then, especially with the brand new Volvo sitting there in the driveway.

Sam admired my new wheels briefly, then wound his arms around my waist. "I miss you," he whispered.

"I'm here." I nestled closer.

"You know what I mean."

I did, of course; and I missed him, too.

"Bob's leaving soon. Tonight I'll find out when. Either that, or I'll tell him he's being evicted."

Good intentions carried me home in a righteous frame of mind. It wasn't late when I arrived, but Davey was already upstairs asleep in bed. In the living room, Bob was stretched out on the couch with his eyes closed. Faith's barking roused him a little He didn't get up, but he did offer me a half-hearted wave.

"You must have had some day," I said.

"Roller-blading," he mumbled. "Your brother thinks he's a teenager."

"Inside, he still is. Was it fun?"

"Davey loved it."

"How about you?"

Bob groaned in reply, and rolled over to face the back of the couch. Now he was just tired. In the morning, every muscle in his body would ache. The thought cheered me enormously. I went upstairs, got a blanket and pillow and tucked him into bed on the couch. I may be tough, but I'm not entirely unsympathetic.

Of course it didn't occur to me that my actions might be misconstrued until I awoke the next morning with Davey and Faith bouncing on my bed.

"Daddy's here!" my son cried. "He spent the whole night!"

Right. So he had.

"He fell asleep on the couch," I said gently. "That's all. You wore him out yesterday. Did you have a good time?"

"It was awesome. Did you know I can roller-blade and eat ice cream at the same time?"

"No, I didn't." The boy had heretofore unplumbed depths. I thought hopefully about knee and elbow pads and resisted the maternal urge to poke and prod for injuries.

"Daddy's taking a shower," Davey informed me happily. "After that, he's going to make me breakfast."

"Lucky you. In the meantime, would you take Faith downstairs and let her outside?"

The puppy's ears pricked at the words and she beat Davey to the bedroom door. After they left, I heard Bob rattling around in the bathroom. I waited in bed and gave him plenty of time before checking to see if things were clear. He'd used up most of the hot water, but he did hang up the wet towels and clean the steam from the mirror.

By the time I got downstairs, the air was filled with the aroma of fresh coffee and Bob was dishing out western omelets and french fries. He met my bland look with one of his own.

"Just making do with what you had on hand," he said.

I helped myself to a mug of coffee, added a dollop of milk, and sat down at the table, wondering if Bob would take the hint. He did. It was nice to be served for a change.

After breakfast I got Davey dressed, then sent him outside with Faith. Bob and I needed to talk, preferably without our son in attendance. Letting Bob stay over hadn't been a mistake necessarily, but it had reinforced how at ease he felt insinuating himself back into our lives. Maybe the way to get him started thinking about going home was to chip away at some of that comfort.

Asking about money ought to start things off on the right foot.

"I've been thinking about the future," I said, as I poured a second cup of coffee and sat back down. "Now that you've got some cash coming in, we'll be needing to set up a schedule of child-support payments for after you're gone."

"I guess that sounds fair," Bob said slowly.

"You guess?" I straightened in my chair. "You *guess?*" My God, I hadn't even mentioned the four years of back support in arrears.

"That's not what I meant." One look at my expression had Bob backpedaling furiously. "It's just that I don't want you to get the wrong idea about this oil well. It's not like I'm rich or anything."

Two new cars, and a three week vacation from work just because he wanted one? Compared to me, he might as well have been Donald Trump.

"Nobody asked you for millions," I said stiffly.

"Sure the well is making money. But the expenses are

high, too. And of course, we lose a lot to taxes, not to mention insurance. You wouldn't believe what that costs . . ."

He went bumbling on, but I'd stopped listening. Taxes. That was the second time that thought had jiggled something in the back of my mind. Taxes and insurance . . . Where had I seen them together recently?

Then I remembered. Monica's files, when Aunt Peg and I had been looking for the Belle Haven Club records. There'd been four partitions in the file box. One for club business, one for bills, and another two for tax and insurance receipts. Except that Monica didn't have any insurance. That's what Joanne had said, and she would have known.

With all the information Monica had gathered about the various club members, it made sense that there would have been some records, somewhere. Like maybe in a file called insurance receipts. It was certainly worth a look.

I pushed back my chair and stood. "I have to make a phone call. Actually, I think I have to go out."

"Now? I thought you wanted to talk about Davey."

"I do. I definitely do." But that could wait, couldn't it? After all, it wasn't as if Bob was going anywhere, more's the pity. "Will you keep an eye on him?"

"Sure, but I wanted to tell you—"

"I won't be long, okay? Thanks."

I called Mrs. Freedman first. Thankfully, she was in and seemed perfectly pleased by the prospect of a brief visit. My second call was to Aunt Peg. I outlined what I had in mind, told her I'd meet her in Banksville, then stuck my head out the back door and yelled goodbye to Davey.

Bob sat and watched this flurry of activity with his arms crossed over his chest and a sulky expression on his face.

With luck, maybe he'd have the breakfast dishes done by the time I got back.

The Volvo made excellent time to Banksville. In the few weeks since our last visit, spring had made its presence felt. The snow and puddles were gone from the Freedmans' yard, and the first green shoots of spring were pushing themselves up from underground.

Because of the stockade fencing, I couldn't see the Beagles, but I certainly heard them. They were in the yard behind the house, howling up a storm at my arrival. Mrs. Freedman apologized for the racket when she opened the door. Ample hips swaying, she led the way down the hall to Monica's office.

"It's a good thing you called," she said. "Tomorrow I was going to take everything down to the tax accountant and let him sort it out, so you're just in time."

As we reached the room, the Beagles began to howl again. Mrs. Freedman ambled out to let Aunt Peg in and I went straight to the cardboard file box near the desk. It didn't look as though it had been touched since our last visit. The three remaining files were just as we'd left them. I pulled out the one marked insurance receipts, carried it over to the bed and sat down.

"Here I am," Aunt Peg said cheerfully from the doorway. "I knew you wouldn't start without me."

She hurried in to join me and I opened the manila file folder, spreading it out across both our laps. On top was a letter from Joanne. It was written on letterhead paper from the Lewis Street Insurance Agency and touted the virtues of the agency policies. I skimmed through it, a lump gathering in my stomach. What if I'd been wrong?

"Go on," Aunt Peg said impatiently. pushing the letter aside. "What else is there?"

Beneath it was a Belle Haven Club membership list, with many of the names circled. All were committee heads, and all had been present on the night Monica was killed.

"Now we're getting somewhere," said Peg.

Under that was a newspaper clipping, taken from the *Westport News* and dated the previous December. "This is about Paul and Darla," I said, reading the first few lines.

Aunt Peg took the clipping from my hand. "What's that fastened to the back?"

It was a note Monica had written to herself, detailing Joanne's involvement in what had happened. Monica had listed three dates on which they'd discussed the topic.

"I never said she wasn't organized," said Aunt Peg, adding the packet to her pile. "What's next?"

More notes. The one on top recorded a comment Barbara had made about Cy's top winning Dalmatian that had aroused Monica's suspicions. The club secretary had apparently followed up by phoning Dr. Rimkowsky, pretending to be Crawford's assistant and needing to verify an appointment.

"Organized and devious," I said, flipping through papers that discussed Lydia's illegal litter and Aunt Peg's Poodle with SA. Penny and Mark Romano's names were noted on a sheet of letterhead paper that appeared to be from a law firm in Greenwich, but with no other explanation attached.

At the bottom of the pile were two snapshots, both blown up to five by seven. I passed one over to Aunt Peg, and studied the other myself.

Both pictures appeared to have been taken from ringside, and each showed a close-up view of a Yorkshire Terrier being posed on the table during judging. The body of a woman handler was visible behind the dog, but her head was out of the shot. In my picture she was wearing a blue dress; in Aunt Peg's, it was red.

"Who do you suppose they are?" I asked.

"Some detective you make," Aunt Peg sniffed. She turned her picture over and read the writing on the back. "It says right here this one is Champion LouShar Lucinda at Springfield. What about yours?"

I flipped it over and read, "Champion LouShar Lucinda at Central Maine. Who cares?"

"Apparently Monica did. I wonder why." Aunt Peg took the snapshot out of my hand and had a closer look. "LouShar is Louis and Sharon's kennel name. Didn't Lydia say at the last meeting that they had finished a Yorkie in Maine this past winter?"

I nodded. "The one she teased them for not bragging about."

Aunt Peg frowned, handing back the photos so I could have another look. "In their shoes, I wouldn't have been bragging either. These two Yorkies aren't the same bitch."

∾ * *Thirty-two* * ∾

"What?" I placed the two photographs side by side and stared at them, hard.

"I'm no specialist in Yorkies," said Aunt Peg. "But when they're together like that, even I can see the difference. The woman looks approximately the same in each picture, but look at the relative size and shape of the dog in comparison. The Springfield show is in November. Central Maine is in January. Unless LouShar Lucinda shrank in size, gained in length and grew a whole new coat, there's no way these two pictures could be of the same bitch."

I nodded slowly, finally able to discern what she wanted me to see. "Are you saying that Louis and Sharon can't tell their own dogs apart?"

"Not at all." Aunt Peg smiled grimly. "My guess is, Monica caught them showing a ringer."

I looked up, surprised. "People do that?"

"It's not a common occurrence, but it has been known to happen. Suppose a dog has almost finished its championship when something goes wrong. Maybe it loses its coat, or gets injured in some way. After all the time and money that's already been invested, it can be very frustrating to be left high and dry just a few points away from completing a title."

"That's got to be illegal."

"Of course it's illegal. It's fraud, for Pete's sake. It certainly would explain why the LaPlantes seemed so flustered when Lydia mentioned their win. They must have thought they'd sneaked off to some little out of the way show, where nobody would ever be the wiser."

"Maybe nobody would have, if they hadn't won the group."

"That's what's so odd," said Aunt Peg. "The only way to pull off this sort of scam is to get the job done quietly. Presumably Louis and Sharon used a very good bitch as a substitute to make sure she'd win. But Best of Breed winners aren't required to go on to the group. I can't imagine why they have been so foolish as to call attention to themselves that way."

"I guess that's Sharon handling," I said, squinting at the picture. With no head and only a small portion of the body showing, it was impossible to tell.

"Sharon's not the brightest woman, but I didn't think she was stupid. And that's exactly what a stunt like this is. No wonder they didn't have any pictures to show off. They probably didn't have any taken."

"Too bad for them, Monica was on hand with her camera."

Peg nodded. "Monica always took pictures at the shows. She said they helped her with her sketching. Presumably, that's why she already had a shot of the real Lucinda at Springfield."

We'd reached the end of the file, and she began to gather up the papers. "Louis must have been horrified when he found out there was a chance he'd be exposed. Of course his chances of ever becoming a judge would be ruined. But beyond that, would you trust your affairs to a lawyer who'd been implicated in a case of fraud? I wouldn't."

She didn't say it, but we were both thinking the same thing. As far as motives went, Louis LaPlante had just shot to the top of the list.

Aunt Peg opened her large purse and slipped the incriminating file inside. "I wonder if Louis and Sharon are home this morning. Let's go find out, shall we?"

We passed by the living room on the way out. Mrs. Freedman was watching QVC on TV. She waved distractedly in our direction and we let ourselves out.

Like me, the LaPlantes lived in north Stamford. Unlike me, they lived in a large colonial on a wooded, two acre lot. Their yard wasn't fenced, but several large, gravel floored pens were visible around the side of the house.

Aunt Peg marched determinedly to the front door and rang the bell. Nothing happened. After a moment she rang again. This time we heard approaching footsteps, and after a minute, the door drew open.

"Yes, what is it?" Louis demanded. He was dressed in corduroy pants and a well-worn sweater, and had his teeth clamped around the stem of his meerschaum pipe. Holding the business section of the Sunday paper in one hand, he used the other to wave back two very fat Yorkshire Terriers who had followed him to the door.

"Oh," he said, looking only slightly less annoyed when he realized who his visitors were. He removed the pipe from his mouth. "What brings you two all the way out here on a Sunday morning?"

"We need to talk to you and Sharon. Is she here?" Without waiting for an invitation, Aunt Peg walked past Louis and into the house. I supposed I was meant to follow along behind, and did. Louis closed the door behind us.

"Certainly she's here. We were just reading the paper. Is something wrong?"

His look of concern was genuine. I wondered whether he was trying to guess what we might have found out.

"Quite possibly," said Aunt Peg.

Frowning, Louis led the way to a sun filled family room in the back of the house. The furniture looked plump and inviting, and sections from the Sunday *New York Times* were spread out over two low tables. A Vivaldi concerto played softly in the background.

Sharon was seated near the window, comfortable in an easy chair with her legs tucked up underneath her. She was chewing on the end of a pencil as she worked the crossword puzzle, and looked up inquiringly as we came in. She reached over and set the magazine section down on the table beside her.

She didn't seem surprised to see us, I realized. Too late, it occurred to me that perhaps I had not given this woman enough thought. I had spoken to Louis and Bertie, but I'd never bothered to question Sharon. It was beginning to look like that was an oversight I might regret.

Sharon unwound her legs and stood gracefully. "Shall I get us all some coffee?"

"I'm afraid this isn't a social call," said Peg. "We've just come from Monica Freedman's house. We found her secret files."

I was watching for a reaction, and got one from Sharon. She paled and went very still.

Louis was clearing away papers. He waved us to a seat, and said, "Files about what?"

"I believe I told you that Monica had been sending notes to some of the Belle Haven members," I said. "She seems to have enjoyed engaging in a sort of emotional blackmail."

"I remember you mentioning such a thing," Louis said, nodding. "I thought at the time, that behavior like that was perhaps what had gotten her killed. But I'm afraid I don't understand what that has to do with us."

Behind him, Sharon cleared her throat softly. "We got a note from Monica," she said. "It came with one of the newsletters. I threw it out as soon as it arrived."

Louis turned and stared. "What are you talking about?"

Aunt Peg and I exchanged a glance. Was it possible he didn't know?

"Monica was in Maine when Alicia finished," said Sharon.

"Yes," Louis snapped impatiently. "So what?"

Sharon's gaze skittered up, then down. She seemed to want to look anywhere but at her husband. It was warm in the room, but she crossed her arms over her chest and began to rub them as though she was freezing.

"I was afraid this would happen," Sharon said finally. She addressed her words to Louis, as if Peg and I weren't even in the room. "She said the plan was easy, that everything would be fine. I should have known she'd be wrong."

"What are you talking about?" Louis demanded. "She who? For God's sake, Sharon, what's going on?"

"You remember how Lucinda got that infected toe nail? And every time we got it cleared up, it came right back? She only needed a single point and should have had it easily, but it seemed like whenever I entered her, she turned up lame. She was due in season in February and I knew how much you were hoping to breed her . . ."

Sharon stopped speaking. For the moment, she seemed incapable of going further. Aunt Peg opened her bag, took out the two snapshots and handed them over to Louis.

"Lucinda," he said quickly, glancing at the first. He looked at the second. "And that's Lorelei."

"Turn it over," I said.

Louis read the words to himself slowly, then lifted his head and stared at his wife. *"What did you do?"*

"I didn't do anything!" Sharon cried. "It was all Bertie's fault."

"Bertie?" I said, surprised. "What did she have to do with it?"

"It was her idea." Sharon turned to me, looking relieved to no longer be facing her husband's wrath. "Bertie knew about the trouble we were having with Lucinda and suggested that she knew a way to take care of it. All I had to do was supply her with two bitches: one to win the point under Lucinda's name and the other one to lose. She said she'd take them out of the area where nobody would notice a thing."

"That's why you didn't want me to come with you to

the Maine shows," Louis said in a strangled voice. He seemed to be having trouble taking it all in.

"I knew it was wrong, but Bertie said the plan was fool-proof."

Louis looked at his wife coldly. "If you believed that, then you're the fool. I can't believe you'd be so stupid as to get us involved in a shoddy business like this. My God, Sharon, what has gotten into you lately? It was bad enough when you lost the club checks—"

"*I* lost the checks?" she cried in outrage.

"You know perfectly well I handed them to you to go in the briefcase. Damn it Sharon, there are times when I think you'd lose your nose if it wasn't fastened on. But this, this is an outrage. This is unconscionable!"

Louis stalked over to a bar behind the door and poured himself a drink. Scotch, straight up. It looked as though he needed it.

"How did Monica find out what you'd done?" I asked Sharon.

"That part was sheer idiocy," she said, shaking her head. "Lorelei won the breed. I assumed we were done, and went off to get some lunch. I ran into Monica, who asked why I wasn't watching my dog in the group. Of course, I told her I didn't have a dog in the group. I was really quite adamant about it. Considering what we'd just done, there was no way I wanted to draw any wider attention to Lorelei by showing her further."

Sharon glanced over at Louis. "Apparently Bertie had scoped out the rest of the Toys, and thought Lorelei had a chance to do well in the group. It was such a small show, you see. I imagine Bertie figured that if she could get another group win on her record, so much the better. Blind ambition coupled with stupidity, that's what that woman is.

"I went running right over to the ring, but it was already too late. Once Bertie had Lorelei in the group, I couldn't get her out. That's when Monica must have snapped the second picture."

"Was that what you and Bertie were arguing about at Francisco's?" I asked.

"Yes." Sharon sighed unhappily. "By then, I'd gotten the note from Monica. This was Bertie's mess. She'd gotten me into it, and I was determined she was going to get me out."

I swallowed heavily and considered the implications of what she'd said.

Aunt Peg wasn't so reticent. "Are you trying to say you think Bertie was responsible for what happened to Monica?"

From the other side of the room, Louis spoke up. "Bertie couldn't have done it," he said quietly. "She was behind us leaving the restaurant. And we'd only just reached our car when the Beagles began to howl. I don't think there's any way she could have gotten to Monica so quickly."

"And you and Sharon were together?" Peg asked.

"Yes, we were," said Louis, glancing at his wife. "We were together the whole time."

Which disqualified all three of them. Or then again, maybe not. Judging by Louis's reaction, this was the first he'd heard of his wife's reckless disregard for A.K.C. regulations. Now that he knew her actions had placed his own reputation on the line, how willing would he have been to cover up for her? Or for Bertie, who might have tried to fix things on her own?

It was all a hopeless muddle. As Aunt Peg had said earlier, it wasn't that we didn't have enough clues; we had too many. The only thing I knew for sure was that trying to get them all sorted out was making my head ache.

Aunt Peg stood. Louis did, too. I glanced down at the two pictures. They were still on the table where Louis had dropped them. Aunt Peg made no move to pick them up.

"What will you do now?" he asked.

"If you're asking whether I'll be talking to the A.K.C. about this matter, I won't," she said. I knew what she had to be thinking. When it came to indiscretions, her own family's record was not entirely unblemished. "You'll have to handle this yourself, Louis. Do what you think is best."

Sharon stayed behind as Louis walked us to the door. We were almost there when I thought of something. "Can I have the file for a minute?" I asked Aunt Peg.

She handed it over and I fished out the note with Mark and Penny's name on it. Louis was a lawyer in Greenwich. Maybe he would recognize the letterhead.

"Walter Crispus," he said, glancing at it. "Of course. I haven't had occasion to deal with him, but he's very well known in certain circles."

"Don't be coy," said Peg. "What you're trying to say is, you don't really approve but he's probably making a fortune. What does he do?"

"He's a go-between," said Louis. "He arranges private adoptions."

ᗧ❋ *Thirty-three* ❋ᗧ

"So that's what Penny meant when she said they were working on it," I said, when we reached the cars.

"I told you she was too old to be having a baby," Aunt Peg sniffed.

The point wasn't worth arguing. But Penny's age did raise an interesting thought. She and Mark were in their forties, old enough to maybe feel that they were running out of time. I wondered how long they'd been trying to adopt. I wondered if they'd been turned down before.

I knew that finding a healthy baby to adopt wasn't easy. In private adoptions, birth mothers often had their choice of applicants. Mark and Penny's ages could be a strike against them. Might they have been worried that two strikes would be too many?

Aunt Peg must have been thinking the same thing, because she said, "Didn't you tell me Mark and Penny's note had to do with her drinking?"

"Yes. And we both said the same thing. Big deal, everybody already knows about that."

Aunt Peg reached out and opened her car door. "Everybody but Walter Crispus, perhaps."

Now we were getting somewhere.

"Let's go," I said.

"Where?"

"To the Romanos'. Do you know where they live?"

"Of course I know where they live. I'm the club secretary, I know where all the club members live. But it won't do us any good. I saw Mark at the show yesterday and he mentioned that he and Penny were showing today at Riverhead."

"Oh."

"Besides, I have to get back and tend to my litter. But later this evening, I know exactly where Penny and Mark will be."

"Where?"

"Lydia's holding her reception for Thelma Gooding, remember? Nearly the entire club will turn out. Why don't you come along as my guest?"

The idea had immediate appeal. I thought about everything Louis and Sharon had said and realized that things were finally beginning to fall into place. It was time to gather all the suspects in Monica's murder together, and and let the situation bring itself to a head.

"That sounds perfect," I said. "I'll meet you there."

In the car on the way home, I thought about Mark's patience in dealing with Davey, and the dreamy expression on Penny's face when she'd told him it wouldn't be long until they had children of their own. Obviously both were very anxious to become parents.

Monica, in her own devious way, had gathered up a treasure trove of secrets. If she'd told what she knew, Cy had stood to lose money; Lydia, her reputation. Joanne had a position on the Board at stake; Louis, possibly his livelihood. On a scale of importance, where did a baby fit into all that? Had the Romanos wanted a child badly enough to feel that the taking of a life was justified in return?

When I got home, Bob and Faith were there, but Davey wasn't.

"Somebody called," said Bob. He barely looked up, he was so engrossed in an old rerun of *Charlie's Angels* on the TV. "He's down the street at Joey Bricklayer's house."

"Brickman," I corrected. I gave Faith a pat, then walked around the couch and switched off the set. "The boy's name is Joey Brickman. Davey's your son, Bob. How could you let him leave with someone whose name you couldn't even remember?"

Bob looked up at me and grinned. He patted the couch beside him, inviting me to sit. My heart used to turn over when he looked at me like that. Fortunately, that was a long time ago. I sat in a chair instead.

"You're not about to run out on me again, are you?"

"No. Why?"

"I want to continue the conversation we started this morning. I think it's time."

"Okay," I said carefully, wondering what was coming.

"I need to go back a bit," said Bob. "I don't necessarily expect you to understand, but I do want you to listen. There are two sides to every story. Maybe I should have told you mine five years ago. Maybe I wasn't sure you'd want to hear it."

"Go on."

"You know I loved you, there was never any question of that."

"No," I agreed softly. "There wasn't."

"I married you because I was afraid I'd lose you otherwise. Even with love, that's a terrible way to start a marriage."

"Why didn't you tell me?"

Bob shrugged. "I thought everyone had doubts. I figured that was just the way it was. The next thing I knew, all the guys I knew were still out cruising and carrying on, and I was stuck with a wife and a house in the suburbs."

"Stuck?" I repeated.

Bob's gaze was unapologetic. "I'm just telling you how it felt to me at the time. I made a mistake, I admit it. I was too young to be married, and I was certainly too young to be a father."

At least we agreed on that.

"I just felt so trapped. I don't know if you can imagine it. There were days when I'd sit in my office and think I was suffocating. I didn't want to come home at night. I didn't want to go to work. I didn't know what I wanted to do. All I knew was that I had to get out."

A shiver skated through me. I'd never realized how he felt. Maybe I'd never wanted to. Faith poked my hand with her nose. I scratched under her chin, and she pressed against my thigh.

"Why didn't you tell me any of this?"

"I couldn't. At the time . . . maybe . . ." Bob's gaze slid away. "Maybe I thought you were the problem."

"So you left."

"I had to. I didn't have any choice."

I slumped back in my chair, feeling defeated. In the end,

we all do what we feel we need to do to save our own lives.

"I've thought a lot about Davey in the last four years. And you, too," Bob amended hastily. "I wondered what things would have been like if I'd toughed it out. I knew I owed it to myself to come back and find out."

What about what you owed your son? I wanted to ask, but didn't. Bob and I were finally talking. I'd let him tell his story his own way.

"And?"

"Being a father isn't exactly like I imagined."

That was a news flash. He hadn't had to drive here all the way from Texas to discover that; I could have told him over the phone. Not that he'd have believed me. Bob always did have a way of seeing only what he wanted to see.

"I've been doing a lot of thinking lately," he said. "And Peter told me that the most important thing is to do what's right for Davey. I think he has a point."

"Of course, he has a point." I stopped, frowning. "Peter?"

"You know, Rose's husband?"

"I know Peter. I just didn't realize that the two of you had met."

"We got to know each other at Frank's house. We had dinner together a couple of times."

"You did?"

"Why not? They invited me, and they seemed like nice people."

Why not indeed? I wondered what Rose had been up to. Like Aunt Peg, she likes to hover in the background and pull strings. The women are two of the world's all-time great manipulators. That's why they make such good adversaries.

"Talking to Peter helped me to clarify some things I was already thinking. I love Davey, he's a great kid. But I don't think joint custody is the best idea right now."

"You don't?" I strove to keep my voice level.

"Maybe when he's older, we'll rethink it. But you know I'm working, and Jennifer has a job, too . . ."

As if I didn't. If he told me children took up too much time, I was going to smack him.

"Davey's too young for the kind of arrangement I had in mind. But now that we've gotten to know one another, we could start out slowly. Maybe he could come to Texas for a visit sometime."

"Maybe he could," I allowed, not making any promises.

"And I could come back here. Maybe even bring Jennifer with me."

"That would be interesting."

Luckily for him, Bob didn't comment on my tone.

I was getting what I wanted, I thought. So why wasn't I happier? Maybe because for the first time, I was seeing what had happened between us from his point of view. For the first time, I was having to consider that maybe it hadn't all been his fault.

There had to have been signs of his discontent. How had I been so wrapped up in Davey that I'd never even noticed? Why hadn't we been able to have this talk five years ago?

"He really is a terrific kid," said Bob.

I smiled. "I know."

"I was thinking about what you said earlier, about working out a schedule for child support?" He got up, went into the kitchen and returned with some papers. "I put this together. See what you think."

I skimmed over what he had written. What I thought was that if Bob kept up his end, I could afford to get the house painted and maybe even take Davey on a small vacation over the summer.

I glanced up at him. "The courts worked out a schedule for us that wasn't as generous as this one, and you didn't stick to that."

"I figured you might say that. I even figured maybe I deserved to hear it." He reached in his pocket and dug out a check. "This is for the first three months. I thought quarterly payments made the most sense."

He wasn't kidding. For a moment, I almost thought he might be. But when I reached up and took the check I saw that it was made out to me in the promised amount. I stared at it for a long moment.

"It won't bounce," Bob said.

"I wasn't thinking that."

"No?"

I shook my head. "No, actually I was thinking how much you've changed."

Bob squatted down in front of my chair. "For the better, I hope."

"Yes, for the better." I looked at my ex-husband with his melting eyes and his easy grace. A man I'd once loved to distraction, a man who would always be the father of my child. I sighed softly. "Maybe we were both too young. It's too bad we didn't meet later. Maybe we could have made a go of it."

"Maybe," Bob agreed. "But now you have Sam."

"And you have Jennifer."

And neither one of us could go back in time to where we'd been before.

"I'll be going home tomorrow," Bob said. "I figured I'd tell Davey tonight. I'll leave him my address. He can send me pictures, if he wants. And I'll send him letters back. Do you think he'll be okay with that?"

I nodded, pleased. "I think he'll be just fine."

Faith jumped up and ran from the room. She knocked Bob slightly and he steadied himself by placing his hands on the sides of my chair.

"How about a hug?" he said softly. "For old time's sake?"

It was just that easy to slip into his arms. And it felt just that good. For years, I'd been holding tight to the resentment I'd felt, nurturing it like a noxious weed. It wouldn't all fade away that easily, but I knew the process had been started.

Bob and I shared a bond as Davey's parents. Now we'd have the relationship to go with it. And who knew? We might even end up friends.

I heard a giggle from the doorway and turned to look. Joey and Davey were both there. Alice Brickman, too.

"Gross," said our son, rolling his eyes. "Mushy stuff."

❧❀ *Thirty-four* ❀❧

Tranquillity reigned for the rest of the afternoon. In my house, that in itself is unusual enough to be worth noting.

After the Brickmans left, Bob and I sat Davey down and told him that it was time for his father to go home to Texas. Davey was sad, but not crushed. I think he'd always realized Bob wouldn't be staying; and now he had the promise of future letters and visits to look forward to.

Sensing his mood, Faith crowded close to Davey, anxious to offer what comfort she could. The big Poodle puppy climbed in his lap and licked his face until he giggled. Davey was cheered; I relaxed. Even Bob was charmed by the puppy's behavior.

I looked around at my family and decided we'd all come a long way in a few short weeks. On that upbeat thought, we trooped out to the kitchen for a mid-afternoon treat of ice cream and chocolate sauce. Faith even got a scoop of her own—plain vanilla—in a bowl on the floor.

At six forty-five, I ran upstairs and changed from my jeans into attire more suitable for a cocktail party in Greenwich: linen slacks and a shawl collared blouse. Bob was staying with Davey one last time, and I promised him I wouldn't be long.

When I arrived at Lydia's, the reception was already in progress. The semicircular driveway was filled with cars and I wedged the Volvo behind Aunt Peg's station wagon. The front door to the house was slightly ajar. I pushed it open and let myself in.

Lydia was in the hall, talking to Barbara Rubicov. She smiled when she saw me. "Melanie, I'm so glad you could make it," she said graciously. "Coats go in the closet, drinks are in the library. I'm sure you can find your way around."

I could, and I did. I didn't see Penny and Mark Romano, but I found Aunt Peg in the living room. She introduced me to the guest of honor: a trim woman in her mid-fifties whose erect carriage and exuberant demeanor were not at all dimmed by the long day she'd just spent judging dogs.

We were pleased to make each other's acquaintance, but I had places to go and people to see and I soon moved on. Louis and Sharon LaPlante were standing near the fireplace. After our tumultuous visit that afternoon, I was glad to see them there together.

"Melanie." Louis nodded briefly in my direction. "I think you should know I've written a letter to the A.K.C., withdrawing my application to become a judge."

"Are you sure that's what you want to do?"

"Actually, I'm quite certain it isn't. But under the present circumstances, I don't see that I have any choice. I hope this whole matter need go no further."

Aunt Peg had relied on Louis to do the honorable thing, and he had. Still, it seemed a shame. He probably would

have made a fine judge. And though he hadn't done anything wrong, thanks to Monica, Sharon's mistake had cost
him what he wanted most.

"As far as I'm concerned, the topic is closed," I told him.
Then I turned to Sharon, who had yet to say a word. "The
night the dinner checks disappeared, who were you sitting
next to?"

She glanced at her husband, as if seeking permission to
answer. I wondered how long it would be until she made
a move without his approval. "I was next to Louis, of
course."

"And on the other side?"

Her brow furrowed as she thought back. "Darla Heins,"
she said finally, pleased to have remembered. "We talked
about needlepoint all through dinner."

"Thank you," I said and moved on.

A teenage waiter came by with a warm tray of hors
d'oeuvres and I felt my stomach rumble. Bob had
promised to take Davey out for pizza, but plans for my
own dinner were still up in the air. I snagged a stuffed
mushroom, a chicken wing, and a napkin on which to bal-
ance them both.

As I was dipping the wing in its sauce, the front door
opened and I heard Lydia greeting new arrivals. A moment later, Mark and Penny appeared in the doorway.

"Are those any good?" asked Joanne, reaching for the
tray.

"Great."

I had to talk with my mouth full, but the effort was
worth it. Joanne held the waiter up long enough that I was
able to get a second piece of chicken for myself. With regret, I watched him move on.

"Joanne, I know you told Monica that you'd reported the Heinses. And I believe you mentioned it to Barbara. Did you tell anyone else?"

"Yeah." Her gaze skittered over to where Bertie was holding court. Seated on a long couch, the redhead was engaged in an animated conversation with Cy and Louis. "Bertie knew. She was really nasty about it, too. As if she thinks she's little Miss Perfect. And, believe me, she's not."

At least Bertie and Joanne agreed on something, if only their lack of mutual admiration. I looked around for Mark and Penny. They'd come into the living room and were talking to Peg and Thelma. I hoped Aunt Peg would manage to wait until we got them alone before bringing up what we'd learned.

I crossed the room to where Lydia stood. "If I were able to return the missing dinner checks, would you take them back with no questions asked?"

The club president thought for a moment. "Would I get an assurance that something like this won't happen again?"

"Yes." The pledge wasn't mine to make. That being the case, I fervently hoped it was true.

"Yes, I would. Do you have them?"

"No. But I know who does. I'll return them to you early in the week. Will that be all right?"

Lydia eyed me assessingly. I knew she wanted to ask. I also knew she was smart enough to realize I wouldn't answer her question. "That would be fine."

Thelma strolled over and placed an arm around Lydia's shoulders. She had a drink in her hand and a twinkle in her eyes. "You've gone to too much trouble. But I love it.

If I'd known you were going to put on a do like this, I'd have come back sooner."

Lydia smiled fondly at her old friend. "I just wanted you to know how happy the Belle Haven Club is to see you again. We hate to let our good members get away."

Over Lydia's shoulder, I saw Penny head through a door at the end of the room. I excused myself and followed her.

The door led to the library, a high ceilinged room that was filled with books. A built-in bar, stocked with a generous supply of liquor and mixers, took up the far wall. Penny was there, making herself a drink. We were the only ones in the room and I pulled the door shut behind me.

"I found Monica's notes," I said quietly. "I know what you were trying to hide."

Penny whirled to face me. The amber colored liquid in her glass sloshed over the rim and onto her fingers. She didn't seem to notice.

"I don't know what you're talking about."

"I'm talking about the adoption you arranged through Walter Crispus." It was only a guess, but as soon as I'd spoken, I knew I was right. Penny's expression hardened. "You said Monica knew about your drinking, but that wasn't all she knew, was it? How long have you and Mark been waiting for a child?"

"Years," Penny snapped. "Someone like you . . . a mother in your twenties . . . you'd never understand what we've been through."

"Maybe I would. Why don't you tell me about it?"

"Why should I?"

"Because I want to know."

I want to understand, I could have said. Because looking at the flat, dark anger in Penny's eyes, I suddenly knew that I was seeing the face of Monica's murderer.

She took a long swallow from her drink. "Mark and I got married when we were in our thirties. We started trying to have children right away, but nothing happened. We saw a fertility specialist. Do you know what that costs?"

"I can imagine."

"When that didn't work, we were stuck." Penny's tone was bitter. "We knew about private adoptions, knew there was a better chance that way than going through the state agencies, but after all the medical bills, we didn't have the money. Ten thousand, just to get your foot in the door. That's what we needed, and we didn't have it."

"So you applied for a state approved adoption?" I asked.

"Along with thousands of others. We ended up on a waiting list. And every year we waited, we were growing older and becoming less suitable in the eyes of the agency. What a catch-22."

Penny tipped up her glass and poured the last of her drink into her mouth. "Then a miracle happened. At least that's what we thought. Our name came up and a baby was available."

When she didn't continue, I hazarded another guess to nudge her along. "They found out about your drinking, didn't they?"

"Yes. We failed the inspection. Mark was devastated. I was . . ." Her hands flailed expressively. "After all that time waiting, the only thing we could do was go back to the beginning and start over."

I knew she wanted me to feel sympathetic, but I

couldn't. I shuddered to think what kind of a mother this woman would make.

"Why didn't you stop drinking?" I asked angrily.

"I tried. Don't you think I tried? But the longer things dragged on, the worse the pressure became. I felt like I was nothing, that I was useless as a woman. My life had no meaning.

"Sometimes I needed a drink or two to help me cope. Sometimes I just needed to forget. But that's over now. As soon as Mark and I get our baby, that will all be behind us. I'll be in control again, and everything will be fine."

I didn't believe that for a minute. But Penny did, and that was all that mattered. Monica had delighted in picking at the scabs of other peoples' wounds. I wondered if she had known how desperate Penny was to have a baby. I wondered if that had made her enjoy the game all the more.

"So when the state turned you down, you signed up for a private adoption where there would be fewer questions. Where did you get the money?"

"We'd been saving it all those years we were on the waiting list. We're not stupid. And neither is Walter. He got a deal put together pretty quickly. We've met the birth mother and the baby's due in a few weeks. This time, nothing's going to go wrong."

I watched as Penny fixed herself another drink, a double shot of whiskey, straight up. "How did Monica find out about your arrangement with the lawyer?"

"How did she find out about anything?" Penny snapped. "She was nosy, and she asked too many questions. I told Mark not to say anything until after the adoption was finalized, but after all the time we'd waited, he was just so delighted he wanted to tell the whole world. It wasn't hard for Monica to get him talking."

I could see how it wouldn't have been. More than once, Mark had told me that he and Penny were about to become parents. I'd misunderstood. No doubt Monica had been quicker on the uptake. Then, once she had the information, she hadn't been able to resist turning the screws.

There was a quiet click as the door opened behind me. I kept my gaze firmly trained on Penny. "Monica was threatening to expose you, wasn't she? Is that why you followed her outside after the meeting?"

"I only wanted to talk to her," Penny said, her voice rising shrilly. "But she wouldn't listen. She said I wasn't fit to be a mother. She said that I needed help.

"I followed her back to her van because I had to make her see that she was wrong. Do you understand? I *had* to. But Monica just ignored me. She was fiddling with those damn Beagles of hers and didn't even have the decency to turn around and listen to what I had to say."

I didn't have to ask if Penny had been drinking that night. I already knew the answer. "So you picked up a rock."

I heard a gasp, and this time I turned. Mark was standing in the doorway, his face ashen.

"No!" he cried. The word sounded like an anguished groan, torn from deep within. Mark started toward his wife, then stopped.

His expression clawed at me. It was both bewildered and disbelieving. He was staring at his wife as if he'd never seen her before. As she started toward him, he backed away.

"Mark, honey . . ." Penny held out a placating hand. "I did it for you, for both of us."

"No!" His voice was firmer, but he was shaking his head violently, as if to negate the terrible truth he'd just learned. He slapped his wife's hand away. "Get away from me."

Penny stopped, confused. Mark spun on his heel and headed for the door.

"I did it for you," she said again, her gaze following him.

Mark's stride never faltered.

"Don't you dare walk away from me!"

Mark kept going.

I was watching him, so I didn't see Penny pick up the heavy crystal decanter from the bar. She screamed as she threw it but there wasn't time to react. The faceted glass bottle hit Mark in the back of the head and he fell like a stone. The decanter shattered beside him on the floor, spilling a thick dark liquor over the polished wood.

I whirled toward Penny who was picking up another bottle. Only three steps separated us, but in the seconds it took to reach her, she'd swung the bottle around to grip it by the neck as a weapon. Chivas Regal, the black label said. It's amazing the irrelevant information the mind will process in times of stress. If I were dead, what would it matter that it was the good stuff that had done me in?

Judging by the look on Penny's face, that's what she had in mind. Clearly she was beyond rational thought. The house was filled with people; doing me harm would only make things worse. Penny glowered at me, teeth gritted in rage, and swung the bottle anyway.

I jumped back, but wasn't fast enough. The bottle missed my head, but glanced off my shoulder, sending a hot lance of pain down my arm and through my hand. It happened so quickly I didn't realize my fingers had gone numb until I tried to grab Penny's arm and nothing happened. She shook me off easily and swung the bottle again.

I'm a fast learner, especially with pain avoidance as an incentive. This time I didn't dodge, I ducked. Then I came up swinging.

I kicked Penny in the shin, then balled my fist and punched her in the gut. Both moves probably hurt me as much as they did her, but at least they got Penny's attention. She dropped the bottle and clawed at my eyes.

I've probably watched too many movies because I reached up and fastened my hands around her throat. I don't know what I was thinking. It's not as if strangulation was an option. Two fingernails raked down my cheek. I yanked Penny's hair, then kneed her in the groin. The combination sent her sprawling.

I heard a commotion behind me and before Penny could get up, Bertie was on her. Penny struggled, screeching like a banshee and Louis jumped in to grab her other arm.

Shoulder throbbing, cheek stinging, I slumped down onto the couch. A low moan came from the body near the door. I guessed that meant Mark wasn't dead.

I glanced over and saw Lydia standing in the doorway, looking horrified. Thelma was beside her. The judge surveyed the scene with interest.

"Things sure have gotten exciting around here since I left," she said.

⊸❀ *Thirty-five* ❀⊶

At the first sound of trouble, Aunt Peg had called the police. Cy stationed himself at the front door so that nobody could leave until the authorities arrived. In the ten minutes that took, Sharon and Barbara applied cold compresses to Mark's head and managed to bring him around.

He was in a chair, groggy, but mostly upright. His wife was in another chair on the other side of the room, with Bertie and Louis standing over her like a pair of belligerent watch dogs. Mark looked her way once, briefly; then firmly looked away. Penny didn't look up at all.

The first squad car was quickly followed by a second containing Detective Shertz. He listened briefly as all the club members tried to explain everything at once, then zeroed in on me.

Even though I'd heard Penny confess to murdering Monica, I'd been afraid it would be her word against mine. It turned out I needn't have worried. Mark still wasn't looking at Penny, and when Detective Shertz questioned him, his version of events was the same as mine.

Mark's voice was flat as he recounted what had happened. He looked like a man defeated; one who has no reason left to care. He'd enabled Penny to keep drinking and now, like Louis, he was going to pay for his wife's mistakes.

The police put handcuffs on Penny before taking her away. Mark went out with them. I heard the cars start up outside and wondered whether he would follow her to the police station, or turn the other way, toward home. I didn't look out to see. I wasn't sure I really wanted to know.

Everybody had more questions, but I didn't feel much like talking. While Aunt Peg held court, I took a moment to pull Paul Heins aside for a quiet chat, then finished up with a conversation I'd needed to have with Bertie. After that, Aunt Peg shooed everybody away and escorted me out to my car.

"You look like hell," she said bluntly. "Follow me home and I'll patch you up."

I felt like hell, too, but a cup of strong, brandy-laced, coffee got the revival process started. Aunt Peg got out a tube of ointment. I could see perfectly well that it had come from her vet, but when she dabbed some on my cheek, the scratches began to feel better. The house Poodles milled around my chair in sympathetic solidarity.

The cosseting lasted at least a good five minutes.

It was followed by a reproach.

"I can't believe I missed all the fun," Aunt Peg grumbled. "The least you could have done was let me in on it."

"Some fun," I muttered, rubbing my shoulder.

She was rooting around in the refrigerator, and came up, after a moment, with a box of Twinkies. Peg set them on the table between us. "There's one thing I still don't understand. Why on earth did Penny steal the club's dinner checks?"

"She didn't. It was simply coincidence that the checks disappeared and Monica was murdered around the same time. The two things weren't related at all."

I eyed the Twinkies, fully aware that it was well past dinner time and all I'd had to show for the meal were a couple of tiny hors d'oeuvres. Finally I reached over and helped myself. The sponge cake went great with my coffee.

"Do you mean we still don't know where that money went?"

Mouth too full to speak, I shook my head, then swallowed. "Paul Heins has the checks. I told Lydia I'd return them to her this week."

"Now I'm confused," said Aunt Peg. "What did Paul hope to gain by taking the club's dinner money?"

"Nothing. He wasn't the one who took it." I paused briefly for another bite. "I'd been thinking about this for a while. This afternoon when Louis accused Sharon of losing the checks, it finally all made sense. Have you ever noticed the way Darla has of absent-mindedly picking things up and carrying them around?"

"Now that you mention it, I guess I have."

"Add that to Sharon's propensity for misplacing things. I imagine she meant to put the checks in Louis's briefcase, but never got around to it. Meanwhile, Darla who was sitting next to her at dinner that night must have picked them up.

"Paul didn't discover Darla had the checks until they got home, and then he didn't know what to do. Already they'd been turned into the authorities for not taking proper care of their dogs. What if people were to come to believe that they weren't able to take care of themselves?"

Aunt Peg nodded thoughtfully.

"Paul feels very protective of Darla, remember. He told me tonight that he wanted to return the checks, but he couldn't figure out how to do it. Especially after the club members raised such a fuss at the next meeting when they found out the money was gone. He saw how they went after Louis and decided there was no way he was going to expose Darla to censure like that."

"Poor Paul," Aunt Peg said, frowning. "He must have felt terrible."

"He did. The night that Monica was killed, he had decided he was going to talk privately to Lydia after the meeting. That's why Bertie saw the Heinses behaving so oddly as they left the restaurant. But he never did catch Lydia, and then Monica was murdered and I started asking questions, which made him even more afraid of being found out."

"Have you spoken to him about this?"

"Tonight, just before we left. Lydia has agreed to take the checks back, no questions asked. I told him I'd keep his secret." I sent her a stern look. "So that goes for you, too."

"Of course it does," Aunt Peg agreed. "I saw you grab a minute to talk to Bertie as well. What was that about?"

"Just confirming a hunch. Do you remember Joanne telling me that she received two notes, one that was signed by a Beagle sketch and one that wasn't? That seemed very odd to me, especially since she was the only one who had gotten a second note."

"Right," said Aunt Peg. "I'd forgotten about that."

"It turns out Bertie was responsible for that second note. She got the idea after Monica sent her one about the Yorkie she showed in Maine. Bertie and Joanne can't stand one another. She told me tonight she was just trying to yank Joanne's chain.

"Her words, not mine," I added with a smile. "That's why Bertie was so defensive every time I brought up the subject of those notes. She didn't want me to find out what she'd been up to."

Aunt Peg frowned. "Don't tell me this means the club has a second trouble maker to worry about?"

"I doubt it. Bertie's tough on the outside, but I think she felt pretty guilty about the way things turned out."

Now that she knew she hadn't missed out on all the excitement, Aunt Peg appeared somewhat mollified. The last Twinkie sat on the table between us, and she eyed it hopefully. "Is that yours or mine?"

"Yours," I said, standing. I picked up my coffee cup and carried it over to the sink. "I've got to be getting home. Bob's there, and Davey will be waiting up."

"Speaking of troubles resolving themselves, isn't it about time for Bob to be heading back to wherever he came from?"

"He's leaving tomorrow," I said. "He's come to the conclusion that full-time fatherhood doesn't suit him." Grinning, I borrowed a phrase from Davey. "Is that cool, or what?"

The next afternoon after school, I piled Faith and Davey into the car and we all took a drive up to New London. I knew I owed an enormous debt to Rose and Peter. Even though I'd made my own plan for handling Bob, their intervention had been key, and I wanted them to know how grateful I was.

Rose and Peter lived in a trim, well-maintained row house in a working class section of New London. I found a space for the Volvo right out front. Davey ran ahead with Faith and knocked on the door. I was the one who held back.

Relationships in our family have never been easy. Just the summer before I'd found myself accusing Rose of stealing one of Aunt Peg's Poodles, then mediating a meeting between the two women that had nearly come to blows. Before it was over, Rose had shocked me with revelations that had forever changed what I thought I knew about my own family.

I hadn't wanted to forgive her for that. If it wasn't for Frank, I probably wouldn't have. Rose and I were related, but we'd never been friends. Now I was uncomfortably aware of the thanks I owed her, and unsure how it was going to be received.

Then Aunt Rose threw open the front door and greeted us with hugs and kisses all around. The uneasiness I'd expected to feel, dissolved. Peter was in the kitchen putting together a stew. He threw some extra potatoes in the pot and invited us to stay for dinner.

A few minutes later, when he and Davey and Faith went out to explore the neighborhood, Rose and I had a chance to talk. I told her that Bob had left, and that everything had worked out fine.

"I was sure it would," she said, smiling serenely. Aunt Rose spent the majority of her life in a convent. Her faith is powerful enough to move mountains, much less sustain her in times of doubt.

"You told me to pray," I admitted. "But I never did."

"That's all right, dear." Rose reached out and wrapped her hand around one of mine. "Each of us does what we can, in our own way. I know God listens when I talk to him. I was praying for you."

I shook my head slowly, wishing I could believe with such utter confidence, but knowing I never could. "Do you really think that's what made the difference?"

"You needed your ex-husband to come to his senses, and he did. Does it really matter why he changed his mind? I see it as the hand of God working his will on earth. You might see things differently."

Rose smiled slyly. "You see, I did talk to God about the situation, but I also had Peter talk to Bob. My husband has spent his lifetime counseling people who are confronted by difficult choices. I knew he'd be the right man for the job. Put your faith in God, dear, but have a back-up plan just in case."

I started to laugh and, after a moment, Rose joined in. We were still giggling like a couple of teenagers when the rest of our group returned. Davey demanded to know what was so funny. Peter slipped me a broad wink over my son's head. Faith just ran around the room and barked.

That note of hilarity set the tone for the rest of the evening. Mindful that we had school the next day, Davey and I started back before it got too late. Even so, it was nearing ten and Davey and Faith were asleep in the back seat before we reached home. The last thing I expected was to find a car in my driveway.

Sam's car.

He climbed out as I pulled in and parked behind him.

"What are you doing here?" I asked.

"Waiting."

"Yes, but . . ."

"Peg called. She told me Bob went home."

"He did."

"It's about time," said Sam. "Did I tell you there's a new pet-sitting service in Redding?"

"Ummhmm." I nestled my head against his broad chest and inhaled deeply. My arms twined around his back. When one hand slipped lower, I felt an unexpected lump in the back pocket of his jeans. "What's this?"

"Toothbrush," said Sam. In the silvery light of the full moon, I could see that he was grinning.

"Oh." I grinned back.

Sometimes it's nice to have things settled just that easily.

The next time a Belle Haven Kennel Club meeting rolled around, I let Aunt Peg go by herself. So far, the club hasn't invited me to become a member. I guess breaking up the club president's reception didn't make the best impression.

Aunt Peg says I should give them time and they'll get over it. She's also mentioned there's an opening for a corresponding secretary. I've told her she's crazy, but that's never stopped her before.

I'm keeping my pencils sharpened, just in case.

Please turn the page for an exciting
sneak peek of Laurien Berenson's
newest Melanie Travis mystery,
HAIR OF THE DOG,
now on sale wherever mysteries are sold!

∽✻ *One* ✻∽

At my Aunt Peg's house, there's often a pot of chicken simmering on the stove. Visitors, however, shouldn't get their hopes up. At least not two-legged ones. The chicken is for the dogs. Peg breeds Standard Poodles and has about a dozen, all of whom eat like royalty. Humans have to fend for themselves.

Which was why I was so surprised when she called one morning in late June and told me she wanted to throw a party. "Maybe a backyard barbecue," she said. "Something simple."

Simple? I wasn't sure Aunt Peg understood the meaning of the concept. The summer before, she'd finagled me into helping find her missing stud dog by insisting that it would be simple. Then last fall, she'd initiated me into the joys of dog ownership by assuring me that that, too, would be simple. Is it any wonder I didn't rush to volunteer my services?

No matter. Aunt Peg merely assumed I'd help out and went on making plans. She's nearing sixty, and in all those years I doubt that anyone has ever said no to her and gotten away with it.

Peg lives in a big old farmhouse on several acres of land that even I had to admit would make the perfect setting for an outdoor party. Her husband, Max, had died the year before, and if you didn't count the dog shows she attended several weekends a month to exhibit her Poodles, she'd done almost no socializing since. Even though I knew it would end up costing me, it was nice to hear her talk about inviting friends over.

"I was thinking fifty people or so," she said blithely. "There are three shows in the area that weekend, and everybody will be around. I'm sure we'll draw a crowd."

I didn't doubt it. Dog people travel a fair amount in their pursuit of the biggest wins and the best judges, and with a trio of important shows in the neighborhood, exhibitors from all over would be converging in Connecticut for the Fourth of July weekend.

"You'll bring Davey, of course," she told me. "And Sam."

Davey was my son, five years old and very full of himself. He'd started morning day camp at the beginning of the week and I was due to pick him up in an hour.

Sam Driver was a friend. Actually he was a good bit more than that, but I still hadn't figured out how to refer to our relationship in polite conversation. Calling him my boyfriend seemed to imply that I was still a girl, which, at thirty-one, I most assuredly was not. Significant other was definitely too unwieldy. Lover got to the heart of the matter, but seemed a little blunt. Not that Aunt Peg would have minded. She's a great fan of Sam's, and a strong believer in speaking one's mind on any and all occasions.

"Faith isn't invited," she told me firmly. "There will simply be too much going on."

"Right," I agreed.

Faith was Davey's and my Standard Poodle. A gift from Aunt Peg, she was fourteen months old and a true adolescent: rambunctious, willful, and growing what, to my mind, was entirely too much hair. Otherwise known as a Poodle show coat.

All forty-five pounds of her was lying draped across my lap as I spoke on the phone. I glanced down and Faith thumped her black tail obligingly. Intelligent as Poodles are, I imagine she knew we were talking about her.

"Chicken and ribs," Aunt Peg was saying. "Mounds of them. Nobody eats dog show food if they can help it. People will be starving by the time they get to us. Then ice cream and brownies for dessert. That sounds easy enough, doesn't it?"

Listening to Aunt Peg chatter on, I almost believed that the party might come together without a hitch. Of course that was before either of us knew that before the weekend was over, one of the guests would be dead.

"Will there be presents?" asked Davey. "And games and goody bags?"

I'd just finished dressing him in a perfectly presentable outfit, and with only minutes to go until we left for Aunt

Peg's, I was hoping he wouldn't find any dirt to attach himself to. With his sandy curls and chubby cheeks, Davey has the innocent look of a Botticelli cherub. He also has the energy, and potential for damage, of a small tornado.

We were in the kitchen, where I was mixing Faith's food. "Sorry, sport, not this time. This is a grown-up party, with eating and drinking, and people to talk to."

"That doesn't sound like much fun." At his age, my son's idea of fun was anything involving cars, loud noises, or fast action—preferably a combination of the three. "Will there be other kids?"

"Not many."

Even that was probably an overstatement. Most of the people Aunt Peg had invited were exhibitors and judges, who would come straight from the Farmington dog show. Aunt Peg had never had children of her own, and while she enjoyed Davey, I knew she held the opinion that one child in the vicinity was often more than enough.

"Sam will be there," I said, setting the dog food bowl down on the floor. "That's someone you know."

Faith sauntered over to have a look at the offering. She was full grown now physically, if not mentally, and the top of her head was nearly level with my waist. A Standard Poodle, she was the largest of the three varieties: strong, solid, and fully capable of retrieving game, as her ancestors had been bred to do. Not that there was much call for that in the suburbs.

"Go on," I said. "Eat."

Faith sent me a look. If I'd been in the habit of ascribing human traits to dogs, I'd have sworn she rolled her eyes.

"She doesn't like it," Davey chortled. "She wants pizza."

"She does not," I said firmly. I nudged the bowl closer to Faith's muzzle with my toe. Grudgingly she took a mouthful of the food and rolled it around her tongue.

She'd always been a finicky eater, and there wasn't an ounce of fat on her. When she'd turned a year old, Aunt Peg had clipped her into the continental trim, which is a modern descendant of a traditional German hunting clip and is required in the show ring. Since the trim mandates a large mane of hair on the front half of the body, and a hindquarter that is shaved mostly down to the skin, it was easy to see just how lean she was. Luckily for me, Faith was taking six months off from showing to grow into her new trim, so her weight had yet to become an issue.

I put the dog food in the refrigerator and patted the top of the Poodle's crate. Obligingly, Faith strolled in, circled once, and lay down. When she was a puppy, we'd used the crate as an aid in housebreaking and to keep her from chewing when we weren't home. Now that she was older and knew how to behave, I usually left the door open. Faith had come to think of the crate as her den, and was perfectly content to nap there while we were gone.

Davey and I live in North Stamford in a snug cape on a small lot. The street was developed in the fifties, and looks it. What we gained in function, we unfortunately sacrificed in charm. Aunt Peg is one town away in Greenwich. Her house is set back from the road in the midst of a meadow studded with wildflowers. A veranda wraps around three sides of the house, and the roof is gabled. A small kennel building out back holds the Poodles Peg is conditioning for the show ring. Though she has neighbors, none of their houses are visible. It's a far cry from my road, where in the summer, with the windows open, I can smell what the people next door are having for dinner.

Davey and I had been at Aunt Peg's earlier in the day to help with the preparations, but now, when we arrived for the second time, the party was already in progress. Cars and vans, most filled with crates and grooming equipment, already lined both sides of the back country road. Since the show site was an hour away, I knew that those who'd stayed through Best in Show had yet to arrive. Bearing in mind what Peg had said about everyone being hungry, I hoped she'd ordered enough food.

As soon as we got out of the car, Davey ran on ahead. Following the sound of voices and the smell of barbecued chicken, he raced around the back of the house. In pursuit of brownies, no doubt.

At six-thirty, it was still fully light. As I followed my son to Peg's backyard, where throngs of people had already begun to congregate around the tables that held food and drinks, I could see perfectly well where I was going. So when I bumped into Sam Driver from behind, and managed to insinuate my body along his, I couldn't exactly say it was an accident.

"Not now," he whispered without turning around. "Melanie will be here any minute. I'll meet you later."

"Hmmph," I muttered, wrapping my arms around him and snuggling my face between his shoulder blades. "How did you know it was me?"

Sam turned, grinning. He was holding a cold bottle of beer in each hand. "It might have had something to do with that three-foot streak of energy that preceded you. Here, one of these is yours."

I popped the top and took a long, icy swallow. It tasted so good going down that I could feel the tingle in my toes. Or maybe that was Sam's doing. It's been a year and he still has that effect on me.

Sam is tall, and built along lean lines; the kind of man who jogs but wouldn't dream of lifting weights. He has sun-streaked hair the color of wheat and eyes as blue as the Caribbean. There have been other men who have made my motor race, but none who have accomplished it with Sam's casual, graceful ease.

"Speaking of the streak," I said. "Which way did he go?"

Sam pointed toward the back door. "I think he was heading for the kitchen. Does he know something we don't?"

"Brownies, stashed inside for later. You know Aunt Peg's sweet tooth."

"There you are!" called a loud voice. "It's about time!"

"Speak of the devil," I muttered.

Sam grasped a bit of skin in a place where I wished there hadn't been any excess, and pinched a gentle reprimand. Next time I'd volunteer him to come early and help set up.

"Hi, Aunt Peg," I said, turning to greet her. "How's everything going?"

"So far, so good. We've really pulled a crowd. Scuttlebutt has it that Austin Beamish's Golden is going to win Best, but no one's arrived yet to confirm that."

Golden was shorthand for Golden Retriever; Best was Best in Show. At its highest levels, the world of dog shows is actually a rather small place. Everybody knows everybody else, from the judges to the exhibitors to the top professional handlers. They've all long since scoped out the strengths and weaknesses of one another's dogs, and they all know which judges tend to prefer what traits. I wasn't surprised that results were being predicted before they'd had a chance to happen; I'd seen other exhibitors do the same weeks in advance of a show on the basis of a judging schedule alone.

Peg lifted the lid of the large cooler beneath the picnic table. She's a tall woman, and had to bend way down to reach. Her gray hair, worn pulled back in a bun for as long as I could remember, had recently been cut and now fell in waves to just below her ears. She tucked back a strand that tumbled forward, and she frowned at the nearly empty cooler.

"Sam, there's another case of beer in the refrigerator in the garage. Do you suppose . . . ?"

"Of course. Be right back." Before he'd even finished speaking, Sam was already heading off to do her bidding. Aunt Peg tends to have that effect on people.

"This is quite a gathering," I said, looking around. I'd been going to the dog shows with Aunt Peg for a year now. Some of her guests I knew, and many others looked familiar. "How many people did you say you were expecting?"

"Too many." Peg sighed, but she didn't look entirely displeased. "At least I had the foresight to call the caterer yesterday and tell him to double the order."

There was a small commotion as a new group of people arrived, two middle-aged men with a strikingly attractive woman walking between them. Aunt Peg followed the direction of my gaze. "Good. If they've arrived, that means the show's over and we'll be able to find out who won."

"Who are they?"

"The couple is Vivian and Ron Pullman. They live in Katonah and show some very good Chows. Their dog won the Non-Sporting group today. The man who came in with them is Austin Beamish."

"The one whose Golden Retriever was supposed to win Best in Show?"

"Quite right. With Ron's Chow winning a group as well, they'd have been competing against each other. Still, everyone looks perfectly chummy." Aunt Peg grinned slyly. "I wonder if that means they both lost. Come on over, and I'll introduce you."

I followed in Aunt Peg's wake as she went to greet her new guests. From a distance, I'd wondered briefly which of the two men was Vivian's husband. Now, as we drew closer, she laughed at something somebody said and twined her arm around the waist of the good-looking man standing to her right. Ron Pullman had long legs and wide, linebacker's shoulders. He was casually dressed in khakis and a button-down shirt with the cuffs rolled back, but his clothes fit his large frame impeccably.

Vivian wasn't a small woman, but beside her husband, she looked petite. Her tawny hair curled in artful disarray and her luminous skin was flawless. She was younger than Ron by at least ten years. That, and the expression in his eyes when he looked at her, were enough to make me wonder if she was a second wife.

"Ron, Viv, Austin!" Peg held out her arms wide. "I'm so glad you could make it."

All three smiled, but it was Austin Beamish who stepped forward and smoothly planted a kiss on Aunt Peg's cheek. He wasn't a physically impressive man, shorter than Peg by at least an inch and bald save for a fringe of rust-colored hair around the base of his skull. It didn't seem to matter. The best show dogs all have presence, and Austin Beamish had it too. Ron struck me as someone who might have played football in college; Austin looked much too intelligent to ever allow himself to be blindsided by a tackle.

"Thank you for having us. This looks wonderful." The merest trace of a southern drawl coated Vivian's smooth-as-honey voice. She lifted her nose to the wind and sniffed delicately. "Do I smell ribs?"

"You can take the girl out of the country ..." Ron teased. "Her mouth's been watering since we got off the Merritt Parkway."

"In a minute, you can help yourselves," said Peg. "But first—"

"Don't even ask," Austin broke in good-naturedly. "Robert Janney's Peke skunked us both. I don't suppose you have a neon sign around here where we could post the news?"

"Don't worry, if you told the group at the gate, it's probably traveled around the whole yard already." Peg motioned me forward and performed the introductions, and we shook hands all around.

Vivian's grasp was surprisingly firm, and Austin added to his by throwing an arm around my shoulder and giving me a squeeze.

"You mustn't mind him," said Ron. "He's like that with all the girls."

"If you've got it, flaunt it," said Austin.

"Oh?" I lifted a brow. "What have you got?"

Austin roared with laughter. "Everything I need," he said firmly. "And then some."

"Don't get him started," said Viv. "At least not while I still have an empty stomach." Linking her arms through both men's, Viv led them toward two big grills, where an abundant supply of ribs and chicken were basting in barbecue sauce.

Now that she mentioned it, my own stomach was feeling pretty empty. I saw that Davey had settled himself in an Adirondack chair. He had a plate holding two ears of buttered corn and a generous mound of baked beans balanced on the big wooden arm. I told myself that it was better than brownies and was about to go get some food myself, when Aunt Peg muttered something under her breath.

Peg was raised in genteel times. Coming from her, "Damn!" meant business.

A new group of guests who'd just arrived from the show was strolling around the side of the house. Among them was Barry Turk, a Poodle handler with low professional standards and even less moral character. I'd visited his kennel when I was searching for Aunt Peg's missing Poodle and found it to be dark, cramped, and filled with dogs that barked incessantly. Turk's prices were right, however, and he did his share of winning in the ring, so he never seemed to lack for clients.

"Don't tell me you invited him," I said, surprised. Turk was not one of Aunt Peg's favorite people.

"I most certainly did not. Obviously he tagged along with everybody else."

Turk hung back for a moment as the group he was with moved on. I saw why when a slender woman, stylishly dressed, hurried around the house and caught up with him. Turk reached out and took her hand.

"Oh, Lord," said Peg, sounding as though she were truly hoping for divine intervention.

"She looks familiar." I frowned, trying to place the woman.

"That's Alicia Devane. You've probably seen her at the shows. She and Barry have been living together since last fall."

I gazed at Alicia with new interest. She was attractive in a quiet sort of way, her dark hair bobbed to just below chin length, her features even and unremarkable. All in all, she looked perfectly normal. That being the case, I wondered what she was doing with a jerk like Barry Turk.

I would have asked Aunt Peg, but it was clear her attention was elsewhere. She was standing on her toes, her gaze searching avidly through the assembled crowds. Considering that Peg's height already placed her above most of the guests, I took this to mean that it was a matter of some urgency.

"What's the matter?" I asked.

"Maybe nothing," she said, sounding relieved. "I don't see Bill. Maybe he's not here."

"Bill?"

"Bill Devane. Alicia's husband."

I told you it wasn't going to be simple.

Grab These
Kensington Mysteries

Get Hooked on the
Mysteries of
Jonnie Jacobs

Get More Mysteries by
Leslie Meier